QUEEN OF THORNS

STACEY TROMBLEY

QUEEN of THORNS

WICKED FAE

Book 5

STACEY TROMBLEY

I

REV

Just when I've earned everything I've worked for, my fated mate burns it all to ash—and it's so like her.

I almost laugh at the thought. It's always Caelynn at the center of it all. Every major event, good and bad, has centered around my lovely Shadow fae.

In the last few months, my world has turned entirely on its head.

Sometimes, the things you dread in the beginning are the very things that make your life worth living.

Meeting Caelynn was like that.

Without her, I wouldn't have an incredible fated mate. I wouldn't be High Heir. And, realistically, I wouldn't even be alive. She's at the center of every bad thing in my life, yet she's the shining light that gives me hope and happiness in a way I've never felt before.

But the haunted look in Caelynn's golden eyes as she leans over the ancient book laying on the coffee table clearly illustrates that our battle is not yet over.

Snow falls in thick waves beyond the large window, blanketing the entire countryside in puffy whiteness.

We've been in the Frost Court for three days, after the High Court was nearly destroyed. It's been a good break from —well, everything. Cae and I have hidden away in our room, with the roaring fire and massive window showcasing the snowy mountains in the distance.

Caelynn spends hours and hours every day conversing with the spell book we retrieved from the Schorchedlands. The book is legendary, but very few souls know the full extent of it. It holds power, yes. It reveals spells long lost to our world, yes.

But it is also a sentient being that holds nearly unlimited knowledge. And it belongs only to Caelynn, the hated assassin fae from the Shadow Court. I'm able to read bits and pieces from the book, but only Caelynn can hear its voice.

While Caelynn obsesses over information from the ancient book, I often attend meetings and dine with our hosts, the Frost Court royals and the High Queen. Every moment between, I am here with my secret mate.

Here, in this cozy room next to the fire, we are far from the conflicts haunting us. Far from our enemies and close to one another. The moment we leave, we'll be dropped straight into a war we may not be able to win. The moment we leave, Caelynn and I will be pulled apart. Maybe permanently.

Snow blankets the hills outside, but we are warmed by the flickering fire. Even so, Caelynn shivers, her muscles tense.

"Caelynn?"

She doesn't move, doesn't breathe. She remains still as stone, staring at the scrawled text of the legendary spell book's open pages with wide, terror-filled eyes.

My stomach twists. There are three words scrawled on the worn page in front of her, but I can't make them out from here.

I step closer.

"Cae?" She still doesn't respond, but she releases a shuddering breath. I lean over the book to read the phrase that has her transfixed.

Hello, my pet.

My stomach sinks. "Caelynn?" I say more firmly, heart pounding. The words fade into nothing, leaving only a blank page.

I crouch and grip her chin, forcing her eyes away from the page. She meets my stare with absolute horror.

"Are you okay?" I don't know what's going on, but her expression has me shaken. "What is it?"

She glances at the now-empty page. "He sent us a message." Her voice is hushed but not panicked.

"A... message?" I frown. The spell book can tell us anything that has happened, even things that are happening now, but it's never been used to send a message. But I suppose someone could if they knew the spell book's power and how to get its attention. The Night Bringer likely knows both.

She nods. "The Night Bringer spoke something meant for me to hear. The book is giving me the option to read it or... not."

I pull in a long breath, thankful to the wise book for giving the option instead of just throwing it at her. But then again, maybe hiding the existence of the message altogether would have been even more favorable. "_Not_ is probably the better option." I can't imagine a single word of their message will be helpful.

There is no negotiating with the ancient evils—if it wasn't for the bargain. To save Caelynn's life in the Schorchedlands I bowed the ancient evil's wishes and freed them, but first forced them to a magical promise—they will never harm us.

Of course, they've already found ways to get around that bargain, and I know it's only the beginning. These creatures want to kill and torture us. Their words will only be baiting and dishonest.

"Show me," Caelynn demands, with a surprisingly strong voice, "the whole damn thing."

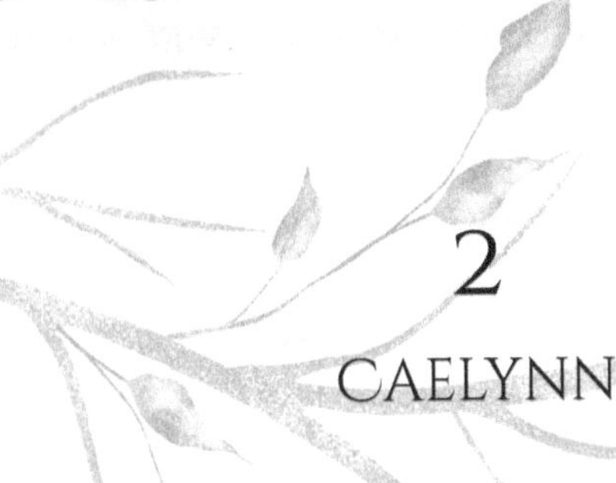

2

CAELYNN

"Caelynn," Rev murmurs, "maybe I should read it and—"

"No. I have to see it," I say firmly. "We will both read it. Together."

Rev's eyes are a dark grey as he holds my stare for a long moment. Then, he reaches out his hand. I cling to his fingers like he's my anchor to life. And maybe he is.

Maybe he always was.

Ink appears on the worn pages of the open spell book.

Hello, my pet.

Have you had a good break from my scheming? Are you ready to begin the game anew?

Breath freezes in my lungs, and every muscle tenses, preparing for the pain I know will result from the words of my worst enemy. My nightmare. Rev squeezes my hand tighter. I can't hear the monster's words, but the echoing memory of his voice reverberates through my mind anyway. I see the darkness surrounding him. Feel his talons.

Your mate freed us, strengthened us. We are both thankful for your help. We could be allies, but it does not seem you've chosen that path, have you? I know that you

plot to destroy us. Foolish, foolish child. Will you never learn?

Your mate bargained for your life. And you will have it. I will grant it to you, my pet. But since you insist on being our enemy, here is my promise—

You will live a long and terrible life. You will be lonely and hated. Death is a mercy you did not choose and so, you will endure pains worse than death. Over and over again.

As for your mate? I will drive you apart. I will ensure he sees you for what you truly are.

I stole away part of your soul when we first met and gave you a piece of mine. If you think one bargain can reverse the damage done, then you are pathetically naïve.

You are mine.

A low rumble pulls my attention from the message. My gaze flicks to Rev. His eyes are pitch black, his expression angry. He, too, is tense, like he's preparing to attack the pages of the book for revealing such atrocities.

You have belonged to me from the moment you stepped into that tunnel so many years ago, right into my awaiting claws. This began all the way back then. You are not free of me. You never will be.

I know everything that is precious to you. And I will take it away bit by bit, until all you have left is me. You will beg me to end you.

And I will not oblige.

You will always be a villain to the world. And soon, everyone will see the darkness within—even your precious mate.

They will all turn on you because that is your fate, oh child of shadow. To live alone in the darkness you created. Empty. Hollow. Abandoned.

***I look forward to that day, when we meet again and you
are no different from me.***

Until then, my pet.

I jerk my eyes away from the scrawled text, heart pounding, mouth dry. Even as Rev pulls me into his warm embrace, I can feel their claws raking down my soul.

"He's just saying what he knows will get under your skin," Rev murmurs against my hair.

I nod into his shoulder. He's right; it's just, that doesn't mean the Night Bringer's words weren't true. I have never been naïve enough to believe that Rev's bargain would keep me from their clutches. Not for long anyway.

I *know* the Night Bringer will attempt to take every precious thing from me, including Rev. And they've already successfully proven just how easy that would be in less than the two weeks since we helped them escape the Schorchedlands.

They have a powerful ally on their side that can very easily hurt us. An ally with massive influence, if not outright control, of a major ruling court. We might be stronger than Drake, prince of the Whirling Court, but he has a lot of influence, and with the added power the Night Bringer granted him for his help...

Raven is with Drake's brother. That's one checkmark on the Night Bringer's list. I love Raven, and he's taken her from me. I don't know if she's still alive or if she's okay.

The spell book has assured me she was well when they left the fae realm last, but it's not enough to reassure me. Its knowledge doesn't extend outside of this world, so she's lost to me no matter what.

The Night Bringer's games have already resulted in me being named a traitor—again—by the ruling courts. I only *barely* convinced the council to reverse that decision when I saved the High Court from complete destruction.

And Rev doesn't see it, doesn't feel it the way I do—how that monster's darkness is still inside of me. His evil shades every move I make. It pulls at me, dragging me down, like a weight I cannot shed.

The desperate bargain Rev made to save me might have halted the progression of my soul's descent—because the Night Bringer can't actively attack—but he's still in me. That cannot be undone.

So, even if his words are classic goading, trying to get me to freak out and lose my shit, they still ring true. I swallow back the stinging in the back of my throat.

He might destroy me like he promises. But I intend to destroy him first.

Perhaps by the end, I will have a long and terrible life like he claims.

But I will not have that sad ending without also putting that bastard in the ground for good.

"What are you thinking?" Rev asks, his adoring eyes still dark, but there is a fragment of soft silver.

"I'm thinking about killing them."

"Good." His voice dips low, and one side of my mouth twitches in what is almost a smile.

He runs the pad of his thumb along my bottom lip and wets his own. I close my eyes and lean into his touch.

"You do not belong to him," he tells me, voice so low it's near a growl. "You are mine."

My stomach flips pleasantly, even as the acid of fear lingers.

Then, his lips meet mine in a claiming, devouring kiss. I melt into him, relishing the zing of pleasure that floods my body every place we touch. His arm curls around my back and tugs me even closer.

Then, he pulls back and rests his forehead against mine, panting softly.

"Are you okay?" Rev whispers.

I nod.

"Don't fall back into old habits, Cae. You are worthy of happiness. You can win this, without losing everything."

I press my lips together.

"Don't give up without fighting. Please."

I suck in a long breath and let it out slowly. He's right. It's hard, and I'm terrified of what may come, but destiny or not, I'll work toward the best possible outcome.

I've been there so many times it's hard not to continue looking down when it feels like I'm falling.

But I won't let that fear be my end.

I will cling to what I have with every breath.

"We'll find a way to kill them without destroying ourselves, okay?" he tells me.

My lips tick up into a false smile, and I rise to my feet, pushing away from the words of my nightmare. The threats have caused the dark power inside my heart to stir. My muscles and mind are restless.

Only a few long strides and I'm standing right next to the massive glass window looking out at the winter wonderland that is the Frost Court. The edge of the town can be seen to the left, but everything else is rolling hills and frost-covered evergreen trees.

It's certainly beautiful here, and the view acts as a small distraction. The bite of cold that reaches me, even from inside these walls, is another diversion.

It's not enough, though. It never is. My mind still considers all the ways the Night Bringer can bring my nightmares to life. The ways he can hurt me and everyone I care about, despite the bargain Rev negotiated to keep us protected.

I shiver.

Rev's fingers drift over my waist, his chest pressed against my back. He pulls me against him, lending me his warmth. He's been like this—caring and devoted—since I came back from my last stint of banishment. After we'd bonded. He's mine, and I am his—for these few days, at least.

It's an incredible luxury that I know I can't keep for long. But Rev was right when he said we should take every moment of happiness we can get before our paths diverge. Because they will. Rev is the High Heir, destined to rule the entire continent for a hundred years. I am the rightful heir to the Shadow Court, and I intend to take my place there. We can't both achieve our dreams and remain together.

Not that duty and distance will change our hearts, but it will never be like *this* again.

"It's beautiful here," I say softly.

"Mmmm," he says in response, nuzzling my neck.

"Are you cold?" he asks.

I shake my head.

"You keep shivering."

I lay my head back against his shoulder. "I'm okay."

Rev is better suited to the cold here in the Frost Court, considering he grew up only a hundred miles away, where snowstorms would occasionally hit his lands.

In the Shadow Court, we had cool winters, but it only snowed a handful of times. And when it did, it was very uncomfortable. We didn't have fur coats or heated buildings to keep us warm. We had a tiny hearth behind rickety wooden walls and old woolen blankets.

"What are you thinking about?" he asks. "Really."

"I'm trying not to think about it," I admit. "But my mind keeps jumping back to all the ways they can hurt me."

Rev grabs me by the upper arms and spins me to face him. The intensity on his face takes my breath away. "Then, focus on how *we* can hurt them."

The problem with that is that we have very few options. I nod quickly, even so. He's right. Focus on the proactive. Create a plan. It'll help me not fall into the panic.

"We need an ancient," I state the obvious. Because the only way we can balance the power difference is by soliciting the help of other beings like them—the ancients.

The Night Bringer and his mate are each more powerful than any fae could ever hope to be, even with the spell book and a bargain. We need more power, or we'll lose.

"There are three other ancients still alive," he says. "The Light Ancient that has already tried to kill you and destroyed the High Court."

"*Almost* destroyed the High Court," I amend. But then again, it's currently unlivable, which is why we're hiding away in the Frost Court.

Rev rolls his eyes. "There are two others."

"The Lady of the Lake and the nomad," I say. These are things we've been through a hundred times—things we've asked the spell book to explain over and over. We know that the nomad is the weakest of all the ancients and most likely can't help us at all. "The nomad is awake and living in the Twisted Forest." Which is nearly impossible to journey through. The vines are alive and will only allow fae with magic of the forest to pass. "He is the weakest of all the ancients, though. Along with the spell book, he could bind *one* of the Night Ancients in a prison-like the Schorched-lands, but he doesn't have enough magic to bind them both."

If we trap one and not the other, we're doomed all the same.

"The Lady of the Lake is strong enough to bind them both, though. That's what the spell book said, right?" Rev says calmly, guiding me in the direction I know he wants me to head.

"She has enough power to bind both the Night Bringer and the Night Terror with the spell book's guidance and power."

Rev nods. "She's our best bet."

"She's also slumbering beneath the lake beside one of your ally's kingdoms."

Rev doesn't react. I don't think King Raijin of the Crackling Court will be very pleased if we were to risk his kingdom. "But the last ancient..."

Rev narrows his eyes, shoulders tensing.

"Is the Light Ancient, who was once king of all the ancients, and is resting beneath the High Court and has the power to *kill* both the Night Terror and Night Bringer."

"Again, he's the ancient that nearly destroyed the High Court the last time someone tried to wake him. And he will almost certainly kill *you* if we talk to him."

I frown. He's not a fan of Shadow fae, apparently. We were able to convince him to go back into his slumber without taking action—aka killing me—but he was still not pleased. Asking him for help would be... a challenge.

"I'd like to know more about him," I say, knowing how Rev feels about this subject. "We very well may require his help." I shrug casually.

"Caelynn," Rev warns.

"Just information," I say, appeasing him. "If we end up needing him, it's best if we know as much as possible."

Rev's resounding sigh is exasperated. "You've heard everything there is to hear, haven't you?"

I shrug. "I doubt it's possible to hear all of it." But he's right, I've heard this story already. The story of how the Light Ancient became king and was betrayed by his own mate. But it's an important one. Not only does it explain the origins of the beasts we're battling and their conflicting motives, but it also explains how his mate betrayed him and why. Maybe I obsess over this too much, but when the key to winning a literal war hates you—well, it sure seems important to understand why.

"It's a distraction," I whisper, against his neck.

"I can think of more preferable distractions." His hands curl around my thighs, squeezing gently. My breath hitches. As much as that would be enjoyable... my stomach is still in knots. My mind still spins. I can't... I have to divert myself with hope of winning this battle.

"I need this," I whisper. "I need to focus on ways to win, or I'll—"

Rev waves his hand. "I get it." His fingers still dig into my thighs as he turns to spell book. "Please tell us the whole story."

3

CAELYNN

Many ages past, at the beginning of all things, there was a tribe of beings blessed by the maker to build their own world as they saw fit.

Most of the ancients believed they were being tested, but not one of these beings agreed on how to pass this test.

Some thought to reign over their creations, calling themselves kings and queens. Some thought to make a successful world with mortal beings that ruled themselves. Some thought the world was their playground, a chance to experiment—they were not afraid to set it ablaze just to watch it burn.

After a few hundred years, the fighting began between the ancients, until only a dozen remained. None of the ancients truly wanted a ruler, but they agreed that the fighting would continue without a clear hierarchy.

Therefore, the Ancient of Light was crowned king of all and given additional power by every other ancient. He ruled along with his mate of shadows.

Under his rule, the ancients' role was to create and oversee a society that could one day rule themselves, and each ancient claimed land, some alone, some sharing with others. They lent their power to soil and stone and water and air. Each province became its own court. The king allowed each ancient to govern their court and only interceded during times of conflict to resolve a dispute.

The ancients had millennia of peace after the crowning of their king. And eventually, the fae began ruling themselves, creating their own laws and customs and cultures. Many ancients believed they had served their purpose and began the process of withdrawing from their creations.

At one final meeting between all the remaining ancients, the King of Light laid one final decree—the fae would have full autonomy over themselves and their lands. The ancients could remain, but they would have no control or say in how the fae choose to rule. They would have their own established hierarchy that did not include the ancients.

To complete this decree, a ritual would need to be completed to magically bind all ancients from interfering with fae royals.

A small group of ancients disagreed with this decision, but they did not speak out during the council, believing the king would not listen and would force the bargain on them. Instead, they plotted an insurrection.

The King of Light's own mate drugged him during the ceremony before the final ritual. The Shadow Queen's brother—the Night Bringer—and his mate led an attack the moment the king was unconscious.

The Shadow Queen did not anticipate that the others would try to kill her mate while he was weakened—a naïve oversight. She fought back against her brother and his mate. She fought fiercely, long enough for other ancients to join the battle. The Night Bringer and his mate were wounded and fled. Many believed them dead.

When the Light King awoke, he was immediately aware of his mate's betrayal and killed her before she could utter a word, then he withdrew from the world and still to this day slumbers beneath the site of the final council.

My head falls back against the cushions of the couch behind me as my mind spins through all the possibilities.

The Light King is the key to this war, I know it. But Rev is determined to find other solutions. He wants to explore the option of the ancient beneath the Black Lake, which is fair, I suppose. But my mind is stuck here—the most powerful being to ever live in this world hates me simply for being a Shadow fae.

The fire flickers softly, filling the room with cozy warmth while snow falls lazily outside the large window.

"So, based on all of that," Rev says, pacing beside the coffee table, eyes cast at the old leather tome, "shouldn't the ancient king desire the death of the Night Terror?"

That's a fair question. Only a week ago, the ancient king from the story was raised from his slumber—and almost killed us. The enemy of our enemy should be our friend... in theory.

"*Should is not always reality, Prince,*" the voice hisses from the magical book, laid open for us.

I frown.

"Did he answer?" Rev asks, turning to me. I blink, *oh right.* I'm the only one that can audibly hear the magic book that apparently knows *everything.* Well, almost everything. He can't see inside anyone's mind. He doesn't know intentions.

"He said 'should is not always reality.' Which isn't really an answer," I chide.

This time, writing appears on the worn pages, and Rev leans over to read his response.

The king does not know everyone involved in the insurrection; he knew only that his mate drugged him. He went to sleep immediately after her death. His slumber was deep —he knows nothing from that moment to the moment he was awoken.

My eyebrows bounce up, filling in the gaps myself. His mate was a shadow ancient, the creator of Shadow fae, and she betrayed him. Whatever her motives or thoughts during all of that—he hates her, and by extension, me. "And he distrusts Shadow fae so deeply he won't believe us if we try to tell him," I guess.

"Correct."

"What would happen," Rev asks, turning on his heel and pacing as he thinks. "If I were to call on the king again? Without Caelynn."

"No," I snarl. "I will not allow you to put yourself at risk without me."

Rev smirks in my direction. "We're talking hypothetical. We need as much information as we can get. Remember?"

I sneer at him but don't say anything more. I hate when he throws my own words back against me.

"Would it destroy the High Court island?" he asks.

No, not immediately, the book writes. **The king has returned to a restful state, but he is not slumbering as before. He is... waiting. Watching. He would only destroy the High Court if that was his desire. He is now aware of how his power affects the island and courts. Assuming his own philosophies have not changed during his slumber, it would stand to reason he'll be careful not to interfere with his creation's ruling structure.**

Which would include the High Court in general.

"Was it the Night Bringer's idea? To raise him?" I ask.

No, the book writes.

"But it was Blane, Drake's brother, that completed the spell." That much we've learned over the last week. "So, it was Drake's idea, then?"

From what I can tell, Blane originated the idea. Drake was unaware, but he certainly used the situation to his advantage and attempted to aid the destruction of the portal to ensure as many powerful fae died as possible.

"He was trying to increase the likelihood of our deaths," I say.

"And he almost succeeded," Rev adds.

"Does Blane still have Raven?" I ask quickly.

Yes. They have fled back to the human world.

I purse my lips. So, Drake nor the Night Bringer seem to have been aware of the spell to wake the Light King—the only living creature able to kill them.

"Are we sure Blane didn't wake the Light King to try to stop the Night Bringer?"

Rev's eyebrows rise, his eyes dancing with amusement. I shrug. May as well ask about every possibility. "That's wishful thinking, don't you think?"

I swallow. I mean, yeah, he has my friend. If he wasn't as much of a douchebag as his brother, that would be great to know.

I do not know his intentions, but I do know he woke an ancient beast, knowing it would kill many fae in the process. Hundreds died that day.

My stomach twists. I know very well where the spell books stands on the concept of raising the ancient king to join our team against the Night Bringer, it's just... we don't have many other options.

And I am willing to do anything required to kill those assholes.

A thud reverberates through the room, and I flinch before realizing it was only a knock on the door. Rev quickly answers, only opening the door a crack and speaking discreetly with the messenger. Rev sniffs as he turns back to face me, his shoulders back and head high. He always gets all proud and formal when High Court duty comes to call.

He wears a gold jacket over a black tunic that dips just low enough to see the outline of his muscled chest. His tattoos are entirely covered, sadly.

His dark hair is growing long quickly, and he has to brush it to the side to keep it from falling into his eyes.

"I'm needed in a meeting. Apparently, something has happened in the Crystal Court."

My stomach sinks. "Go."

Without waiting a beat, Rev is out the door. "Tell me," I say firmly to the book the moment the door clicks shut. My mind jumps immediately to Kari, the princess of the Crystal Court. She's one of my few true friends.

"*You should really work on your manners, young one.*" The book's low voice floats through the air, along with a sizzle of magic.

I roll my eyes. "Please, tell me what happened in the Crystal Court."

The book hums in pleasure like a damn kitten, and then a few pages flip. My eyebrows furrow—he doesn't usually show anything written when it's only me.

I scooch in closer to the table.

An image sketches itself in black ink. It's the inside of a temple, with statues and plaques on the wall, but it's in ruins. The statue on the right lays in three pieces. The one in the middle is decapitated. Rubble is scattered all over the floor.

"What's this?"

"*An ancient Crystal Court place of worship. It is not currently in use, but it is a protected historical monument.*"

"What happened to it?"

"*A band of Shadow Court rebels destroyed it.*"

My heart drops to my feet. Blood suddenly cold. "What?"

Shadow Court, as in my people. My court. My heart clenches, stomach roiling so hard that my knees buckle and I slump to the ground beside the table.

I know everything that is precious to you. And I will take it away bit by bit.

4

REV

I hold my head high, shoulders back, as I march into the meeting room. Ice drips from the ceiling like stalactites, causing flickers of light to scatter across the room. The walls are shiny—more ice—with a slight blue hue.

The High Queen sits on a cushioned armchair. Red light from the flickering fire bounces off her eyes. Her mate, a fae from the Glistening Court, sits to her right draped in furs, and the Queen of the Frost Court sits to her left. Before them are a few fae I don't know—all Frost Court advisors.

"What's this about?" I ask just before I take an empty seat beside the Frost Queen.

"The Shadow Court has attacked the Crystal Court," the High Queen says. Her chin remains up, but she won't meet my stare.

All I can hear is my pounding heart as I drop into my designated seat beside the High Queen. My mind races through all the implications of this news. The Shadow Court was once a strong, ruling court, but it is now weak and discarded. Its citizens have been openly angry about it, to the point of celebrating the death of the last High Heir—my brother. But they haven't outright attacked any court in the five hundred years since they've lost power.

"The Shadow Court? Or a few rebels?" I ask calmly. There is a difference, though it may be small. The pit in my stomach grows.

"Rebels," the Frost Court Queen says quietly. Her long white hair is braided down her back and her silvery blue eyes are soft. "But there is more."

My eyebrows rise, but I wait.

"There was a wraith attack on the Crystal Court as well," the High Queen says, her eyes narrowed. "It began in unison with the rebel attack."

Several things whip through my mind as this new information settles. The wraith attack had nothing to do with the shadow rebels, I am confident of that. But perception is reality, and that's exactly what my enemies are banking on.

Control of the escaped wraiths from the Schorchedlands, we've learned, was gifted to the Night Terror's new ally. Drake. It's not a leap to suggest he sent the wraiths to increase the rebel attack and further vilify Caelynn's Court—to make them seem more dangerous than they are.

The Shadow Court is nearly in ruin since its fall from grace a few hundred years ago. They're weak and poor. A battle against them would be a catastrophe, but Drake could easily convince the fae realm at large that the Shadow Court is deserving of punishment if they are not only attacking one of the High Courts but also have a large amount of power on their side. No fae is a fan of wraiths.

I know everything that is precious to you. And I will take it away from you bit by bit. I blink back the panic rising in my chest. I pull in a long breath and force myself to think logically. Drake controlling the wraiths is an issue but not one I can tackle here and now. It's unlikely Drake pushed the *rebels* to attack. His monstrous allies likely tipped him off and he only used the situation to his advantage. Which means the rebel attack was legitimate, and that is the issue we must focus on now.

"What did the rebels attack? What were they after?" I ask, forcing my chin up.

"They were making a point, surely," one of the Frost advisors chimes in. "A message that they are not friends of the High Courts."

"They've sent messages in the past. Threats. Marching soldiers," one of the advisors adds.

"Those were protests, not attacks," another advisor says. "This is a serious escalation."

The group murmurs in agreement.

"If this was only motivated by anger—a message, as you say—do you really think they'd choose the Crystal Court to attack?" I ask, pivoting to the dark-skinned male. "The court whose princess has openly allied with Caelynn, their hero."

He purses his lips.

"Kari was injured in the wraith attack," the High Queen says softly.

My blood runs cold, and then my attention whips to her. "Is she alright?" I finally manage.

The High Queen dips her head in a small nod.

I pull in a breath and hold it for a few moments. The High Queen and the rest of the ruling courts do not like that I openly defend Caelynn. They think I'm biased. So, I withhold all of the things I long to say—to scream at these fae about how wonderful Caelynn is and how those evil monsters will continually try to vilify her and her people.

In reality, we do not know what the rebels were after. I know very little of the rebels in general, and Caelynn likely doesn't either considering she hasn't been to any inhabited part of her court in a decade.

I, however, have heard many rumors of unrest within the Shadow Court in that time. The Shadow fae are enraged at their standing within the court system and their general treatment. And from what I've heard from Caelynn about life in that region, I can't blame them.

"I'd like to look deeper into why and how the Shadow Court rebels attacked rather than simply label them terrorists," I tell the group.

The High Queen's nostrils flare, her fiery auburn eyes flickering. "They attacked a monument, destroying statues and stealing the gemstones that decorated their eyes."

"Magic-filled stones?" I ask quietly.

The queen nods.

"They are building up power?" the Frost Court Queen asks. "That is concerning."

"Or simply trying to survive," I add. "Are we up to date on the poverty levels in those lands? They are considered poor and weak, but do we know the full extent of it?"

The Frost Queen blinks.

The High Queen lifts her chin. "There is poverty in every court, the Shadow Court especially, but—"

I hold up a hand. "I don't mean to say that it excuses their actions. But I don't think our first assumption should be that they are building power to attack. A starving father will easily resort to theft to feed his family. The Shadow Court has a mere fraction of the magic that the other ruling courts have by this point, and a few old gemstones will do little to even the playing field. From what I understand, they don't even have enough to fuel their own palace, let alone the ability to access heat in the winters, clean water, or the ability to feed their crops. I don't think we should be worrying about their power to attack but rather what put them in the state of desperation to begin with."

"But if they have wraiths on their side, that certainly makes them a dangerous enemy."

I hold back a sigh. "We should certainly begin an investigation about the wraiths. There is an increase in wraith activity in general, so we should begin tracking that. We may learn a lot." There, impartial with the vague possibility of uncovering where the true control of the wraiths lies. "However, I don't believe for a second that the Shadow Court has control over more than a few wraiths. I believe the wraiths are a secondary issue. We must deal with the Shadow Court delicately. Punishing them could exacerbate the issue."

"And what would you do? Negotiate with the rebels?" one of the advisors says, his nose in the air.

I shake my head. "Certainly not."

"With the Queen of the Whisperwood?" one young advisor asks more sincerely.

"We do not know how deeply the rebellion is rooted in the royal court," the High Queen answers for me.

I nod. "We should investigate the wraiths and the rebels separately. We will prosecute any guilty parties caught. But we shouldn't punish the court as a whole with so little information. Even just a gesture of good faith from the High Courts may help absolve some of the unrest."

"It's a short-term solution," the Frost Court Queen says. "If the Shadow Court is as desolate as you claim—and I admit to hearing rumors to that effect—then it will take much more than good graces to get them into a healthy position where rebels will not be an ongoing issue. And if rebellion continues, retaliation will occur. War may be imminent. And with our own conflicts hanging over our heads we cannot afford to give a poor court charity..."

"They do not require our charity," I say, head high. "You're right that we do have very important issues to handle that outweigh the conflict with the Shadow Court. However, I do have a possible solution, assuming you agree with my assessment that poverty is the core motivator of the unrest."

The room quiets, all eyes focused intently on me.

"We will give them a new queen." My lips curl up in a wide smirk.

5

CAELYNN

I pace in the room while I wait for Rev to return from the meeting.

My stomach is in knots, the power in my chest coils. This is what he promised.

I know everything that is precious to you. And I will take it away bit by bit.

The Night Bringer is behind this. I know it. I feel it.

They attacked one of my personal allies. Wraiths hurt Kari.

That alone is enough to boil my blood and make me shake in my boots at the same time. No one that cares for me is safe.

No one and nothing.

He's going to use this conflict to destroy my court. Part of the bargain was that he couldn't attack our courts, but his allies can attack us—especially if there is provocation.

Kari may not retaliate against the Shadow Court, but there are others that would gladly go to war against my helpless court. *This is only the beginning.*

"Is Kari okay?" I ask the book. He pauses long enough to cause nausea to roil through me. "Is she okay?" I repeat.

"She is not currently dying, but she was bitten by a wraith. There are few fae in the realm able to heal that sort of wound."

I nod quickly, even as my teeth chatter. She needs Rev.

"Was it Drake? The attack?" I begin hastily tossing things into my backpack. I make a lot of assumptions, but I've come to learn that it's better to check because sometimes things are more complicated than they appear.

"Drake instructed the wraiths when and where to attack, yes."

"I'm going to kill him too," I tell the book.

"The world would be better off without him," it agrees.

I store the spell book in my bag, forcing it in between rolled up items of clothing. "Is it a trap?" I ask, stilling as the idea crosses my mind.

"I do not know intentions," the book tells me again, speaking slowly, *"but I see no specific actions that imply they are preparing for an ambush. They do know you will immediately help Kari, and anytime you follow their expectations, there is risk."*

I nod and finish closing the bag. "Thank you," I tell the book. "For all of your help."

"It is my duty."

"I know. But you don't have to give advice or kind words, yet you often offer them. Even when I'm less than polite to you."

The book chuckles. *"I appreciate the appreciation."*

I shrug and head out into the hall to find Rev. He's probably still in the meeting, but I'll be ready to head straight to the Crystal Court when he's through.

6

REV

I am the first to burst from the meeting room to find Caelynn. In my three days here in the Frost Court, I've spent most of my time in our rooms and the rest at a few meals and meetings. I've tried my best to show appreciation to our hosts—after the near destruction of the High Court island, the Frost Court offered us their hospitality. For the High Queen and I, that's not a surprise. But even after Caelynn's actions that saved us, most of the rulers do not look kindly on her. The Frost Court was one of only three that offered her a place as well.

But even so, I frequently receive looks of suspicion when I head back to my room, where they all know the Shadow fae is hiding. I don't know what they think of us lodging together. I don't really care.

Today is no different. I rush up to our rooms to find Caelynn and tell her we've got to go straight to the Crystal Court. But then again, I suspect she's already aware. Especially considering when I enter the bed-chamber, her backpack and the spell book are nowhere to be seen.

I grab my own bag and rush back down to find her.

Whispers halt the moment I enter the entrance hall, but I don't stop to eye the fae. I don't care who is talking about Caelynn and me. Or the Shadow Court. I only care about finding Caelynn to ensure she's okay after such shocking news, and to get to Kari as quickly as possible.

I force open the heavy front doors. Cold bites into my fingers, and I silently curse how *everything* here is covered in ice.

Once there is enough space for me to sneak through, I let the doors close behind me. Icy cold wind slams into my cheeks, and I wince at the sharp pain. It takes a moment for my eyes to adjust to the shockingly bright palace grounds, but then I make out the dark clothing and rustling blond hair.

My shoulders relax immediately, and I approach her calmly.

7

CAELYNN

Snow flutters from the blue sky, and I shiver, watching the flakes dance. I try not to think about the ash fluttering in the same way in Schorchedlands. I try not to think about what it felt like when they landed and seared my skin.

A fur jacket drops onto my shoulders, and I wince at the sudden weight, but then its warmth infuses into my body and I close my eyes. In my rush, I hadn't prepared for the short time we'd spend in this wintry court. In less than an hour, we'll be in the Crystal Court, where it's warmer, but the between time would have been very uncomfortable without a fur jacket.

"Better?" Rev asks, a small smile playing at his lips.

"Better."

"We'll be out of the cold soon," he says, like we're going on some pleasant trip.

I don't know if we'll be back here. I don't know what will happen next.

I turn back to the palace, where the royal family watches us from the front steps. The Frost King and Queen wear their glistening crowns of pure ice, their smiles polite and demure.

Their two children, a young boy and girl, are maybe fourteen at most. They whisper and laugh.

The High Queen also watches us with a flat expression from a balcony two stories up.

I'm not quite sure what the queen thinks of me now, after everything. She'd been fairly supportive of me during my time in the High Court, but then again, she had needed me. I was an important part of ending the scourge—a plague spreading across the land.

But the moment the scourge was gone, she banished me. Again. The queen knew I had nothing to do with the wraith attack, but that didn't matter. She knows quite well that the Night Bringer and his mate will not rest until I am destroyed. She'd rather be rid of me and the target on my back. But she was foolish to think that's all it would take to be free of their evil.

"You alright?" Rev whispers, his warm breath sending shivers down my spine.

I nod, though we both know it's a partial lie. I am eager to get to Kari. Part of me just wants to shadow leap—forget waiting for a damn carriage—but it wouldn't get us there much faster and it would leave me vulnerable. The last time I was in the Crystal Court, someone in the crowd tried to attack me. *Good times.*

I've always been hated. Ever since I was a seventeen-year-old convicted assassin. Every court except my own has vilified me. For good reason.

Rev sniffs and stands up straighter. "We're going to destroy them," he tells me as the carriage pulls to a stop right in front of us. "We will." He keeps repeating it because he knows I need to hear it. I need the reminder that we are working together to stop this. It's the only thing that's keeping me from spiraling into panic and rage.

I nod as Rev pulls open the door, and I slip into the small but cozy carriage. The seats are covered in gold velvet; the curtains are patterned with gold and silver embroidery depicting trees and flowers. Fae scramble around us, grabbing our bags from the palace steps and packing them all away.

It's strange to have this kind of treatment, but Rev is now the High Heir. The second most important fae in the entire realm.

I pull in a long breath through my nose and out my mouth. The carriage jerks forward, and we begin the short trip to the Crystal Court, back into the spotlight in a court that will hate me on sight. Just like usual.

8

REV

The carriage rattles as we pull off. Caelynn's chest rises and falls heavily, her hands wringing together. I drop to my knees on the ground of the carriage and lean in. She opens her legs to give me more space, and I press my cheek to her shoulder.

"She'll be okay," I tell her. "We'll be okay."

Her arms wrap around my head, squeezing gently. I can feel the slight tremor in her body.

"It feels so impossible," she admits.

My stomach churns. Caelynn appears so emotionless much of the time. She's determined and strong, but deep inside is a well of emotions so deep it's hard for me to fathom. She is deep where I am shallow. And while that's an incredibly beautiful thing, it also terrifies me because Caelynn is full of darkness and pain. How deep does it go? Is it ever possible to fully weed it all out?

"One step at a time, Cae."

The ride to the Crystal Court is short. We simply have to reach the edge of the Frost Court grounds and go through a portal, then it's a short way to the front of the Crystal palace. The trip is only a couple miles but we travel thousands.

"What if Kari isn't okay?" she whispers.

"She'll be okay. I'll make sure she's okay."

"What if Drake attacks the Shadow Court? He'll dismantle them before I even get the chance—" Her voice breaks, and I squeeze her tighter.

"This is a long game, Caelynn. He won't attack yet. And I intend to make the next move."

She leans back, a sad frown marring her beautiful features. "What move?"

"I'm going to put you on the throne."

Caelynn blinks rapidly.

"I have thought ahead two steps. First, we stabilize the situation with the Crystal Court. That means healing Kari and smoothing over any strains. Then, we take you to the Shadow Court and make you queen."

"What?" Caelynn breathes. Tears well in her eyes. "I don't... that doesn't—"

"We have a lot of work to do Caelynn, but if they're attacking the Shadow Court's reputation, I intend to counteract it. I will openly support your rise to the throne, and we will fight against our enemies from there."

"They'll... they'll be angry."

"Let them be," I growl. I'm not sure who she is concerned about, to be honest. The Night Bringer? The courts? The people? Her people? But it doesn't matter. At the end of the day, if anyone is angry about Caelynn living out her destiny by taking her place as Shadow Queen, let them be angry. It will not stop me.

"It's what you want, right?" I ask just to be sure.

She swallows and nods softly.

"Then, we take it. Now. Before anyone can stop us."

One shaky breath leaves her lips, and then she crashes

into me with fiery passion. Her hands clench at my jacket as her lips claim mine. Her knees are around my waist.

I kiss her back and resist the urge to chuckle as she attempts to devour me in this tiny carriage. Her hips buck against me. My blood boils with desire so thick it's hard to think past it. "We don't have much time," I force out.

"I'll take every moment I can get," she says between kisses. Her hands claw down my chest, over my now wrinkled golden tunic. I push the furs off her shoulder and then sweep her up, twisting so that I'm sitting on the cushioned bench and she is straddling me.

Have I mentioned I quite enjoy this mate-ship business? Her taste and scent wrap around me, burning through to my very soul.

Mine. She is mine, and I will not allow anyone to harm her. I will give her every ounce of happiness she deserves, and the very stars in the sky could not stop me.

The carriage jerks to a stop, and Caelynn lifts her head suddenly. Reality crashes back into us. This will be our first time out in public after the incident at the High Courts. The general public will not have changed their minds about her. For all they know, she's the one that controls the wraiths. In too many of their minds, she is the source of all this conflict.

I still have a lot of work to prove them wrong.

The mark on my forearm burns, but I remember to keep it hidden. The silvery magic of our bonding is only visible to us —so long as that is what we desire. And while it's not what we want, it's what we both need.

One day. One day, I'll shout to the world that she is my mate and I adore her.

Our rapid breathing mingles together, warming the coach to a near uncomfortable degree. Then again, it's not below freezing outside the carriage any longer. Caelynn pulls in a long breath, straightens her shoulders, and then pushes her way out of the carriage. Sunlight streams into the coach, and I blink rapidly. She turns everything off so easily.

Me? My face is red. My chest heaving. My eyes are probably still dilated, and I definitely have to adjust my pants. I try to channel Caelynn's ability to slip on that mask. I puff out my chest and become the High Prince, powerful and self-assured, when I step out of the carriage, but inside my body is still so wound up.

Caelynn stands still before a crowd of silent staring fae with purple eyes. The last time we were in this court, we ended the largest bout of scourge, where an entire city was at risk of being devoured.

And someone tried to attack her. I clench my hands into fists, remembering that moment and the rage that took over me, even then. Now, I don't know if I could control myself if someone were to come after her.

And they've certainly got more reason to hate her now that her court just launched an attack against theirs.

A large male with deep brown skin pushes through the small crowd and rushes forward. His cloak is silver and purple, his eyes large and full of obvious concern. "Welcome!" he says cheerily, louder than I think is necessary, but then I wonder if he wants to make it very clear we are not the enemy. Particularly Caelynn, with her black dress and golden eyes.

"Come, guests of the High Court!" he says in a near squeal. "Follow me quickly!"

I place my hand gently on Caelynn's back and guide her forward. Her body is stiff, and her expression hard. "Now may not be the best time to present anger."

She swallows and wipes the stress lines from her face like a painter has just entirely redone it. How does she do that so easily? Even so, her eyes are hooded and her mouth flat. Indifference isn't all that much better.

Instead of dwelling on how I want people to see her, I follow our guide past the small throng of people and through a back door of the huge Crystal palace. No one says a word to us as the fae ushers us down the hall. We rush up a set of steps and through another corridor.

"How is Kari?" Caelynn asks after another moment. We haven't passed a single other fae.

"I'm sorry, miss, I am not privy to much information. I was simply urged to ensure you arrive quickly and safely."

"We understand," I assure him.

"Here." The fae waves to a near translucent lavender door with uneven ridges. Gemstone. One of the most precious materials in our world. It is the source of our wealth. And the Crystal Court uses it as basic decoration.

I push open the purple stone door and then pause the moment the cool air hits me. It's quiet. Deadly still.

There are around a dozen people in the medical wing. Only three of the patient beds are occupied, but there are three healers and several visitors. The Queen of the Crystal Court is easy to pick out of the small crowd, with her glittering purple crown.

Her eyes narrow on me immediately, and I straighten my shoulders.

"Where is she?" Caelynn asks before anyone else reacts.

The Crystal Queen blinks, eyes shifting to Caelynn with a grimace. Several sets of angry and accusatory gazes shift to her. Two seated fae stand slowly, their fists clenched.

"Caelynn?" a soft voice croaks.

Cae's breath catches just as I notice Kari lying beneath the white sheets of the bed at the farthest end of the room. She rushes forward, paying no mind to the sneers and shocked expressions of the fae around her. Every single one shows open disdain and accusations toward Caelynn.

An urge to keep Caelynn safe pulls at my gut, and I follow right on her heels. I glare openly at every fae that would dare threaten her, even only in expression.

"Are you okay?" Caelynn whispers.

Kari responds with a cough, and for the first time, I allow my attention to shift to our friend. Her curly hair is matted, her eyes sunken. "I'll be alright," she finally answers and then winces as she shifts.

"Show me the wound," I demand.

Kari winces again as one of the healers leans from the other side of the bed to pull back the sheets, revealing an open grey wound on Kari's stomach.

Caelynn frowns, but she gives away no other emotions.

"We've done what we can, but it keeps spreading," the healer says in a near whisper.

"Caelynn had a similar wound in the Schorchedlands." I suppress a shiver at the memory.

Kari and the healer both stare openly.

"It was less than pleasant," Caelynn admits. "Rev healed me, though."

The healer's eyes brighten as he takes me in. "You can?"

I nod. I give one glance to Caelynn, noting her dark eyes and sad expression. With no effort, light flickers in my palm. When I focus on Kari's injury, the light brightens. Her back arches at the first contact of her skin with my magic. Caelynn squeezes her hand tightly.

It's always a strange feeling, to send one's magic into another, and that's certainly true now with Kari, but I realize how different it is, and has always been, with Caelynn. Before the trials, I wasn't well versed in healing. Healing Caelynn's arrow wound was my first time healing a serious injury in another fae, and I remember being shocked at how intimate it felt.

But now, now I wonder if that was because she is my mate. I didn't know it then, but my magic did. With Kari, there's a small sense of intimacy. I feel her magic and her essence in a way that's unusual. But more like breathing in her scent. With Caelynn, it was like… bathing in her soul. As strange as that sounds, I was immersed in her.

Everyone crowds the bed, peering over Kari, staring at the now bright pink flesh of her wound. I remove my hand gently.

"That's… incredible," one of the fae with the queen whispers.

"You made that look so easy," the healer says, voice full of awe.

Caelynn makes it easier to use my healing abilities, but I'm not sure how to explain that even if I could tell them she is my mate—which I can't. Kari knows, but with the High Queen's bargain that we never be publicly bound…

I just smile bashfully.

"How do you feel?" the Crystal Queen asks Kari, her eyes searching her daughter's face.

Kari takes in a long breath. "All right," she says. "But I'm tired."

The queen's shoulders relax. "You should rest."

The healer nods in agreement. "The other healers will want to come and see. But yes, yes, I imagine you'll need plenty of rest now. This… this looks as if it will heal entirely within a day."

"That's wonderful news," the queen says, her mouth tense, but her eyes are soft. Her gaze turns to me. "We have some other matters to discuss as well. If you're able."

I nod, and as the whole group prepares to leave the medical hall, Kari calls out, "Mother!"

The queen spins back, eyes wide.

"I trust Caelynn," Kari tells her with a firm but hoarse voice.

The others whisper frantically but hush quickly.

"I know," the Crystal Queen says, her eyes soft.

9
CAELYNN

I'm barely able to keep my shield of disinterest in place as I enter the meeting room with the Crystal Queen. My fingers tremble against Rev's palm.

The Crystal Queen doesn't like me—none of them do— but that's not what has me rattled.

The image of Kari's ashy face—the open greyed wound on her stomach—is stuck in my mind.

The room we enter is dark and still. The windows are covered by thick curtains. No servants follow us into the room; it's only me, Rev, and the Crystal Queen. It's a weird feeling to be alone with a queen, but then again, I'm holding hands with the soon-to-be High King.

The Crystal Queen pulls a lever, and a small fire erupts in the fireplace, casting the room in a warm glow, then she takes a seat in the stone chair at the end of the meeting table.

"I have a lot of questions," the Crystal Queen says.

I shift my weight from foot to foot awkwardly. Do we sit? Am I even welcome?

The Crystal Queen waves to open seats. "You may sit. The council is gathering as we speak, and once they arrive,

Caelynn may have to leave. They didn't expect your time in the medical wing to be so *brief*, however. So, we have some time."

Rev guides me forward, and we take seats beside each other near the queen at this massive table.

"What would you like to know?" Rev asks, his shoulders back, chin up.

The Crystal Queen sighs. "I'd like to know what the hell I'm supposed to do about shadow rebels attacking my court."

Rev and I both pause.

"Nothing," Rev finally says. "You should do nothing."

"Nothing?" Her voice pitches high.

"Yes," Rev says again. "The High Court is—"

"I disagree," I blurt out. Both Rev and the Crystal Queen stop to stare at me. "Obviously I don't want you to retaliate, but you should capture any guilty parties."

The Crystal Queen nods. "We've begun investigations."

"Good," I mutter.

Rev watches me closely for another beat and then turns his attention back to the head of the table. "There are a few nuances to these events that should be made clear before decisions are made. One, the source of the wraith attack was not the Shadow Court."

The queen's lips part, but Rev continues before she can speak.

"Not everyone will believe me about this fact, but Kari would and I am hoping you will as well. The Shadow Court does not control the wraiths. The Night Terror does."

The queen flinches.

"The ancient beast had an army of them at her disposal inside the Schorchedlands, and that has continued now that she is free. The wraiths are being used just as they were during the ball when Caelynn was arrested. To frame the

Shadow Court. Or in this case, make them seem like a significantly more dangerous foe than they are."

She frowns. "So, you believe this whole attack was orchestrated—"

"No," Rev says quickly. "The rebels are a real concern."

I lean forward. "But please understand that the Shadow Court is weak and poor. We don't have the ability to feed ourselves, let alone defends ourselves."

"Then, explain how and why rebels would attack my court if they are so weak. So in need of aid."

I bite the inside of my lip.

"We believe the band of rebels attacked the temple to steal the gemstones," Rev answers for me. "You could liken their attack to a father stealing to feed his children. Is it wrong? Yes. Is it understandable? Also, yes. No father should ever be put in such a situation."

The queen frowns. "Some in the council are concerned the Shadow Court is building power for an attack."

Rev nods. "I find that notion foolish, if I'm honest. They do not have enough power to fuel their palaces or their people. Their power is lacking, and their structures are failing. Such a court may be angry, there may be discontent that fuels some small acts of aggression, but—"

"If *any* court was to retaliate, it would be a massacre," I say.

The Crystal Queen blinks. "The High Court has a plan then? If this is true, and the Shadow Court is this desolate..."

Rev nods. "We have a plan."

We've got a lot of work to do to fight against the Night Bringer. We don't have the time right now to seek out the shadow rebels or resolve their poverty issues unless... he did say he intended to put me on the throne.

My stomach flips pleasantly and nervously all at once. I

have the power to reverse some of the damage that has been done to my court. But can we really do that and fight the Night Bringer at the same time? We are on the verge of war with an ancient power.

A squeal jerks my attention behind me where light floods the room.

The door to the meeting chamber swings open, revealing several imposing fae royals, each with a crown on their heads.

I stand, heart hammering. The High Queen's eyes flit up and down my body as she passes but says nothing. Rev's father is right on her heels, followed by several other kings and queens.

They file right into the room. The Crystal Queen greets all the others with a soft smile and firm embrace.

"Kari is well, thank you," she murmurs, to the Frost Queen as they embrace.

I scooch away from the table, toward the door, until a hand on my back stops me. I look up to King Raijin's soft yellow eyes. "Stay," he whispers.

I pull my hands behind my back to hide that they're trembling. This nervousness, this fear, is new for me. I'm used to being able to handle myself, even in the most stressful of situations. I never let them see me riled up.

But right now, I can't get that crawling feeling out of my stomach.

"*It's what he wants,*" a hissing voice floats through the air. I flinch before realizing I'm the only one who can hear it. The spell book speaks only for me.

I don't respond to the book because they'll all think I'm insane. No one other than Rev knows that the spell book is sentient, let alone that it speaks to me.

"*The Night Bringer wants to unravel you. You're letting him win.*"

I curl my lip, but I cannot react. These fae already hate me, and I'd prefer not to add certifiably insane to their list of reasons to mistrust me.

The spell book knows what is at the core of my anxiety, though. The Night Bringer is targeting everyone and everything I care about. Kari being injured was not a coincidence. Who is next?

I close my eyes as the council settles into their places. Rai is the last to sit, leave me standing alone.

"Caelynn." The High Queen nods in my direction.

"I can leave..."

"Not yet," Rev says quickly. "I have something to say before Caelynn takes her leave."

"Go ahead." The High Queen nods to Rev, who stands. Again, his shoulders are back, his chin high. He is so proud to be the High Heir. I'm happy for him, but it still makes my stomach sour because I'm selfish and stupid.

"We are all aware of the shadow rebel attack, and it is an issue we must address, even while we are in the midst of conflict with powerful beings. The Shadow Court has been a topic of conversation for hundreds of years. They were once a powerful court, but that is no longer true, in part due to the action of the High Court and the council. Both Caelynn and I understand the reasons for the dismantling of the Shadow Court's power, but I am here to declare that it is no longer necessary. The blood of the shadow heirs was the key to the curse that kept the Night Terror chained. But The Night Terror is now free, and there is no longer any risk in allowing the Shadow Court to regain their true rulers, their true power."

"You want to make the Shadow Court powerful again?" someone whispers.

"No," the High Queen says, "but we do believe the

Shadow Court is at a breaking point, and we must facilitate some healing or these conflicts will only get worse."

"Your plan, Reveln, is to reward the Shadow Court's violence?" the Luminescent Court king curls his lip in disgust.

"Not reward," Rev leans back in his chair. "We are simply going to give back some of what was unjustly stolen from them."

"Caelynn," the Crystal Queen says. "You grew up in the Shadow Court. What was your experience there? Did you witness rebellion or discontent? Were you truly as poor as we are being led to believe?"

"I—" I pull in a long breath. It's been a long time since I spent deep thought on my childhood. It's a painful subject. "I, technically, am a countess. You all will know what wealth and power that usually entails. However, I grew up in a shack without running water."

I let that truth sink in for a moment. The room is still, but the expressions tell me they are listening intently. Some give me shrewd stares, others sympathetic gazes, and the rest stare wide-eyed in disbelief.

"My father owned a small castle a few miles from the village where we lived, but we had no magic to fuel it. I assume it remains abandoned. Even in the village, we were poor in the truest sense of the word. I don't recall ever fearing that I would starve, but I do remember being cold. My whole family would cuddle up in one bed in the winter. It was the only way to keep warm. And my mother took me on trips into the Whisperwood weekly to forage for berries, even during the cold winters." The shadow sprites would lead us to areas where we could dig up roots to make stew. In the warmer months, we'd harvest blackberries, and that was most of what we ate for months. I'd never thought much about those things, it was simply our reality, but now

I assume we needed to forage, or we'd have starved. "We survived only on the natural magic of the Whisperwood. Our natural magic is fairly strong, and that cannot be siphoned from us. But even our farmers were barely able to make enough food to feed themselves, let alone the whole town. Some summers, the harvest was generous enough that we'd hold a festival where food was plentiful, but I only remember two of those in my seventeen years in the court."

The room is quiet, the kings and queens of the realm shift awkwardly and stare at me.

"Is there no wealth left anywhere? Are they on the verge of magical collapse?" The Crystal Queen finally asks.

"It has been a long time since the Shadow Court has reached out to the High Court for aid," the queen admits. "We generally assumed the Queen of the Whisperwood finally accepted their place as a lesser court and that their former wealth and power would never be reestablished. But because of that, we are not up to date on the state of their power or poverty."

"If the entire court is as desolate as it seems, wouldn't she have asked for help again? Swallow her pride and tell us her people are starving?" the Frost Court Queen asks.

The High Queen locks her jaw, eyes cast to the table. I look up to the ceiling to stop myself from reacting to the realization that the High Queen knew.

She knew the Shadow Court was full of poverty, and she still denied any aid to facilitate rebuilding even basic structures. She knew and did nothing.

"It's not our fault," I whisper.

All attention shifts back to me.

I blink. "We are poor. But it's not our fault. You did this." I stare at the High Queen. "You forced marriages, taking the most powerful fae from a powerful court until we had nothing left."

"We didn't realize it was this bad," the Crystal Queen whispers. "Reveln's comparison to a father stealing food to feed his children feels much more apt now that we've heard your story. I'd like to know what your plan is. How do we reverse their course?"

"You mentioned the shadow heirs," Rai says slowly. "I assume you mean the Shadowspell line, but it has been lost for hundreds of years."

Rev shakes his head. "It is not lost."

The room stills, but it's the High Queen who speaks next. "We knew one family with Shadowspell blood remained in the court; we just didn't know where. It's why we continued to force marriages that weakened the court."

"You admit to this?" the Twisted Queen says, her eyes darkened.

The High Queen nods. "I'd like to remind the room that none of this was my decision. All of these events and decisions happened before any of us were born."

"No, you just continued the unjust rules." I release a shuddering breath.

It was that sacrifice that broke my ancestor, Darren. When he completed the spell, he didn't know the full repercussions. Or perhaps it was never intended at all. Maybe it was all a result of the botched magic. The Night Bringer was never imprisoned fully as they had intended. With him free, the courts knew he would forever seek out the right fae to free his mate. So long as the Shadowspell line existed in the Shadow Court, there was risk. So, they systematically weakened them.

Darren Shadowspell did what he could to save his children, but in the end it only got worse. His hatred for the next

High King's decisions turned him so dark he became a wraith for nearly five hundred years.

"The Night Bringer is the one who uncovered the Shadowspell line," I say quietly. "He never stopped seeking a way to free his mate. Your tactics to weaken the court worked for a time. He was unable to use other fae of Shadowspell blood to break the curse on his mate. They weren't strong enough."

"Until..." the Luminescent Court king says like an accusation.

"Until he tricked me into a bargain and gave me the power to complete it. It was all a big chess game."

"So, you." The Luminescent Court King stands, leaning over the table toward me, expression full of rage. "You are the culprit after all. We all suspected it, but we were so desperate for the cure we..." He shakes his head. "You were the only fae able to break the spell and release those evils beasts, and they are now free. You did this."

"No," I whisper.

"No," Rev says over me, his voice strong and proud. "I did."

I release a short breath. My stomach plunges. The Luminescent Court King was going to use this to try and bury me. To convict me of another crime I am not guilty of. But Rev jumped right in front of it.

"How?" someone whispers.

"While I was in the Schorchedlands, I met a wraith," Rev continues as if he didn't just drop a major bombshell. The kind of truth that could not only cost him his role as High Heir but get him arrested. "The spirit of the once High King. Darren Shadowspell."

"Truly?" the Crystal Queen whispers.

"He was... well, he was a wraith, and he had questionable morals and tactics. But he cared for Caelynn. He sacrificed to save her—and me, in the end. I did what I had to in order to retrieve the cure."

"Was he freed too?" the High Queen asks, her eyes glittering. She's as fascinated as much as the rest of us. "The wraith of Darren Shadowspell?"

"No. His soul was redeemed." Rev puts his hands in his pockets. "But he helped us to escape the Schorchedlands with the cure. And it was through him that we learned that Caelynn is his ancestor."

The room stills.

"And this long story was all to explain that we are going to help the Shadow Court by giving them a queen. Their true queen. Caelynn Shadowspell."

10

CAELYNN

After the shock of Rev's declaration died down, I was finally allowed to leave the council meeting, but that didn't mean that I had calmed down.

My heart still pounds so hard it's hard to think straight.

Caelynn Shadowspell.

Caelynn Shadowspell.

Caelynn Shadowspell.

Rev told the entire council that I am going to be the Queen of the Shadow Court. I will be expected to not only rebuild a court on the verge of collapse but put a stop to the rebellion.

I can do that, I remind myself. I have the power to refuel the magical well in the Shadow palace. That would be a great start to assisting the healing of my court. I've imagined that moment more times than I can count. It's just hard to imagine it could really happen.

And the thought that I could live out something I want that badly honestly gives me anxiety. The Night Bringer won't let me be happy. He's going to do anything and everything in his power to ensure I fail.

I shake my head and begin pacing in the hall. What now? Now that Rev has declared me the rightful Queen of the Shadow Court. Will we go there now? Or will we wait until after the war with the Night Ancients?

He said during the meeting that it's something we need to do even during the conflict. So, he means now? Like now now?

I shake my hands out before I explode from excitement and confusion and nervousness.

"Cae?"

I whip around to find a dwarfish fae standing at the entryway to the hall I've been pacing in for the last several minutes.

"You... alright?"

I release a breath. "Kinda," I answer Tyadin's question. "Not really." Ty is yet another friend at risk from the Night Bringer. *I know everything you care for...*

I can almost see the big red target painted right on his forehead.

He approaches slowly. "Kari is alright," he says. "I just saw her."

I nod quickly. "Rev healed her." But that doesn't mean she's safe. That was just a warning. The Night Bringer will taunt me before he begins plucking away the things that are important. Like Kari and Ty. Like the Shadow Court. Like Raven. Like Rev.

"So, what's got you so upset?"

"I—I don't know. I'm freaking out, I guess. Rev just told the whole council that I'm a Shadowspell, ancestor to the last Shadow Court High King, and that I'm going to take the shadow throne..."

Ty's thick eyebrows rise, but then his sweet smile spreads across his face. "That's fantastic news."

I nod. "I suppose it is."

"But…"

I shrug. But everyone I know is at risk.

"Cae? I know something else is wrong."

"The Night Bringer sent us a message." The words rush from my mouth before I think better of it. "He told me he was going to start taking away everything I care about. And that was minutes before we found out about the shadow rebels and wraith attack."

"You think this is part of his plan?"

"Kari's injury was." Again, her sickening wound flashes into my mind. If it weren't for Rev's healing ability, she may have died. I saw it in the healer's face. They didn't know how to handle that kind of cursed injury. "And the shadow rebels… well, he wants the High Court to turn against the Shadow Court."

Ty bumps me with his elbow playfully. "It doesn't sound like he succeeded."

I close my eyes and try to calm down—think this through rationally. "No. I suppose not. Not yet."

"You know how they play, Cae. Moves and countermoves. This was Rev's countermove, and it sounds like a good one."

I pull in a long breath. He's right. It's a countermove. "It's a chess match," I mutter.

"You'll never win if you begin to fear the game. Even if you don't want to play, it's important to keep focused."

I want them dead. I hold on to that anger. It's a weight that keeps me grounded. Hope is a new feeling, one I'm unsure how to maneuver.

Rev is placing something I desperately want right in my lap, and I'm afraid that will derail me from my war against my nightmare. I can't let that monster live, even if it means sacrificing the Shadow Court.

"What's your next move?" he asks.

"Take a walk outside," I say.

Ty smirks, amusement dancing in his eyes. "Can I join you?"

I nod quickly and allow Ty to hook his arm in mine. Part of me feels nervous to be near Ty, like I'm only making his risk higher, but I also recognize the need for a kind council. He's very good at advice. We walk down the hall and out some side door I wouldn't have known about. Guards lets us pass without question which seems—odd.

"You know your way around here," I note as we twist around a pathway and into a small garden, following the lavender and white stone pathway. We are in the castle court-yard, surrounded by mile-high crystal walls of varying colors.

"I've been spending a lot of time here."

"With Kari?" I ask, voice pitching high.

He smiles again. "Not like that," he chides. "We are making plans to merge our courts."

"Really?" I stop, shocked at this news. "That's fantastic." Lesser courts have fewer rights and privileges than High Courts. The Crumbling Court broke away from the Crystal Court due to fae rights issues. The dwarves were not treated well under Crystal Court rule, and the Crumbling Court was formed to create a safe place for them. But being a citizen of the lesser court automatically makes you considered lesser in our world. Merging the two courts would have a big impact on the fae in the Crumbling Court, like Ty.

"Kari is working toward a treaty that would keep the Crumbling Court council but make them an official part of the court. As well as a law that would ensure equal rights for dwarves and other fae species."

"That sounds amazing." A chill washes down my spine with a rush of renewed affection for Kari.

He nods again, his cheeks turning red. "She promised me a place as an advisor when she takes her mother's crown."

I suck in a surprised breath, more chills, the hair on my arms stand up straight. I'm used to those things as fear responses, but this.... this is pure joy. I turn and wrap my arms around Ty's large middle. "I'm so happy for you."

"And I'm happy for you too, you know," he says against my shoulder.

Then, I release him just as quickly and keep walking, maybe faster than I should.

"We've done all right," Ty says, rushing to keep up with me. "After the trials."

I allow a small smile. "So far."

"If anyone can do this, Cae, you can."

I swallow but say no more until we've curled all the way back around the courtyard, and I push my way back through the door into the palace. I stop suddenly, noting the confusion on Ty's face. "I'm really proud of you, Ty. You're going to do amazing things." I squeeze his arm affectionately.

"Why does that sound like a goodbye?"

I force a smile. "I'll see you again soon," I say, but I taste the lie.

I just hope that when it all comes crumbling down, some pieces can remain. Like Ty and Kari. I feel honest hope that if I step far enough away from them, even if everything else falls apart, that they can remain standing at the end of the story.

"It was good to see you, Ty." I tell him over my shoulder as I rush away. He skips forward, making to follow me, but I turn a corner, pull at my shadow magic, and disappear from view.

I wait quietly until he passes by, looking around in confusion.

He asked me what my next move would be. And this is it.

Step away, quickly and quietly, like the wraith that I am. I can only hope that keeping distance between us will help cushion some of the backlash they'll get just by caring for me.

II

REV

The meeting drags on, as all council meetings do. The kings and queens of the realm diverge from serious issues into court dramas and bragging competitions.

Until finally, the queen declares the meeting over. I eye the door eagerly but know that I can't always be the first to leave the room. My reputation as High Heir is already at risk with the fae in this room. If I'm always cutting out as quickly as possible to find Caelynn, that will not go unnoticed.

But even so, my stomach twists uncomfortably. I only have so much time left with Caelynn at arm's reach. Precious days before she's off ruling her own kingdom.

This is exactly what I'd planned, it's what we both want, but I am not eager for the moment I must let her go.

"You can go, you know?"

I jerk my attention to Rai. His yellow tunic and the blue metalwork lining his shoulders has him looking both ready for a political meeting and battle at the same time. His white locks are pulled back into braids and tied behind his head.

I take in a deep sigh. "I could, but I shouldn't. Not yet."

Rai smiles. "The queen will not strip you of your title for

eagerness to see a friend. Even if it happens regularly." He winks.

"No, but she won't be happy about it. And it's only moments. Besides—" I clear my throat and straighten my shoulders. "I did have something to discuss with you."

"Did you?" His eyebrows rise, revealing more of his golden eyeshadow. The Crackling Court has always been one of the more ostentatious courts. Somehow, they pull it off without looking like complete fools, but it's not exactly to my taste. "Then, that calls for a glass of scotch." He laughs and calls over a horned fae to fetch us a set of drinks.

I release a breath and sit back in my chair. This is good. A productive excuse not to rush from the room.

"You have a busy next few days ahead of you. Do you plan to set out for the Shadow Court immediately? I assume you intend to... escort her."

I frown at the use of that word. Will it seem like the High Court is planting a new queen for the court? Will that even matter at the end of the day? I suspect not. "I do intend to go with her. But I suppose that's up to her. If she'd rather go on her own..." My stomach twists at that thought. I find that I want to be a part of it.

I want to have a place in her new life, even if it's not a permanent one.

"But there is something I'd like to do before we set out. A stop on the way."

One of Rai's golden eyebrows rises as he takes a sip of his new beverage, just delivered moments before.

"Caelynn and I would like to visit Black Lake," I say, taking a long gulp of my own drink.

"Honeymoon?"

I snort. "Not exactly."

Rai leans back in his chair. "You're welcome to come visit

my court any time of course. Come now; stay for a few days. I have something I'd like to show you anyway." He swirls the gold liquid.

I simply nod. It's a good plan. "I'll just need to have our things sent to the Crackling Court. We didn't pack much due to the rushed nature of our morning."

"Do whatever you need, but I can provide anything the two of you may require."

"I appreciate that."

"I'd offer you to ride with me, but I didn't bring a carriage."

I smile. "And I'd say we don't need one, but given Caelynn's reputation, it's safer in the High Court carriages. Especially here, so soon after a Shadow Court attack."

"Then, it's settled. I'll travel back to my court and be ready to greet you when you arrive. No rush."

I stand and grip Rai's forearm "Thank you."

"It is my honor." He bows his head, squeezing my arm tightly.

12

CAELYNN

The surface of Black Lake is so smooth it looks likes one massive shard of glistening glass. The lake is larger than I'd pictured—I can't see the other side. This is a massive sea.

I was surprised when Rev suggested we go to the Crackling Court next, but it makes sense. This is where the ancient we need lies, slumbering beneath the eerily still waters.

"Is it always this calm?" I ask.

Rai stands beside me, admiring the lake, his hands folded behind his back. "Almost always, yes."

"What are the exceptions?"

"When a storm rolls through, the water—dances."

"Dances?" Rev asks.

Rai nods. "It begins as a gentle ripple, as expected. But at the height of a thunderstorm, the waves rise in unnatural formations. From the shores, it honestly looks like two figures dancing together. No ships ever successfully make it out to sea during these times to find out exactly what's happening. We only have legends to explain the phenomenon."

"Your element is lightning," I say. "You can't control the storm?"

He shakes his head. "We can control the lightning, but not the wave's reaction. Even the fae from the Glistening Court have been unable to control the lake when it rises in this way. It's as if it's protected by a great power."

"I suppose it is."

Rai whips his gaze to me. "It is?"

I purse my lips, unsure how much information to give to Rai. We're trying to make him an ally, but how much do we trust him? "There is an ancient slumbering here," I say quietly.

His eyebrows rise. "A beast like the one that destroyed the High Court?"

"*Almost* destroyed the High Court," Rev amends.

I nod. "One not unlike the being that rose in the High Court. One not unlike the Night Bringer."

Rai's eyes flare. "And how do you know this?"

"I simply do." That is where my trust will end.

He narrows his eyes and glances at my backpack. He suspects the truth, but I will not tell him that the spell book, which only answers to me, holds knowledge of every event that has ever happened in our world. The council knows the book has power and can grant me spells no one else has access to. Members of the council have made it clear they deem control of the spell book to be too much power for one —untrusted—fae to hold. And they don't even know its full ability. I don't plan to let them in on this secret.

"And you intend to raise this ancient power," Rai says calmly, but his jaw clenches. A soft breeze blows over us, rustling my hair. The water doesn't so much as ripple.

"We haven't decided."

"We would take your opinion into account," Rev tells him.

"Into account," he says through gritted teeth. "We all saw

what raising one of these beasts did to the High Court. And you would take my *opinion into account*."

"What happened to the High Court will not happen here," I say. "And yes, if we believe raising this power is the only way to save the entire realm, we'd complete the act with or without your blessing".

"But that would be a last resort. We both believe you to be a wise fae. You'll hear us out, and we'll honor your wishes."

"For now," he says, voice low.

"For now," Rev admits.

Rai shakes his head and runs his fingers through his hair. "How can you be sure it will not destroy my court?"

"The High Court relied heavily on the power of the king, and he was slumbering directly below the island," I answer. "It affected the very structure of the island when he rose. In your court's case, the ancient is miles off. There is plenty of space between your capital and the lake. I can't promise to be able to control the being we raise. But the rising itself will not affect your court."

"You cannot promise to control the being," he repeats.

"Raising any of these beings is a risk," Rev says, "but it is the only way to even our power with our enemies. If there was another way, I'd do it."

"Are there any other ancient powers in our world? There is nowhere else to risk?"

"There is one other, but he is the weakest of them all— not strong enough to aid us in battling two ancients. Which means we must raise the power beneath Black Lake regardless."

"Was it you?" Rai asks, eyes still cast out over the smooth water. "Did you wake the ancient power beneath the High Court?"

Rev whips his head in his direction. "Is that what you think?"

"I am simply asking."

"No," I say. "We had nothing to do with the destruction at the High Court. I didn't arrive until the attack began."

"Then, who did?"

I glance to Rev; our eyes meet for one beat, then he looks away.

"A prince from the Whirling Court," Rev answers.

Rai faces him. "You do not know which?"

"Does it matter?"

Rai takes in a deep breath. "What happened at the High Court? The being was roused. He spoke with you both. Nearly killed you both. What happened to him?"

Rev pulls in a long breath through his nose. "He settled back down in his resting place."

"And went into a deep slumber as before?"

We both pause, unsure if we should answer him honestly. "He is sleeping. How deeply... is up for debate."

A partial lie. He is not sleeping as deeply as before. He is resting, according to the book. But paying attention.

"Is it out of the question to request his help?"

"It would likely destroy the High Court for good," I say.

He nods. "That's not my question."

Okay then. "He hates me," I answer. "Convincing him to work for us... would be challenging."

"He would kill her," Rev says, voice grim.

Rai narrows his eyes but says no more.

"Can we take a boat out to sea?" Rev asks after several moments pass.

"Not without me, you won't," Rai answers sharply.

Rev chuckles and holds his palms up in surrender. "We wouldn't complete the ritual without your knowledge."

"Yet."

"We respect you, Rai," Rev says. "Truly. I will not make any decisions that could hurt you without either your permission or having no other choice. Do you believe that?"

"I believe it, but I do not like it regardless."

I hold up my hand. "I will promise to do everything in my power to inform you of our decision before completing the spell to rouse this ancient."

"You would make a vow?"

"No," Rev growls.

Rai narrows his eyes.

"A vow would make us too vulnerable," I say. "If you were incapacitated in any way, we'd be bound, and that makes us vulnerable to control. You'd become a target."

Rai shakes his head. "Logic is very frustrating sometimes."

"We are your allies," Rev says. "You will simply have to trust us."

Rai takes in a long breath, holds it for several seconds, and then releases. "All right, come on. Let's get that boat."

13
REV

The bow of the ship carves through the black water, which ripples like a sheet of silk. There are no waves. The ship does not even rock as I would have expected. This lake is impressively calm.

"This seems unnatural," I comment, staring at the sleek surface of the dark waters. Raijin's gaze darts to Caelynn on the other side of the ship as she also watches the water.

Rai nods. "There are no tides, no uncertain shifts. The water is as still as death."

A dark chuckle falls from my lips. "Death is not always so still."

Raijin's eyes meet mine, and they are softer than before. "I suppose you'd know more about death than any other."

My mind jumps to Caelynn. We both have faced more death than any single soul should.

"Tell me, what is your future with the Shadow fae?" Rai's shoulders relax slightly.

I hadn't expected that question in the slightest. "I don't know." I sigh.

His fingers clasp over my wrist, and he pulls my arm up to

examine it. The lines of our bonding shimmer in the sun but should only be visible to Caelynn and me. My eyes widen.

"You've made a choice," he says.

I rip my arm from his grip.

"I can sense it," he answers my unspoken question. "Can see it in your eyes. I may not have noticed if I hadn't already known…"

I didn't tell Raijin that Caelynn was my mate, but he must have read between the lines and figured it out during our heart-to-heart a few weeks ago.

"I will support you, you know. Support your union." His hard eyes find mine again. "Just don't destroy my court," he says, voice suddenly low and fierce. Then, his lips tick up into a smile.

I shake my head. "I appreciate that, but it won't be necessary."

He frowns, golden eyebrows furrowing.

"Caelynn will never sit beside me on the High Court throne for several reasons."

He crosses his arms. The wind picks up its pace, rushing and whipping our tunics back. "And what reasons are those?"

"For one, she vowed not to marry me while I am king. The queen forced her into that bargain."

Rai lets out a sharp breath. "Cruel, conniving…"

I wave him off. "It's not the only reason. Caelynn does not wish to be my queen. She wishes to be her own."

Rai purses his lips. "So, your plan to put Caelynn on the Shadow Court throne is not a temporary solution. She plans to be a true ruler."

"And she will. I will ensure it."

Rai is quiet for a time, and we stand there, side by side at the bow of his small fishing vessel, watching the smooth waters of Black Lake. Soon, we cannot see land on either side.

"It will be tricky. To be High King while your mate rules another kingdom. But I will support that too." He nods to himself, as if he just made a solid decision. "If any of the other kingdoms find out that you are mated while you both rule separate thrones, they won't be pleased. They'll assume you can't be impartial—which of course is true but irrelevant. No High Ruler is ever truly impartial. Regardless, you will have an ally in me. I promise."

"Thank you," I whisper. "Kari also knows. And my father... well, my mother knows. It's likely she's told him."

Raijin nods. "I doubt the Luminescent King will be eager to share that news. And you trust Kari?"

I nod. "Kari is a close ally."

"Well, I'd try to keep the list of those in the know to only these three. I—" He frowns and pauses. "I do wonder if it's a mistake. Being separated from a mate after you've bonded." He shakes his head. "I cannot imagine the agony."

I force a smile, even as an ache shudders through my heart. "I know. But I'm not going to take this from her, no matter the sacrifice I must make."

14

CAELYNN

I sit on the banister of the ship, my backpack nestled between my feet, and watch Rev and King Raijin talking. As the conversation continues, Rai's shoulders relax more and more.

"Tell me about the ancient here," I say quietly. A few of the crew eye me warily, and I hope me talking to 'myself' doesn't add to their suspicions, but I suppose, it won't make much difference.

"*What would you like to know?*" the book whispers.

I wrinkle my nose. "You're trying to make me have to talk more, aren't you?"

A fae with long auburn hair eyes me, brow furrowed, and then marches past.

"*Whatever could you mean by that, child?*"

I roll my eyes.

"What is her story? Her personality. Who were her allies, her relationships, her enemies?" Rev and I both have read a decent amount about the two remaining ancients. The being in the Twisted Forest roams quietly in the form of a massive wolf. The being here, beneath Black Lake, has not interacted with any living beings in a few centuries.

"Many called Rose dramatic. That's an understatement. She was an assbag, if you ask me."

I hold back a choking laugh, which of course causes more glances in my direction. I ignore them, giving up on acting normal. They hate me *and* think I'm insane, it's fine.

"She was beautiful and expected attention from all. She did not respect mated pairs and sought adoration from every being around, regardless of if it harmed relationships. Many of our kind disliked her for her attitude, and others frowned upon her many relationships with mortal fae."

"So, you disliked her because she slept around?"

"No, I said some disliked her for that. My issue with her was that she constantly attempted to seduce my own mate."

My lips part. "Your mate?"

The book quiets and remains so for a long while.

"Who was your mate?" I whisper.

"Her name was Aisling."

My stomach sinks, mind spinning. "What happened to her?"

"She was lost during the fight with the Light King. She sacrificed her life to stop the Night Bringer and his mate from killing the king. I later sacrificed my soul and free will to contain the Night Bringer and his mate. I do not blame anyone for the events that have taken place."

I press my lips together, trying not to let my mind twist down the path of guilt and shame.

"Death is not the end, child. It is simply the end of now. She is at peace."

"But... will you ever get the same?"

"That, I do not know."

"And you made this sacrifice... for what? The Night Bringer and Night Terror are free."

"They were not the only beings we fought against. They were

simply the last. And I am confident, that with you, we will finish this battle for good."

I close my eyes, lips trembling. Then, I let out a long breath and stand.

"I believe in you, Caelynn of the Shadow Court. You will complete my legacy."

No pressure or anything. My heart swells with fear and pressure but also pride.

I release a long breath and rise to my feet. I don't think I want to hear any more about these ancient histories. The relationships and sad stories. So many hearts and souls and lives have been lost to battling these beings that only wish to destroy. To control those weaker than themselves. I pull my backpack over my shoulder and stride toward the front of the ship.

Rev turns to me as I approach their spot at the bow of the ship. His brows furrow. "Are you alright?"

I force a smile, but my limbs still feel weak. *I believe in you.* His words echo in my mind. Very few souls have ever truly believed in me, my own included. Even my own parents didn't really believe in me. Or maybe they did, I don't know.

"*She is beneath us now,*" the book whispers.

I suck in a breath. "Stop the ship."

Rev blinks, and Rai spins to face me. "What?"

"Here, this is where we need to stop."

Rai marches toward the back of the small vessel, shouting orders to the crew. The sails are lowered, an anchor dropped. A fae in a blue cloak leans over the edge of the ship and waves his hands at the water. A water fae, I realize. Hired by the crew to aid in sailing. A convenience that is more luxury than necessity.

We may be with the Crackling Court, but the Glistening

Court is nearby, on the other edge of Black Lake, the Whirling Court above them, and the Shadow Court below.

The ship quickly comes to a halt in the middle of the lake; smooth unmoving water surrounds us on every side.

Rai marches back to Rev and me. "What now?"

"Have him use his magic. But no touching the surface of the water."

I pause, unsure what that would do. We're not trying to wake the ancient yet, not unless Rai is comfortable doing so. And I also don't want to ask the book for more details because that would look rather strange to a fae who doesn't know the powerful spell book is sentient. A fact I still don't want him to know.

"You don't know?"

"No, I do," I say slowly. "I'm just trying to figure out how best to move forward."

"She feels the magic when used near her. We'll get a small reaction if you use your magic near the surface. It won't wake her but will recreate what happens during a storm."

"She isn't entirely asleep," I tell King Raijin. "She feels the magic near her. Which is why you see that phenomenon during storms. We'll get a small reaction if you use your magic near the surface in the same way."

Rai takes in a long breath. "I don't know how I feel about this."

"I know."

"If it was your court at risk... how would you feel?"

I blink, surprised he'd ask such a question. I glance to Rev, whose soft gaze and smile is reassuring. "I would be nervous, but it is necessary."

"Is it?"

"Yes," I whisper. "You understand the threat at large, correct?"

Rai nods.

"Then, you know we can't do *nothing*. And we do not have the power to defeat them. Not without help."

He nods again.

"We did not complete the spell to rouse the ancient beneath the High Court," Rev adds, speaking slowly. "Someone else did. So, what happens if it's not us that rouses this one? What if someone beats us to it?"

Rai frowns at that. "I hadn't considered that."

"This is quickly becoming a war surrounding ancients," I say, frowning at the still waters beneath the ship. "We need allies. These powers will either choose us or our enemies."

"What happens then, if the response we get today is unfavorable?"

"Then, we increase security on the lake, keep a close eye on Drake, and plan according to the increased risk," Rev says.

"If we deem it an unworthy risk," I add, "to use the Lady of Black Lake for our cause, then we'll know we only have one recourse."

"Caelynn," Rev warns.

"What is that?" Rai asks, spinning to give us his full attention.

"I'll have to risk my own life, and the High Court, by approaching the ancient king a second time." I cross my arms and keep my chin high. They will find no fear within me.

The spell book growls. The vibration so strong, my bag even vibrates with his anger. Rai's eyes widen, staring at the bag. "Someone doesn't seem to like that answer."

"Neither do I," Rev says, voice low. He steps closer, leaning down over me. "I will not sacrifice you to that being —he will want you as a sacrifice."

"We don't know that."

"*Yes, we do*," the book says.

I roll my eyes, and my lips part, ready to tell the book off but then remember Rai. He may suspect more than we've told him, but I won't give it away entirely. I'll reprimand the spell book later. He doesn't know what's in the mind of the ancient king or what his intentions are. He's making assumptions just like the rest of us.

"So, those are our only options?" Rai asks. "We rouse this ancient power and hope she'll aid us in a war? Or we sacrifice Caelynn and the High Court island to the king, and use him in the war instead?"

I nod. "We wouldn't use this ancient for war, though. She won't be strong enough for that. We'll simply need her power to complete a spell to trap the Night Ancients again. But yes. We need an ancient on our side, or we have no hope of containing this evil."

Rai covers his mouth with his hand. "All right, what are my instructions for this test?"

15
REV

My stomach squirms uncomfortably as Raijin holds his hands over the railing of the ship. We'd decided on pulling up the anchor just in case we need to make a quick escape. The water fae stands at the ready beside Rai.

Lightning sparks in the Crackling King's palms and then flickers out.

He waits, watching the still waters glistening in the bright afternoon sun.

He takes in a deep breath and then lightning sparks again, crackling and sparking between his open palms.

I turn my attention to Caelynn. Her wide eyes are a dull bronze, her muscles tense.

Ever since she came back from the human world, she's been only half here. Her mind is constantly moving, thinking through all the what-ifs. I know she feels as though she can't truly rest until the Night Bringer is gone from this world.

The Lady of the Lake is only a backup plan to her. I know she wants to raise the ancient king beneath the High Court because that's the only way to kill her monster, instead of only banishing him.

I know Caelynn's tendencies to disregard her own needs to complete what she deems a worthy cause. She'd easily kill herself to complete her goals. And I am praying against hope that she won't resort to that again.

But part of me knows that raising the ancient king may be our best option. I just can't bear the thought of putting her at risk again.

Another flicker of bright light pulls my attention back to Raijin. His streak of electric magic rises twenty feet over the ship and then dissipates in a snap.

A breath releases from my lips as a rumble begins beneath my feet. The ship groans, wooden boards trembling.

Caelynn leans back, fear and anticipation in her eyes.

The once-still water ripples gently.

"Again," Caelynn whispers.

Raijin lets out a long breath through his nose and then holds out his hands again. He releases a bolt of lightning into the sky. It's flashes and crackles and then disappears just like the last.

"*Mmmmm.*"

Caelynn frowns. "Did you hear that?"

I nod.

The ship rocks to the side, knocking me into the railing. I grip it tightly, holding back a yelp of surprise.

"What's happening?" Rai calls out over the rumbling that is growing with each moment.

"*Hmmmmmmmm,*" the sing-song voice calls again.

Water sloshes several feet out. Black water rises in a smooth glistening bulge, like the crest of a monstrous crea-ture is rising. Around the figure, water swirls in a circle.

A sound suspiciously like a growl releases from Rai's lips.

"Just like during a storm," I call to him. He told us a figure would rise.

"Move us farther out!" Rai orders his crew. The wide-eyed glistening fae leaps into action and pushes his hands out toward the water at the bow of the ship. The ship groans as the water beneath us stirs and sloshes. We begin moving away from the rising black waters slowly. So achingly slow.

My breaths come out in pants as I wait. We all wait. Within the rushing black water, a set of glowing white eyes flash open.

A female with a head the size of an elephant stares at us from behind the smooth layer of dark waters. Her eyes are distant, hazed. Her expression lax. Her skin is dark with a near golden sheen.

She lifts her chin, gazing up into the clear skies above us and then whines. A shrill but sad sound. She's... disappointed? She usually only rises to dance during thunderstorms. It's what she expected when she rose from her watery grave.

She turns her attention back to us, only her neck and head are above the surface of the lake, and still, water remains in a thick layer between her and open air.

"The Lady of the Lake," Raijin murmurs, leaning toward her as if mesmerized. He holds out his hand, palm up.

I grab his upper arm and force him to face me. "No more magic."

"It's what she wants."

"You may wake her," I say quickly. "We don't want to wake her."

Rai blinks and recognition returns in his gaze. "Keep moving away," he says, eye glancing over my shoulder. "Faster!"

The water fae pushes harder and harder, and finally, the ship picks up speed. The dark female curls a lip in what appears to be annoyance. She rises higher, exposing shoulders and collar bones, and then a hand rises. She flicks two fingers in our direction. A whip of cracking white magic slams into the boat. Splintered wood flies about, sending the ship reeling, tipping sideways. Everyone onboard falls at once, screaming and clawing at the wooden boards. I cling to the railing as the ship evens out and smashes back down to the water, sending a wave at the ancient.

The massive female begins laughing. A haunting tune echoes through the waves like a sadistic melody.

"Below deck!" Raijin cries out. "We're taking on water."

The crew shouts in dismay as they rush below deck to check out the damage. The waters of Black Lake shudder. The ancient rises until her entire body is exposed. She is a hundred feet tall at least, but now she spins, her water rustling out like a flaring skirt.

"She's dancing," Caelynn says, crouching low but her eyes are intent. She too is mesmerized.

As the Lady of the Lake picks up speed, her form is no longer recognizable, and soon it's just a spinning waterspout, rising higher into the sky.

I rush to Caelynn just as the waterspout reaches the side of the ship, but Caelynn steps out, her eyes still unfocused. Her hands reach wide, and inky black magic blasts from her open palms.

A shield of solid black curls around the ship in a protective orb just as the twisting water reaches us. The crew scream in horror but then stop, staring at the black magic surrounding us. Protecting us.

Most fae only see shadow magic as secrets and destruction. Their expressions are full of awe as they realize what Caelynn has done.

The watery cyclone spins, slamming into Caelynn's

shield, shuddering. I grab her forearm to steady her and then turn to Raijin. "Get us out of here, now."

16

CAELYNN

I step off the ship and onto solid ground, teeth chattering. Salty water drips from my tunic.

"What do we make of that?" I murmur.

"*She has always been a fickle beast.*" Well, that's not going to help in convincing Rai to allow us to rouse her from her restless slumber.

Rai sheds his jacket and tunic, standing on the docks entirely bare-chested. A small redheaded fae scampers toward us, carrying his replacement clothes. My eyebrows rise, but then I turn my attention to wringing out my own clothing. Water splatters onto the uneven wood by my feet.

Rai marches to meet us at the end of the peer.

"Well, that was fun," Raijin comments. "You two owe me a ship."

The ship is half sunk, water now reaching the top deck. We were able to make it back to shore thanks to the help of the water fae. The hull had several cracks and even outright holes that were irreparable.

There are several more water and crackling fae on the docks, rushing to help all of the sailors from the sinking ship.

"She was disappointed there was no storm to dance in," I say.

Raijin nods. "But she's powerful. She could have destroyed us without a second thought."

I nod. "But she didn't."

Rai narrows his eyes.

I smirk. "We won't wake her. Not yet." If I'm honest, I'm not convinced it makes sense to wake her at all. But this is the course the spell book thinks makes the most sense. He openly dislikes the idea of approaching the Light Ancient.

"Anything else you two need from the Black Lake?" His eyebrows are high, he's hoping this business is done for now.

I shake my head.

He nods sharply. "Good."

~

Rai takes us back to his palace a few miles south of the lake where we change into fresh clothes. Rai seems in a decent mood considering we'd just barely survived an interaction with an ancient.

He invites us to a small meal with him and his mate, a lovely red-headed female who smiles shyly.

The palace is bright and bustling, covered in yellow and blue décor. The lights flicker with electric power, buzzing through every hall and chamber. There are no fireplaces, only the buzzing lights along the walls.

We sit at a small round table in a quaint dining hall where serving fae deliver plates of finger sandwiches and fruits. Rai recounts the story of our adventure on the lake to his mate who's eyes are wide. He seems to enjoy telling the shocking tale, though.

"It's a mystery we've always wondered about but never

thought we'd uncover. It is exciting to know the truth, even if I do fear the repercussion of having an ancient so near to my court."

"What do you think her reaction means?"

"Honestly?" I say, "I don't think it means much. She wasn't truly conscious. She wanted to dance in the storm and we were just in the way."

Rai frowns but nods slowly.

"Well, now that you are finished harassing the ancient powers in my kingdom—" Rai side-eyes me. "What is your next move?"

I consider what kind of surprise he could have for us as Rev tells Rai of our plans to eventually travel to the Twisted Forest, where another ancient is said to dwell, but that our next stop is the Shadow Court.

"We are taking Caelynn to the Shadow palace."

Rai's eyebrows rise, but his lips quirk. "As I suspected."

My lips part in surprise. "Really? Do you really think it's a good idea *now*?"

"It's a good idea for several reasons," Rev says, eyeing me like he expects me to argue again. Of course I want to go to the Shadow Court, like yesterday, but with everything else going on it feels... selfish.

The Night Bringer is out there plotting ways to destroy us all, and I'm intending to indulge in wish fulfillment. Even so, my mouth dries at the thought of walking through the gates I've admired only from afar.

"Caelynn has never been to the palace she is meant to rule. It is a wrong I intend to right."

Jaw clenched tightly, I keep my gaze away from the two males examining me. I won't show them the emotions welling inside. We have so much to do. Things we must focus on.

"Well, I have something to show you that may be of interest to you then."

I bite my lip and resist the urge to ask anything more.

After our short meal, Rai escorts us back into a carriage and we ride around to the north of his palace. The Black Lake can be spotted through the trees, glistening in the distance.

We follow a pathway into a small forest of massive trees stretching a hundred feet into the sky with thick pine-like branches. Little rooftops can be seen down the hillside beyond the copse of giant trees.

Rai stops at the entrance of a circular clearing surrounded by stones with lightning-filled lanterns swinging gently. There are several empty archways facing us, the insides rippling like water. They're portals. My brow furrows—he's taken us to the Crackling Court portal system.

The stone of the archways are all a smooth dark blue, with streaks of yellow inlaid, but at the crest, each has a carving representing the different ruling courts. Each of the ruling courts has a High Court portal within their palace gates, and a portal circle for the rest of the courts a few miles out. There are also scattered portals throughout the realm that are more for trade or recreational travel. These portals are made for royals.

I take slow steps toward an archway empty of the rippling magic of the others. Near the top of the archway is a plaque made of shiny black obsidian, with a raven carved into the stone.

The breath catches in my throat.

"You rebuilt it," Rev says, voice hushed.

King Raijin nods. "There were bits and pieces lying around haphazardly. It was a safety hazard." He shrugs casually.

The stone appears perfect. Brand new. No evidence at all

that it was in pieces recently, likely days before, besides a few small pieces of rubble scattered within the dirt around it.

"When was it destroyed?" I ask, and I run my fingertips over the cool stone.

"Oh, at least a hundred years ago. All of the courts destroyed their Shadow portals by then. Some destroyed them the moment the Shadow Court was removed from the ruling courts. Some waited to see if the decision might be reversed. But eventually, every court gave in and accepted this new reality. I've heard that even the Shadow Court destroyed their portals out of spite—not that they'd work with no connecting portal."

I sniff. "Why did you rebuild it if there is no place to connect it? If there is no magic?"

"Because I intend to finish it. I have a set of workers readying to travel to the Shadow palace to build the Crackling portal in the shadow lands and complete the spell to bind them. If you wait here for three days, we should have a portal ready to take you home."

17

REV

A chill washes over me as Raijin's words sink in. He's creating a portal from his court to the Shadow Court. A royal portal.

Caelynn is still as stone.

So many thoughts rush through my mind at this revelation. This is incredible for Caelynn, and for her court. I don't think even Rai could fully comprehend the kind of hope this will give them.

There are some interesting political complications here—complications that Rai is willing to take on because he knows this means a lot to me.

He's doing this for me.

I know how he feels about Caelynn. He has never acted kindly toward the Shadow Court in general. He made this portal because he knows that I love her. And he did it even before he knew Caelynn would choose to rule the shadow throne.

I can't even fathom the level of courage and heart and sincerity this shows in a fae that has quickly become someone I consider a true friend.

After moments of standing in shock, I throw my arms

around Raijin, pulling him into a tight embrace. He stumbles back with a laugh and then returns the hug.

"Consider it a gift to the new High Heir."

I pull back, hand still firmly on his shoulders. "It's incredible."

"I don't understand..." Caelynn whispers.

"We've all had our differences," Rai says. "But I trust in Reveln's judgment. And as I considered what a new High Heir would want as a gift—jewelry, gems of power, spell books, stags. They make good gifts, but they are not things you need or really desire. You'll have your fair share of those as prince and eventually king. So instead, I decided on something more personal."

Caelynn absently stares at the glittering rigid stone. In a few days, she'll be able to step through the stone archway to go home.

Her home. Not mine.

"It's a wonderful gift," Caelynn says with a nod, then her eyes turn sharp, one side of her mouth upturned. "But it's also a political move."

I flinch. "What?" I turn to Rai, expecting him to take offense, but he only smiles right back at her.

"Creating something of use for the High Heir," Caelynn explains slowly, carefully, "that no one else yet has. It connects him to your court in a profound way."

Rai chuckles. "Do you blame me for it?"

"Not at all," Caelynn answers.

"You will make a good ruler, Caelynn."

I have to resist the urge to hug Rai a second time.

Rai clasps his hands behind his back as he steps forward, toward the soon-to-be portal. "To be honest, I didn't know what kind of impact a portal might have when we started the project two days ago. It may only have been a symbol of good faith. Or perhaps it was a chance for the mate of the High Heir to travel home periodically. Now that I know you will be ruling your own court, I realize it will have more use than I'd initially anticipated."

I shake my head. "You have no idea what this means to us."

Rai smiles sincerely, his eyes sparkling. "You're wrong about that. I know what it means. There is no greater gift than to simply make your mate happy."

My heart twists in the most beautiful way.

"Thank you," Caelynn whispers.

"Yes," I say firmly, "thank you. I doubt anyone could top this gift."

"The queen may have forbid you from marrying, but she cannot take away affection or connection."

"Is the rest of the council going to figure it out?" Caelynn frowns. "How will they react if they do?"

I sniff. "We'll deal with it as it comes." The politics in all of this will get interesting, I'm sure. Perhaps once, I would have cared. But now, there is little I care about except Caelynn and winning this war. I refuse to fear the judgment of a few powerful fae.

"Some will scramble to support the Shadow Court to earn the High Heir's favor. Others will push back at every turn. With war already looming... Well, things will get worse before they get better. But I hope that this gesture will bring you some hope."

Caelynn steps beside me and curls her fingers in mine. "It does. Thank you."

My heart soars at just that small touch. At just the smile on her face.

"We won't be waiting for the portal to be complete,

though," I say quickly, eyes still on my beautiful mate. Her smile so rare it takes my breath away

Rai frowns.

"We will travel to the Shadow Court the long way. We have a few things to attend to on the way."

Raijin nods. "Would you like to travel with my workers? They will be leaving in a matter of hours, and there will be space."

I slip my hands in my pockets and rock back on my heels. "So long as they're okay with a short stop in a Whisperwood village, that would be wonderful."

18

CAELYNN

Rev and I walk hand in hand through the dark forest. The black leaves of the shadow maples glisten and dance in the wind, almost like they're waving at us as we pass by.

The ride to the Whisperwood was several hours in a cramped carriage with three other fae. The portal workers were more than willing to agree to a detour so Rev and I could stretch our legs and take a walk through the Whisperwood.

The shadow sprites bounce through the trees, whispering and cheering. The occasional wisp of a kiss tickles my cheek, and I shiver. But the sprites don't seem to have anything to say to me today. They whisper to each other, excited and hushed, but I can't make out the words.

We crest another hill, and the Shadow palace can be seen just on the horizon. The sharp peaks veiled behind grey clouds. My chest squeezes, not for the first time. I'm going there, now. For the first time in my life, I'll see my court's palace. I'll walk through those gates.

I half expect something to happen, to stop me from completing this lifelong dream. The Night Bringer will show

"

up, just in time to stop me, and swallow me whole. I don't get to be happy.

But I force down those fears and insecurities.

A blackbird flies overhead, screeching. I follow its descent through the leaves until it disappears, blending into the dark forest. I smile, thinking of Raven, even as my stomach sinks. I miss her, and I long to know where she is and that she's all right.

An inky black shadow about the size of my fist drops onto Rev's shoulder. He flinches and then laughs as the shadow sprite hops to his head and then back into the tree line.

"Have they spoken to you?" I ask Rev, nodding to the shadow sprites, leaping through the trees.

"Not much," Rev answers.

Well, that's more than I've gotten. "I haven't made out a single word. But they do seem excited." A group of about a dozen sprites leap after us, chattering eagerly. They bounce and twist and chuckle.

Rev smiles. "They are definitely excited."

My eyebrows pull down. "What did they say to you?"

"Home," he says, voice low. "That's all. Just 'home.'"

I meet his stare, his silver eyes soft. Then, I turn back to the Shadow palace just before it disappears behind another hill. "Home," I say softly, testing the word.

Several shadow sprites leap straight at me, and I wince as they latch themselves to my arms and shoulders. *Home. Home. Home*, they agree.

I chuckle. "I guess they liked that."

"They did indeed."

Rev pulls me to a stop suddenly. I frown, about to ask him what's wrong, but before I can get the words out, his lips are on mine. I gasp and stumble back, but his arm snakes around my waist, and he pulls me in tighter.

Heat floods my whole body, and I allow the feeling of being adored to fill me. To own me, here and now. Because I may never feel it again.

The bittersweetness of going home, gaining what I've truly wanted since I was a child, means losing something I didn't know I needed until I had it. The sprites squeal and cheer, and their cool magic tickles over my head and shoulder and back and legs.

Rev pulls away, leaving me breathless. He too is covered in little wisps of shadows. His smile is smug. "I think they liked that too." He holds up his arm to examine two of the little creatures holding tightly to him.

"What was that for?" I ask, still in a daze. My chest is buzzing as much as the shadow sprites. Fluttering and wonderful.

Rev's smile fades quickly, and his eyes turn intense. "I love you, Caelynn."

I suck in another breath, mind dizzy.

"And we don't get many chances to do this. We probably won't have many more." The pad of his thumb drifts over my jaw. "I just didn't want to let another opportunity pass by."

I try and fail to hold back a bashful smile. "I still can't convince myself that I deserve this."

He grips my chin between firm fingers. "You do," he swears fiercely. "You deserve so much more than I can give you." He kisses me again, quick and soft.

Then, Rev links his hand back in mine and tugs me to continue our stroll through the Whisperwood. The sprites follow along behind, like a little train of fans.

"I love you too, you know?"

His smile is amused. "I know."

We continue to walk the final mile through the forest,

shadow sprites and phantoms alike following along inside the tree line. When we finally reach the last tree, I stop.

Down below, past the valley and field of tiny black flowers, the village is visible. Smoke puffs up from a few chimneys, but otherwise it's still. Just a few dozen rows of rickety old cottages.

"Is this it?" Rev asks.

I nod. My heart is heavy, stiff. Fear and pain and regret and hope and nostalgia, and many more emotions I couldn't name, weigh down on me. "This is the village I grew up in."

19
REV

We pass the Crackling Court carriage in the valley just before the village. Charles smiles and waves as we pass. We're taking a bit of advantage of these fae, but they don't seem to mind waiting for us to enjoy our small moments between. I'll have to show them my appreciation later.

The trip from Crackling Court to the Shadow Court would normally take at least two days, but we took a shortcut through a portal to the east of the Crystal Court which cut the trip into less than half. Even without detour, we hope to be at the Shadow palace before sundown.

"This is where my classes were," Caelynn says, pointing to a large tree in the middle of the field.

I had private lessons with several tutors inside the Luminescent palace. She had hers in a field of tall black grass.

We continue up the small hill then reach the first row of wooden, hand-built houses, and the air becomes stagnant. Three fae up the street freeze, eyes turned toward us, their dark clothes little more than scraps. Caelynn keeps walking down the soggy pathway, and so I follow her lead.

My heart pounds as we pass the staring fae with gaunt faces.

At the next street, wafting smells of sewage reach me, and I recoil.

"No plumbing," Caelynn tells me with a sad smile. "My family had an outhouse, but not all do."

My eyebrows rise, but I don't ask any additional questions. The high-pitched squealing of windows pulling open catches my attention. Heads pop out from several windows lining the street.

"It's a small town," she tells me. "They notice when someone doesn't belong."

Heads with pointed ears and scraggly hair pop out of the windows. Dark eyes watch us, their expressions blank.

"Do they recognize either of us?" *Will we be safe?* Is the question I don't ask. Because I know there are people in this part of the fae realm that celebrated my brother's death. The death of the High Heir.

Caelynn shrugs, but I don't suspect she grasps my meaning. She seems unbothered or at least too distracted to dwell on it. Her eyes flicker with bright golden light. She must feel some pain or worry being back here after so long, but obviously the good outweighs the bad.

A murmuring crowd gathers, watching us. No one approaches.

"It's Caelynn," I hear someone say in the crowd.

"What's she doing here?"

"Who is that with her?"

I keep close to Caelynn as she walks slowly toward the center of town, nearer to the small crowd. They're so thin, I realize. Children with bloated bellies but nail-thin limbs. Adults with sunken eyes, gaunt faces, and raged clothing.

I don't comment. I don't dare let my eyes linger too long

on any one of them, even the children that laugh and point in our direction.

The crowd shifts to the side as one as we pass through the town square. There is a tiny, dry well. Dirty streets, lined with trash and weeds.

I have so many questions. Was it like this when she lived here? I heard her speak a little bit about her life in this village, but not enough. There is so much more to know.

But now is not the time to ask it.

The crowd doesn't move to follow us, but their eyes never leave us as we venture down a side street until we reach a small home with a thatched roof and crooked wooden door.

Caelynn stops in front of the door and goes entirely still. I don't have to ask if this is it, her childhood home.

I let her stare for several moments while the crowd still watches us. Then, finally, I knock. The gentle pounding echoes through the quiet streets.

Without even a moment of pause, the door swings open, and I hold my breath as a female with pitch-black eyes and long black hair opens the door.

Caelynn releases a breath. "Hello, Mother."

20

CAELYNN

My mother doesn't look the same as I remember. Her eyes are so dark they appear black. Her hair is matted, and her clothes hang off her.

My heart pounds, but I'm not sure I'm breathing.

With an expressionless face, my mother steps back, holding the door wide for Rev and me. Somehow, I find the strength to step through the door and into my home from ten years past.

Rev steps in after me, his hood still up over his head.

I blink in the memories as my sight quickly adjusts to the darkness inside. Curtains cover the windows, keeping all light out. Dust lingers everywhere. But otherwise, everything is exactly as I remember it.

A small curved cot sits in one corner, and two waist-high shelves, still filled with books, create a nook in the other. My books. I almost smile as I recognize a few of the titles on the spines. But there are too many bad thoughts to allow it.

My heart is heavy with so many what-ifs, and the fear my mother still hates me.

"What are you doing here?" Her voice is quiet but unkind. Or maybe that's my imagination.

I spin away from the spot that was once my comfort, the corner where I used to hide away from everything for a while, reading about fae of the past. I face my mother. Her expression is hard now. Angry. She stands next to the hearth, rusted and full of discolored water.

"Nice to see you too," I whisper.

"Oh please, Caelynn. Don't act like you aren't at fault for all of this."

My breath catches. "I didn't say that."

"How is she at fault?" I blink as Rev's deep voice registers. Rev is here, with me. Defending me.

Her attention jerks to Rev. "Who are you?"

Rev pulls his hood down, but my mother doesn't immediately react. Her eyebrows pinch together as she takes him in. "My name is Reveln."

Her eyes widen, and her shoulders stiffen. "You..."

He nods.

"You're his brother."

I swallow, and then force myself to take in a long breath.

"You're the High Prince."

"Thanks to Caelynn, yeah."

My mother's eyes narrow, but she doesn't speak, though I can tell she wants to.

"Don't give me credit for that," I murmur.

Rev shrugs, his soft eyes turning to me. "You saved my life. You are the only reason I succeeded in retrieving the spell book. I shouldn't have even won the Trials. All of that was you."

I open my mouth to speak, but my mother beats me to it. "She killed your brother," she spits. "Murdered him."

"Yes," Rev says, his eyes still haven't left mine. There is no shame or anger left there. Only unconditional love.

"She released those beasts. She failed at what her father gave his life to keep from happening."

My limbs feel suddenly weak, but I can't show any of that now. I can't fall to the ground the way my body wants to. I will stand for the next few minutes. I will survive this.

This, this is just another repercussion of my actions. A parent who will never respect me again.

Did my father die hating me the same way my mother does now? Or did his death increase her anger?

"She didn't free them," Rev says. "I did."

My mother blinks. "No, you don't understand—"

"I understand it all," he says quickly. "Your husband gave his life to stop the Night Bringer from using him. Caelynn gave her life for the same cause, only I didn't let her."

I close my eyes against the wave of emotions, both good and bad that rush inside me now.

"I used her magic through our bond and freed the monster in order to save her."

My mother's mouth parts as she stares at him. "You..." She shakes her head. "Your bond?"

Rev nods, his eyes soft, but it's me who answers. "We're mates," I whisper.

~

"How?"

Rev snorts. "Hell if I know."

"Rev," I chide.

He quirks a brow. "You don't choose your mate," he says more seriously. "I would never have chosen Caelynn for mine, but the fates know better than we ever could. She's everything."

I pull in a breath and hold it.

The moment lingers. Rev holds my stare, and I don't know how to react. Finally, Rev smiles again and then turns his attention to my mother. "We didn't come for your forgiveness. Closure, maybe. But we also came to warn you."

"Warn me," she repeats.

Rev nods. "The Night Bringer has made threats to destroy everything that Caelynn loves."

I release the breath I'd been holding. Her face doesn't change. Not even a slight shift. Her expression is frozen.

"And despite what you may think or feel about your own daughter," Rev continues, "she loves you. You are at risk."

"The... the Night..."

"The Night Bringer."

She blinks and then shakes her head. "He is targeting people you care for?"

I nod.

"Why?" she whispers. "I thought..."

"Because we are and will forever be his enemy," I say, more confident now. "We're going to kill him."

21

REV

Caelynn's mother didn't exactly warm up to us being in her home, but we finished telling our story—the basics, at least —and then left her stunned. We offered her protection, whether in the Shadow Court palace or the High Court, but she declined any help at all. She said she'd go into hiding and did give a quiet thank you for the warning. That seemed significant given her other reactions.

I didn't mention this to Caelynn, but I intend to confront her a second time, offering my aid.

Our "visit" was a shock to her, and we gave her more information than she could possibly register at one time. Though I am unreasonably angry that she seemed to have no grace or love for her own daughter, I am hoping that can change over time. And if not, Caelynn never has to know.

The moment we're back in the Crackling Court carriage, I pull Caelynn into my arms. "I love you," I tell her. "I love you. I love you. I love you."

The three other fae look the other direction, their eyes wide, but I don't care. They can know I am in love with Caelynn. That part doesn't matter.

She chuckles softly as she melts into my arms. "Why are you saying that?"

"Because it's true. And because I get the feeling you didn't hear it enough from them."

She stills in my arms, and I swear I can feel her heart break.

"They were plenty loving when I was a child."

"That probably only makes it worse." I nuzzle into her neck, taking in her scent. "I love you. I trust you. I believe in you."

"Thank you," she whispers. Her fingers dig into my shoulders, and we stay like that for the next few hours as the carriage rattles forward.

"We'll be home soon," I tell her eventually.

"Home," she whispers, testing the word like she doesn't even really know what it means. What it could mean. "I'm already home. Here." She snuggles in closer, as if to show me what she means, but I already know.

We're home in each other's arms. It's the only home I'll ever need.

22

CAELYNN

The images of my childhood home haunt me for the next hour as we bump down the uneven roadways covered in weeds and overgrown bushes. Even with Rev's arms around me, my mind cannot keep those heavy thoughts and feelings from suffocating me.

The carriage stops eventually, and Rev squeezes me. "We're here," he whispers.

My stomach drops to my feet. I blink back my dark memories to see the three Crackling Court fae staring at me. Here.

Home.

Rev exits the carriage first. The sky is dark grey behind him as he holds out his hand to me. I take it and step out into the world of shadows. My home.

I pull in a breath as I look up to the massive castle looming ahead. Dark spires stretch into the sky over sharp-edged stone platforms. The palace looks like a mountain carved into a gothic castle.

I struggle to force air through my lungs. There is a stretch of cobblestone road lined with buildings between me and the stairs to the palace gates.

Rev stands beside me, a constant comforting presence, but he doesn't push. He just waits for me to be ready. The shadow sprites swirl around us, leaping down the pathway toward the shining black steps that lead to two huge iron gates.

The Crackling Court carriage is a few yards behind us, watching. They too realize that this is a big moment for me. For the court. And the presence of a ruling court carriage has brought the attention of many townspeople all around, even as the sun sets.

The chattering of distant fae grows quickly, and soon, crowds begin pooling at the edges of the alleys.

They're waiting. Waiting for me to do something, say something.

It doesn't take long for my name to scatter through the crowd, though I'm surprised I've been recognized that quickly. As much as I'm famous here, most Shadow fae have never seen my face, and I'm still a few dozen yards from the gathering crowds down the hill.

The shadow sprites are less patient, though, and they leap down the streets, bounding and chattering excitedly. Maybe they're the reason the crowds have caught on to who I am. Maybe they already know why I'm here.

I've been fairly infamous in the fae realm for a full decade, but this is the first time I've really had the opportunity to experience my fame in the court that actually likes me. My muscles tense, heart pounding. I half expect to be attacked at any moment because that's the kind of treatment I'm most used to.

I hide every emotion behind a mask so carefully

constructed it's hard for me to tell the difference between me and who I pretend to be.

My feet are frozen to the spot, my eyes glued to the dark stone that's visited my dreams for decades now. Everything here is dark, and not in the way that I expected the Shadow Court to be.

In my dreams, the wonderous Shadow Court is glorious and majestic. Shining, poised, and smooth. But this place is... dull. Large and impressive, but haunted.

This is closer to what the courts who hate us picture. Old and dingy. Lifeless.

At some point, it became a reality through neglect.

The spires on the outside of the massive building are faded, translucent. Like a dark ghost. Like the phantom I see in myself.

The center of the palace is solid black, but even there, dirt and scorch marks streak down the stone walls. One of the pinnacles is bent. Pieces of the tallest turret is crumbled.

The city even smells stagnant. Old. Dirty.

There are so many emotions running through me as I just stand here, staring at the castle that my ancestors once ruled from. The castle that has represented hope for the court I adore. Represented dreams I would have bet my life I would never achieve. But now, I stand here on the precipice of something new, something beautiful, something great, and I can't even make my brain believe that it's true. I cannot conceive that, moments from now, I will be standing inside the palace I've never stopped dreaming of.

But I'm also sad. My heart aches for the pain of my people. I grew up in this court, and I know what it's like to be poor and belittled. The frustration of knowing it isn't your fault, but you're blamed all the same.

I know what it's like to feel determined that you could be

powerful if only given the chance—but no one ever will. I know what it's like to be cold. I know what it's like to be hungry. I know what it's like to be dirty all the time.

For hundreds of years, hope has been stolen from the people of the Shadow Court. And it boggles my mind to think that I might be their new hope. It's so insane that I spent ten years believing I was a villain and here I stand trying to be a hero. Trying to be what Rev believes me to be.

And there's such a vast difference between being a hero hidden in shadow—doing good things but knowing no one will ever appreciate them—and standing before crowds of people who admire me.

I don't know if I can live up to their high expectations. I don't know if I can be the leader they need.

Rev nudges me with his elbow. "You belong here."

"Home," I whisper again.

23

CAELYNN

You belong here.

I try to believe him. I want to believe him. But my heart aches.

Rev seems to read this on my face because he grips my chin and stares down at me. "You are incredible, Caelynn. You've faced monsters with your chin high and heart pure. This is no different. This is only a new obstacle."

My heart pounds. "This is different," I whisper. "No one has ever expected anything from me before."

Rev releases a quick breath from his nose. "You're used to exceeding low expectations, not meeting high ones."

I nod.

"Well, if there is anyone used to striving to meet high expectations—and often failing—it's me. It's hard, Cae; I won't pretend it's not. But you—there's not a single being in any world that I could believe in more. You will be an incredible leader, to a people that need you."

"What if I fail them?"

"Then, they will be no worse off than they already are."

I swallow, that truth hitting me hard. Rev releases my

chin, and I look around at the stacks of crooked buildings with rusty hinges and trash piles in the streets. The dirty bare toes and rags covering children.

"They need you," he tells me again.

I pull in a long breath. They do. I know that. I've always known that.

"This is what I've wanted... forever. There's not a thing I can remember ever wanting more. To belong here. To give power back to this court."

Rev's smile is sad. "And you were born to do it. This is your destiny." Rev swallows, his eyes darkening as he turns to stare at the palace again.

I watch him for longer than I should. His eyes distant, pained. It was a quick change.

"Our destinies are separate," I murmur, realizing the source of his pain. How wonderful would it be for us to have a future together? As one. But we don't have the luxury.

Rev doesn't respond.

"Thank you," I tell him.

"For what?" His voice is lighter, almost amused.

"For bringing me here. For believing in me." Forgiving me, trusting me, bonding to me, loving me. All of it, really.

My heart is full, even though I know it's short term, him being here with me is everything. "You're welcome," he whispers. "In the Schorchedlands, I made a decision. I saw all your sacrifices. I saw the pain you'd endured for so long."

The back of my throat stings.

"And I decided I wanted to give some of it back to you. Any bit of happiness I can grant to you, I will."

"Well, this is it. This is—"

"I know," he whispers. "Now, go and take it."

24

REV

I stay at the hillside and just watch as Caelynn takes long purposeful strides toward the Shadow palace—my mate approaching her destiny. The people gather to watch her ascent to the gates. Uncertain murmurs scatter over the crowd, but the shadow sprites leap through the streets.

The swirling darkness of those playful creatures bound onto shoulders of the fae lining the path toward the massive structure covering the horizon.

"Queen?" a few people murmur.

"She's going to see the queen?"

"No," someone says. "She *is* the queen."

Uncertain understanding seems to settle in some of the onlookers, others remain dubious or concerned. Some eyes turn to me. Hatred and curiosity swirl in stormy dark eyes, but the focus remains on Caelynn. Her dark cloak billows dramatically.

I realize that this is something I'll never have. Taking the High Court crown will never be like this. This is something more. Something bigger.

Something so *right* I'm shocked I hadn't seen it before.

Caelynn could have never remained in the High Court, and I think it took me seeing this place firsthand to understand that. I wanted to give her what she wanted, to grant her wishes, even if they pained me, but this, I realize now, is and always has been fate.

Almost like… her kingdom—her court—is her true mate.

She belongs to it, as much as it belongs to her.

I'm not jealous that something else has as strong of a claim on her—if not stronger—as I do. But I am jealous that I don't have the same sense of belonging.

Which is maybe a silly thought considering I'm the High Heir. I'll be the High King in a few years. I'll have more power than anyone else for a full century.

But somehow this, this is more meaningful.

My twinge of jealousy is fleeting, though. I am so incredibly happy for my mate, who is finally getting what she deserves.

I don't want to distract attention from her right now, but I ache to follow. To witness this.

I slip into the crowd, moving down the alley below the palace, where hundreds now wait, watching.

"It's Caelynn," they whisper.

"Caelynn the assassin?"

"The hero!"

My stomach twists as the people whisper excitedly about Caelynn's most famous act—killing my brother. Not that I blame her for it, not anymore, but there is still an ache in my gut when I hear people speak of it with glee.

I try to understand. To them, my brother was a symbol of power that was stolen from them. He was a powerful prince from far away that none of them had ever seen. A prince that would not have cared for them.

That was true for Reahgan, but not for me.

Though, I admit to not understanding the full scope of what's happened in this court. Or why. Without Caelynn, I wouldn't have ever realized.

I push forward, closer to the gates.

The ground trembles, and my heart plunges. A crack appears straight down the middle of the Shadow palace gates, growing steadily as it swings open.

Gasps reverberate through the crowd, and still more than a hundred feet away, Caelynn stops in the middle of the street. The crowds file in but leave a wide-open gap where Caelynn stands before the gates.

At the top of the steps, a female in a billowing black dress and shining black crown stands.

"The queen," someone whispers.

The Queen of the Whisperwood, the current Queen of the Shadow Court, is waiting for Caelynn.

25

CAELYNN

The breath catches in my throat when I realize the gates are opening. The crowd lining the streets stills, eyes wide.

These gates only open once per year, and even then, only a small group are allowed in. We're months away from Yareakh, when the queen welcomes citizens in.

Steps echo until a form appears on the platform above. I see her crown first, shining black spikes. Harsh and beautiful. Then, her wrinkled face and black gown.

The Queen of the Whisperwood.

I met her at the Trials. She treated me like a daughter, but I'd been so cold with my court then. They were so proud of my deeds that it sickened me. Even while I loved the Shadow Court, I couldn't accept their praise.

And I haven't yet had the chance the meet the queen here. Where I should have the first time. She would have welcomed me into the court and offered me a drink from the shade fountain. That would have completed my rites and made me an official member of this court.

That was one of my dreams, that I never accomplished.

I never got the chance. I was banished to the human world before I could fulfill it.

I don't know why the queen would publicly greet me like this now. Yes, I'm well known here, well liked. Most consider me a hero. I expected to be welcomed, to be allowed in. But the main gates don't need to be opened to allow me access. The queen herself does not have to be here.

They didn't have to make it a spectacle.

The sprites continue their swirling and dancing, their joyous whispers leaping through the crowds.

I take another deep breath and then continue my walk to the palace. In only a few moments, I reach the steps. Slabs of uneven black stone, with shades of purple and blue twisted in. Like the feathers of a raven.

The moment my boot hits the first step, the murmuring of the crowds stops. There's a stillness everywhere. Or maybe, it's just that my mind has blocked everything out.

There is only me, this moment, and the waiting queen.

A soft breeze eases the nervous heat creeping up my neck and face. My chest rises and falls rapidly, but I keep my mind focused and calm. This walk feels like an eternity of in-between.

At the top is my destiny. A fate I'd didn't dare believe was possible.

After several minutes of slow walking, my thighs burning, I reach the platform before the massive stone gates and I face the queen.

I don't know what to expect. I don't know what she sees in me now. A predecessor? Her court's hope? Or a threat?

I stop. My expression is not at all the poised female I am meant to be, ready to take control of an entire kingdom. Instead, I feel like a child, internally begging this queen to accept me.

I am desperately hopeful. Pathetically so.

The queen approaches with slow deliberate steps. Then, her lips curl into a kind smile as she stops before me.

"I've been wondering when you'd come."

The Queen of the Whisperwood, with her long, raven black hair and wrinkled face places both hands on the sides of her black crown.

My eyes widen as she pulls the crown from her head and falls to one knee, holding it out to me.

26

CAELYNN

The crowd is no longer silent.

Gasps and shouts give way to chattering so loud that for a moment, it's hard to hear. It's certainly hard to process what's happening.

"Take it, child. Let them see this. Then, the work can begin."

My heart swells to the point of pain, and I cannot control the tears now. They fall freely down my cheeks. This is... this is so much more than anything I'd ever imagined.

I take the outstretched crown with trembling fingers. But I don't dare place it on my head. Not yet. Not like this.

The queen stands and then motions for me to follow her through the gates and into the palace.

The smell of stale dirt and distant rot greets me first as I enter the Shadow palace. I blink, taking a few moments to adjust to the darkness of the first chamber. There are no lights or windows, just a high ceiling made of the same shining black stone as the stairs.

Our footsteps echo through the dark chamber. I stare up at the gothic architecture. Near the arched ceiling, lined on each side, are stone gargoyles. I blink. I hadn't expected those, or even knew they were here.

In the center of the massive room is a large, curved basin —bone dry. This was once the shade fountain, pouring with the magic of our ancestors.

I knew it would be empty—it's been drying for a hundred years or more due to lack of power in our lands—but it still hurts to see.

If it were flowing the way it should, our people could have running water and lights and heat in their homes. They could create power-filled gemstones and trade with other villages and courts. The people themselves can be strengthened by this source.

The old fortresses crumble without the infrastructure the rulers are supposed to supply. The people must rely on the magic they can gather from natural sources, like the Whisperwood. In the fae realm, magic fuels everything. Without a power source, we are only able to barely survive. We make do, but we can never thrive without it.

Any Shadow fae with power could fuel the magic. Most courts have several strong fae that give and take from their power source often, keeping the magic strong. In the Shadow Court, those who take are unable to give back. Except me.

"I'm sorry."

I jerk my attention to the Whisperwood Queen, her eyes cast down at the empty fountain, shame written on her wrinkled face.

There is a tiny canal that leads up to a bowl on a platform. I follow the empty canal, curving up to the chalice. There is one trickle of power dripping down to the fountain's well. Single drops every few seconds. That is all that's left.

"It's not your fault," I tell her. "You were only holding on until…"

"Until you could come."

The hair on my arms stands up straight, and I take in a deep breath to stop my teeth from chattering.

A few feet beyond the fountain is a bowl on a stand. I approach and stare at the tiny bit of magic swirling inside.

I look down awkwardly at the beautiful black crown in my hands. This, unlike everything else, is polished and lovely. It's been well taken care of.

"You can place it here, for now," the queen says, motioning to a stand next to the back wall. I obey and place the glistening crown on the plate gently then turn to the bits of dark magic swirling in the bowl.

"Wait," the queen says. Her heels click on the stone flooring as she marches toward me. "Take first. Then, give."

I frown. "But—"

"You have never tasted from the fountain. It is customary that you complete your rites."

"Okay," I whisper. She grabs the small silver ladle hanging off the side and scoops a small bit of frothy black liquid. Carefully she brings the magic up to my mouth and tips it until the smokey magic pours in.

The moment it touches my tongue, all my senses explode. It's bitter and sharp and, somehow, delicious. The magic soars through my veins, stretching, pulling, and filling. I stumble back, shocked at the effect. I had expected such a small amount from a weak source to be timid.

This is—incredible.

My eyes fly open, strength and magic more alive and purer than I've ever felt it before. I stare down at the last bit of magic in the bowl. My fingers tingle, ready to complete the ritual, but I pause.

"He'll know," I whisper. The moment I do this, the Night Bringer will feel it. He'll know.

"Who, child?" the queen asks.

"The Night Bringer."

The queen stills but otherwise doesn't react.

It is time, the voice floats from the bag on my back for only my ears. *It must be done.*

"Let him know." The queen's harsh voice surprises me, but then my lips curl into a grin, and for the first time, I am excited.

Let him know, I think. He'll be angry. He might act out. But for now, this is the rebellion that I've been waiting for. This is the moment he used as temptation before our bargain, the desire he used against me.

This was supposed to be the purpose of the power he granted me. It was always what I intended to use it for, and finally I will.

I hold both palms up, and black power explodes from them. There are rumblings of surprise and awe from the crowd below. Honestly, I was so distracted by the moment I didn't even notice that some of those from the city had followed me in. There are nearly two dozen fae watching me.

I ignore them and focus on the darkness crawling from my hands. It expands quickly, covering the entire room in black shadows. The crowd gasps, but I can't see anything but my body, the bowl, and my magic surrounding me.

The blackness breathes, a low growl reverberating from it. Someone below whimpers, but I don't even blink. This magic may be angry and fierce, but I own it. And I am worse.

"You are mine to wield," I tell it.

It stills, and when I press my hands into the bowl and curl

my fingers, the magic obeys. The bowl rocks violently at the sudden rush of magic. It swirls like a tiny cyclone and filters quickly into the canal, down to the fountain.

The room lightens enough for me to see the shadowed faces of the onlookers, their eyes wide as they watch the magic pass from me to the bowl and quickly fill the fountain that has remained empty for a century.

The walls that were dull and dingy now shimmer—their darkness no longer a detriment but instead impossibly beautiful. The cavernous room is brightened and swells with life. Like the castle itself has taken its first breath in a very long time.

Power still floods from my hands. The fountain is not yet full. But I turn my gaze up to the domed ceiling, watching the palace reveal itself, bit by bit. Like a veil has dropped, this room has become something entirely new.

Near the ceiling, the lines of gargoyles shake dust from their leathery skin but then return to their stoic positions, eyes shining bright.

Black water bubbles up in the fountain until three streams of magical water shoot up and down in a gentle curve.

"Drink," the queen tells the crowd. And as if a barrier was dropped, the people rush forward. Desperately, they claw at the water, like it's the very source of life. They drink greedily, some scooping with their hands, others dunking their face into the magical waters.

The magic continues to flow from me, and my fingers tremble. I lick my dry lips.

"We have entered into a new era." The queen's voice booms over the crowd. More bodies press into the room. "Caelynn has the blood of the old kings, and the magic needed to rebuild our power. Caelynn Shadowspell will be your new queen."

My head spins suddenly, knees weak. I blink and brace myself on the stand holding the bowl.

"Well done, child."

I don't know who says those words.

Darkness peppers my vision, and my knees buckle. And then, I fall into strong, gentle arms just as the power takes everything.

27

REV

I force air through my lungs as I watch magic returning to this neglected palace. It's palpable, the hope and power and love filling this large room. Around a hundred Shadow Court citizens have made their way up the steps and into the palace by the time the fountain began truly flowing with magic. The rush to taste of the power sends a wave of urgency through the crowd below, and fae began running for the palace steps.

Just a few sips will strengthen their own magic, increase their healing speeds, and sharpen their existing skills. It will make a big difference for these fae. But there are many thousands more in need.

Just witnessing this beautiful exchange causes my heart to soar because I know this is everything to Caelynn. I turn to watch her, stunning and ethereal, but... her face is pale, her eyes unfocused.

She's giving too much, too fast. Without thinking, I rush forward while the queen gives her small speech. The people don't react to her declaration that she's a Shadowspell the way I would have expected, but I suppose they assume this queen is a Shadowspell. They don't know that her line has been a replacement for several hundred years.

I reach Caelynn just as she collapses. Her limp form falls into my arms. I pull the bag off her back and sling it over my own shoulder, and then I stand, cradling her.

The queen faces me, the crowd still swarming the fountain below.

"Is there somewhere I can take her?"

She frowns, eyes examining me. "Reveln?"

I nod.

Her eyebrows rise in surprise. "This way," she says in lieu of any additional questions, and I follow her down a corridor off the back of the great hall. Our feet echo through a stone hallway, and she swings open a wooden door to expose a small room. It's stale and dusty, but there are couches and tables and a bare fireplace in the corner.

I lay Caelynn on one of the couches and squat beside it. Her lips are cracked and dry, and her skin is clammy.

"She'll be fine in a few hours," the Whisperwood Queen says.

I nod, but it still bothers me to see her like this. And it worries me that she'll continue to put too much of herself into that fountain. The more she can give, the better off her people will be. She'll kill herself if it would help them.

"She'll need to be instructed on how to control it. She can't use all of her magic every time."

The queen nods.

"You will likely need to regulate it for her. She… she's more than willing to kill herself to help people she cares for, and I worry she won't know when to stop."

My magic flickers against my palm, seeking a way to aid Caelynn. She has no injuries, but even so, I press my hand against her belly. Light sears its way into her skin, and her back arches, then she relaxes. Her cheeks are flushed imme-diately.

An audible pull of breath catches my attention, and I turn to see the queen's wide eyes, swirling with curiosity.

"What was that?" one of two males standing behind the queen says, his face sharp and unkind.

"And who are you?" the other says, shorter than the first but with similar features—sharp cheek bones, dark hair, and small, near-black eyes.

"This is Prince Reveln. The High Prince," the queen says.

Both men's lips part. I stand and brush my pants of the dust clinging to them.

"Why are you here?" the shorter male asks cautiously.

I consider many possible responses. "I have come to deliver your rightful queen."

"Deliver?" one asks.

"Rightful queen?" The other frowns, eyes cast to the ground. "Caelynn is powerful. We'd welcome her as a queen," he says, brow furrowed but no longer accusatory. "But that is a right given, not forced. If you are placing her here as a—"

The Whisperwood Queen holds up a hand, and the male stops mid-sentence.

"Caelynn is truly the rightful ruler of our court. Even if I wished it, I could not stop her from taking the crown."

"Wh—how?" the taller male asks.

"It's a long story," I answer, and the queen's lips quirk up in a small smile.

"It is indeed. I am glad to know you are aware of the truth in her blood. It will make this transition easier. And there is no longer any risk to her taking the throne, I presume?"

"There will always be risk." I shrug. "Those creatures are not our friends nor allies. But the deed is done. The curse no longer exists."

The queen nods.

"I've been introduced," I say. "But I'm sorry, I don't know who you are."

"Of course!" the queen says. "These are my nephews, Rian and Cillian. And you may address me as Emberly. As I am no longer queen."

Rian and Cillian flash a look to their aunt. "You are queen," the taller says.

Her chin remains high. "I am relieved to shed this responsibility to the rightful heir. But first, we have much to discuss."

28

CAELYNN

"You're certain this is safe, Emberly?" Hushed voices rouse me from a deep slumber.

"We've heard many stories about the curse of the royal family."

My heavy body resists as I try to force myself up. My head throbs as I open my eyes but my body remains limp on the soft surface.

"As safe as it will ever be."

Gentle fingers slide down my cheek, and I turn to find Rev looking down at me with a soft smile. I blink, and realize my head is in his lap. "Morning, Angel."

My heart flutters. I try again to sit up but pain shoots through every muscle. Rev's steady arms guide me up, and the voices quiet. My vision flickers, but then it finally clears and I am able to take in my surroundings.

We're in a small room, dark and cold, with several strangers. One is the Queen of the Whisperwood, but there are two young males and three older fae, all watching me like a damn science experiment.

"Caelynn," the queen says softly, "this is your existing council. There should be more but—well, that's a problem for another time."

"She woke quickly," an older male says, his back straight, eyes unkind.

"*She* is right here," I say, voice groggy. My head still throbs.

"You extended quite a lot of energy today," the elder male turns his sharp gaze to me. "To the point of collapse. But you woke in only an hour."

"And how long was I supposed to remain unconscious by your calculations?" I regard him with hooded eyes. His hair is dark, his features severe. Not unlike the portrait of Darren Shadowspell, if I'm honest.

The male doesn't answer.

"She had some help," the queen says simply. "And that is really not the point, Luscious."

"Luscious?" I repeat.

"Something wrong with my name, child?"

I shake my head; they won't understand *Harry Potter* references, so there's really no point.

"That is your queen you are speaking to," the Whisperwood Queen says, rising to her feet. I blink. The female I know as the Whisperwood Queen— called *me* the queen.

Images flash through my mind of her taking off her crown and handing it to me.

"Not yet, she isn't," the male says.

"As queen," I say slowly, "will I have the opportunity to... adjust my council members?" I flick an eyebrow but resist the urge to study the unkind male's expression.

Silence stretches through the room.

"We have a strong tradition," the queen answers, finally

breaking the silence. "And long held positions by families of old. But yes, you can make—adjustments."

The harsh male does not speak again.

"I am glad you're awake, Caelynn." The queen approaches and then crouches down beside me. "I've been waiting such a very long time for you. I wasn't sure it would ever happen, or if my family line would simply be burdened with watching the slow suffocation of our court until no magic remained at all."

I pull in a long breath. "We were very close to that fate, weren't we?" I whisper.

She nods, a small smile on her face. "You have given us hope. Let me introduce you to your current council."

She walks to the side of the room and motions to the two younger males, dark hair and sharp features. "These are my nephews, Rian and Cillian. And these are the remaining counts and countesses still *willingly* in favor. Luscious." She waves to Mr. Stick-up-his-ass. "Tameria." She motions to a female with sandy blond hair and sallow cheeks. "And Octavia." A female with curly brown hair and beautiful dark skin, wearing a green velvet gown.

"Nice to meet you all," I say.

The male rolls his eyes. The younger two simply frown. The women smile, but it doesn't reach their eyes.

"What now?" I ask softly.

"Well, I'd like to plan an official coronation for one week from now."

"She will continue to fuel the fountain, yes?" the dark-skinned female—Octavia—asks.

The queen nods. "That is up to her, I suppose. But ideally, yes. Even with Caelynn's impressive magic, it will take weeks for her to rebuild the foundation of our court's power—to obtain any sort of long-term impact. The well will dry in a matter of hours at this current rate."

"She cannot do that every few hours," Rev comments.

"Of course not. The court will require less and less over time as the power cycle rebuilds itself."

"How long?" I ask, eyebrows furrowed.

"In a week, the fountain will likely be able to hold its power for a few days. After one month, I'd estimate it will be strong enough to keep for weeks. If we work out a structured plan, we can solidify our court's magic using yours without draining you, as per Prince Reveln's *impassioned* suggestion."

I raise my eyebrows at Rev, but he just shrugs. I guess I know what they've been discussing for the last hour.

"Then what?" I whisper.

"As you've obviously guessed, a magical fountain is not enough," Luscious says with pursed lips.

"Well, that will do an incredible favor to the people," Octavia says softly.

The queen nods. "Our people's lives will improve greatly with the healing of the fountain. And if we accomplish nothing else, it is a great deed done."

"It is not enough," Luscious says firmly. "A bit of power to aid the people will not reestablish our power among all the courts. It will not undo what has been done to us. Our people have had power bred out of them. It will take much more than a trickle of magic to reverse the damage."

"I agree with you." I resist the urge to wrinkle my nose at having to admit that I agree with douchebag Lucious. "But I am curious, what would you intend to do?"

I don't trust this male. His harsh eyes and aggressive tone tell me his priorities will not align with mine. But it's important to know his intentions before I fight him on them.

His eyes narrow, and then his sharp gaze flashes to Rev and back. He doesn't speak.

"You'd like to continue rebellion," I answer for him. I'd already suspected this could be the case, and his obvious refusal to elaborate due to Rev's presence confirmed it for me.

One of his brows quirks up, but he doesn't answer.

I stand on wobbly feet, and Rev quickly joins me, hand firm in mine.

"I understand the desire for revenge. The desire to make the ruling courts regret what they've done to us. To show them why they should fear the Shadow Court." I'd had those thoughts and more when I was younger.

His chest puffs up, and I wonder if he was one of those that praised me for the murder of the High Heir.

"I understand the pain our court has had to deal with. I've lived it. And I have seen my fair share of disdain from other courts. But I have also learned why we had to endure it."

He frowns.

"I hate that our court was sacrificed to conquer an ancient evil. I hate even more that, after five hundred years, that battle was lost. And I promise I will do everything in my power to reverse our course and make this court powerful once again. But rebellion and hatred may make you feel better for a time—revenge often does—but it only serves to destroy, never to build. We cannot become the powerful court we should be with a vengeful mindset."

"And how do you propose we do that? Rebuild, as you say. One powerful young fae is not enough. Other courts have dozens and dozens of young fae as powerful as you."

"Not as powerful as her," Rev says, his lips tugging into a smile. "She is the most powerful fae I've met, aside from the High Queen. And believe me, I have met the most powerful out there."

The angry male's face softens slightly; a small light of pride shines in his eyes.

"But you are right," I answer. "I am not enough to rebuild the entire court. It will take time. We must have patience. But in my time back in the fae realm, I have developed allies. True friends, who desire my success and believe in me."

"Like the High Prince?" Octavia asks.

My stomach flips pleasantly. "Yes."

"The High Courts will give us favor?" Luscious asks dubiously.

"Caelynn's allies are still in the minority," Rev answers. "Even as High Heir, I cannot suddenly place her on the council. As Caelynn said, it will take time. But I promise I have every intention of helping your endeavor to reestablish your court. I too have learned the reason behind the Shadow Court's fall from grace. If only that were enough to convince the rest of the realm, but it isn't. The world will have to see your strength and honor and come to trust you as I have come to trust Caelynn."

"We need marriages," Tameria says quickly, her voice hushed.

Rev frowns. "What?"

"The other courts weakened us," she says, voice nearly shaking it's so frail, "by taking our strongest fae by forced marriages. We need powerful unions."

"We must reverse that trend and give *us* strong fae," Octavia says.

I pull in a long breath through my nose.

"I agree," Rev says.

"You agree?" Luscious asks slowly.

He nods.

"So, you will arrange powerful unions for the Shadow Court?"

"Wait." I hold up a hand. "Bringing in strong magic into our bloodlines is a great idea—a necessity, even—but I will not allow forced marriages."

The room stills.

"It is not fair to either party. If both are willing, that's great. We can facilitate and promote this, but even if it means it takes longer, we will not arrange a forced marriage."

29

REV

Caelynn and I are escorted to a hall with bedrooms, dark and dingy like the others, and each assigned a room. Separately.

I press my lips together but don't comment. I'll let Caelynn take the lead on this.

The queen explains that there are more luxurious rooms in the palace, but they are unsafe for now. As the magic broke down, the palace residents condensed to only the central hall, closer to the source.

Once Caelynn's magic refuels more of the palace, she'll be able to move to several other areas of the massive castle.

The queen takes her leave, and Caelynn and I stand there in front of our doors. I curl my fingers over the handle of my room's door but wait. Finally, Caelynn turns to me and nods for me to follow her.

I release a breath as we both slip into her room.

My hands curl around her waist, and I pull her back into my chest as we get our first look at her new bedroom. The bed is large with a faded black bedspread and an iron headboard, inlaid with tarnished gold, with twisting designs carved into it. The walls are entirely black, and there are three small, faded windows, peaked at the top with elaborate metal framework.

There is a round table in the corner and two green velvet chairs in front of a small fireplace.

"Not quite what you're used to," Caelynn says.

I shrug. "It's not bad. Just needs a cleaning. And," I lift my palm up, and four balls of light rise to the ceiling, "light."

Caelynn sighs and lays her head back against my chest.

"This is yours now," I whisper in her ear.

She shivers. "I hardly know what that means."

"You'll learn what it means."

She nods. "I can't believe I'm here. Can't believe I actually made it. Can't believe I fainted my first time using the fountain." She smacks her palm to her forehead, and I chuckle.

"What you did was absolutely incredible." I glide the tip of my nose down her neck. "You are incredible."

Her fingers dig into my thigh, and then she pushes her back into me.

"You're supposed to use this time to rest, Cae," I whisper, but it comes out huskier than I'd intended.

"Believe me," she says, spinning to face me. "You give me more energy than you take." She places both hands firmly on my chest and shoves me back against the closed door without breaking eye contact.

I pause for one beat, heart pounding. Then, I quickly grip her waist and claim her mouth with mine.

My hand drifts down her neck, fingers curling under the hem of her tunic.

There's a knock on the door.

"Sorry to bother you," a soft female voice calls, "but there are visitors from the Crackling Court looking for you."

I curse under my breath. I'd forgotten about the Crackling Court workers sent to build a portal.

Caelynn chuckles, pushing her lips against my shoulder, and then slipping from my hold. "We'll be right out," she calls.

My heart is still pounding and my body still buzzing. I grab her and kiss her fiercely, pulling her against my chest. "We'll finish this later," I promise against her lips.

"Yes, we will."

The two Crackling Court fae are in a waiting room near the main hall.

"Apologies," the yellow-haired fae says with a bow. "We couldn't make it through with the carriage due to the crowds." His eyes linger on Caelynn, eyes wide, then they dart to the floor. "We had to come on foot."

"Not a problem," I answer. "We should apologize too. We'd honestly forgotten about the portal in all the excitement."

"Yes, it was rather intense," the taller fae says. "I feel honored to have witnessed it if I am honest."

I grin.

"That's kind of you to say," Caelynn answers.

The queen enters the meeting room and smiles; her eyes are dull, though. It's rather late by this point. "There was something you needed?"

"Yes," Caelynn says sweetly. "The Crackling Court has come to build a portal to their capital. Would you help us with that? Is there a designated place? An old, unused portal somewhere?"

The queen's eyebrows rise. "You consistently surprise me, Caelynn."

She smiles. "You can thank Rev for this one."

"I suspect the Crystal Court will not be far behind," I say.

Caelynn laughs. "Kari will be angry she wasn't the first."

"And the Luminescent Court?" the queen asks cautiously.

I still. "That ... will be unlikely."

Her eyebrows rise. "Oh?"

"I may have forgiven Caelynn for her past actions, but my father most certainly has not and never will. The people of my court are also unlikely to forget any time soon."

"I see."

"One step at a time," I offer. The Shadow Court already has more allies than anyone would have expected.

"Indeed. One step at a time."

"Did you have a place in mind, your Highness?" the tallest of the Crackling Fae interjects.

"Yes, I will show you to the old portals. There may be something you can use there, but let's do that in the morning. It's late."

30

REV

I nuzzle into Caelynn's chest, as we wake in each other's arms.

Very little light streams through the windows of Caelynn's new room in the Shadow Court, only barely enough to tell it's morning. Caelynn is still, her chest rising with even breaths. We have a lot to do today, but I also don't want to wake her until she's ready.

But as I pull my body from hers, she groans and her eyes flutter open. "Is it morning?"

"Yes." I place a soft kiss on her forehead.

She looks up at the discolored molding on the walls above. "It wasn't a dream, was it?"

I smirk. "No. It wasn't."

She closes her eyes and sighs. "I don't even know what to think about that."

"It's going to be a lot of work. But take time to enjoy the process too. This is incredible, Cae. Honestly, truly amazing."

She snuggles in closer. "You're amazing."

"I know," I answer quickly.

She snorts.

"Ready to get the day started? Or would you like to rest longer?"

She sits up quickly and runs her fingers through her tangled locks. "No, we should get moving."

"I can get the Crackling Court started on the portal while you rest if you want."

She shakes her head. "No, I can't sleep anymore."

I pull myself out of bed and change into fresh clothing. Caelynn chooses a silk blouse and tight-fitting pants. I choose a black tunic and pants, nothing showcasing my role as Luminescence fae or High Prince. That choice was specifically to avoid any potential conflict but part of me is happy to feel like I do belong here, despite knowing it is not at all true. My place here is temporary, Caelynn and I both know it.

But that doesn't stop it from hurting.

We meet the queen and Crackling fae in the main hall, already chatting and waiting for us.

I hold onto Caelynn's hand as the Queen of the Whisperwood guides our group out to the formal portals. She is achingly slow, but it gives us all time to examine every inch of the palace that we pass. The main hall is still flooded with Shadow fae desperate for a taste of the power Caelynn has given. I suspect the fountain is already dry but the queen doesn't mention it, which I appreciate. Caelynn needs to keep her strength for a bit longer.

We pass through a corridor so dark I need Caelynn to guide me through. I'm now grateful for the slow pace. I can't see a thing.

A crack of light forms just ahead, and a door swings wide, exposing the sunlight, blasting us. The queen and Caelynn shield their eyes, and even the Crackling Court fae blink to refocus.

We continue forward to a small pathway lined with

shadow maples. Their leaves are shiny black and wave in the gentle breeze. We've come out on the side of the castle, I realize. And soon, we come to an open field, filled with ruins. Crumbling boulders and gravel is scattered over the dark weeds.

"This was once our portal field," the Whisperwood Queen says softly. "This was once the High Court portal." She points to the largest boulder right in the front. The stones are all dark, nearly black, but a small High Court crest is visible on the side of a stone lying on the ground.

"I'm unsure which was once the Crackling Court portal, but it was here somewhere," she says, shifting a piece of rubble with her foot.

We stare at the rubble littering the ground, but most of the stones are indistinguishable from the rest.

"The magic to use these portals was disbanded one by one over three hundred years ago, but the structures remained until my father grew frustrated when every attempt he made to strengthen our court left us weaker. Every attempt at communicating with once allies disintegrated."

Caelynn's eyebrows rise. "He threw a tantrum and destroyed them all?"

She nods.

"Here," someone says, and we all turn to the Crackling Court fae. His blond hair falls into his face as he leans over to examine a set of stones. "This was ours." His fingers grip a large black stone and holds it out. A streak of yellow paint reveals the partial crest of the Crackling Court.

"Can you use anything?"

He shrugs. "We can try. But we have the necessary supplies to build without the original stones."

The other fae leans down and digs his fingers into the soil. "The magic remains."

The blond fae nods. "We should be finished by sundown tomorrow."

I press my lips together and nod. The resurrection of this portal will signal my necessary departure. Something I am not eager for. My stomach aches and I'm not sure the feeling will dissipate until... well maybe never,

"Thank you," I tell them, but the two fae are already working, maneuvering stones into an area they'll complete their project.

"The restoration of a portal to a ruling court is... significant," the queen tells Caelynn.

"It is," Caelynn agrees.

The queen's smile is small, but the hope in her eyes is immense. "I've always hoped for the return of the royal family," she says as we walk back toward the shadow maples. "If only to relieve my burden. But no family in our kingdom has held enough power in their blood to make a real difference in... well, longer than I've been alive. The magic you hold is more than I'd have ever dared to hope for. But I knew the courts would continue to hate you for your actions. I believed —I believed I'd never see any real progression for our court in my lifetime, but in a matter of days, you've changed that."

Caelynn swallows.

"Caelynn is incredible," I pull her hand into mine. "I'm glad she'll have some place where people see that. Where she'll be truly appreciated."

"She'll be more than appreciated," the queen says casually. We turn around a bend until the city spreads out before us. I blink at the massive crowds gathering. "She'll be worshipped."

31

CAELYNN

I hold my breath as a dozen fae kneel before me, their heads bowed, fists over their chest. Swearing fealty—to me.

The shadows of gargoyles shift above me, watching. Their purrs of approval reverberate through the stone palace.

I don't know what I expected when I thought of taking the Shadow Court throne, but this is so overwhelming. The magic part is easy. Draining, but easy. I was made for that. The rest is... surreal.

"We've been waiting a very long time for you," one of the fae before me says.

Two of the others nod fervently.

"Why did you not serve the Whisperwood Queen?" I ask.

Nervous eyes dart to me, but I just wait. "My brother swore fealty to the Whisperwood Queen," a young male tells me, "but he was turned away. She would only allow a select few in her service."

My lips part. The power of this palace was degrading quickly. It was well known that the queen limited those who had access to the palace due to that fact, but I didn't realize it also included guards and servers and maids. Families who have served the Shadow royals for millennia.

I take two steps down to the dozen fae waiting on one knee. One at a time, I place my hand on their shoulder. A spark of black flickers from my palm, and one by one, they look up to me, grinning. "Thank you," the young male whispers.

The fae stand and then scamper off to the eldest guard who wears a grim expression. He's going to have a challenge ahead of him, training a barrage of new recruits.

I resume my spot, standing beside the Whisperwood Queen as I prepare to give more magic to the fountain. "There will be no shortage of fae who desire to serve the new queen," she tells me. "Citizens have already felt the difference in the magic throughout the kingdom. I've received word that there are caravans of fae coming to witness your rise, to drink from your fountain and see for themselves that there is hope yet for the future of our kingdom."

I stand before the chalice, magic pulsing in my palms. Eager. Ready.

I smile out at the wide-eyed fae watching. "The rightful queen," someone whispers. Chills scatter over my arms.

But before I can let their words distract me, I send my power into the bowl. It swirls and pulses, flickering with purples and blues and dark greens.

I watch as the magic spins and swirls and dances, as if celebrating. My heart throbs in the best possible way as the people gasp and then rush forward to the edge of the fountain. More fae press in, trying to get past the front gates, where three guards stand watch, blocking the rest from entering too quickly. Only twenty fae are allowed in at once.

The fae inside now, laugh with tear-filled eyes as they

reach into the fountain. The magic tickles and dances against their fingers. They drink.

One girl with dark skin looks up at me, her eyes shining golden. After a moment, the gold hue fades into a pretty bronze. I give her a nod. Magic still flows from me to the fountain, and I want to do more. Give more.

But then, a calloused hand rests on my forearm. "That's enough, Cae."

I swallow and pull my hand back, the magic cutting off. I watch as the final bits of magic flow to the fountain.

"Thank you," one of the fae below says to me. "Thank you!"

This group is ushered out of the hall, and another set is allowed in.

"They'll all get a chance," Rev tells me. "It'll just take time."

I nod, but I'm unable to pull my eyes from the newcomers. Their awe is palpable.

"Let's eat and rest, and you'll do it again when you're refueled."

After another long breath, I take Rev's hand and follow him from the hall.

We dine at a long, metal table with the entire set of Shadow Court advisors. My advisors.

"We are getting reports of record-breaking migrations. They're all coming to the fountain. To see it for themselves."

I take slow sips of salty stew and barely register the words as they chat about all the changes in the palace and in the lands. The Whisperwood Queen and her nephews are working hard to hire more staff now that the magic in the palace can sustain it. They're hiring cooks and cleaners but mostly guards.

Tameria and Octavia are searching for the most eligible

fae in the land that we can bring in to prepare for a season of marriages. Rev promised to invite a few to each High Court ball he holds and mentioned asking a few of his closest allies to do the same.

My mind is hazy and unfocused with exhaustion, though. All I can really think about is how grateful I am that the former queen is taking such control when I am obviously unable, and I hope that it doesn't make me look weak.

After dinner, Rev walks me to my room with his hand pressed gently to my back, quietly guiding me like a lost puppy. But I appreciate that too because I can barely remember which hall is which.

This is my home now. I'm supposed to know where I am, right?

"Are you all right?" he whispers, leaning in close as we walk down the dark hall.

"Mhmm. I'm just tired."

"I'm worried about leaving you. You're going to run yourself into the ground."

I sigh. "I guess I'll need you to keep coming around to check on me then."

Rev pauses, and I stop to look at him. He's smiling, eyes full of wonder and fear and hope.

"I love you," I tell him before he can say it first again.

His grin spreads, and he leans down to press a feather light kiss to my lips. But that's not enough for me. I grip the back of his neck fiercely and drag him back to me. He chuckles against my lips as we stumble back.

He kisses me like it'll be the last time, soft but demanding. Slow and yet desperate. "You're mine, Caelynn," he tells me. "No amount of time or distance will change that."

I sigh. How will we survive this? Even if we win this

impossible battle, we'll be parted. How do I live this new, extraordinary life without Rev?

Rev pulls me along the rest of the way to my room, and we slip inside quickly. He has me against the door the moment it clicks shut, lips on mine. I'm gasping and writhing against his hard body pinning mine, nails digging into his back.

I plant my hands on his chest and shove him, hard. He stumbles back, panting, eyes full of wonder and lust. He watches greedily as I pull off my shirt and pants. Then, he returns, hands sliding up my waist to my breasts. "You're supposed to be getting rest," he tells me through desperate breaths.

"Well, then, make this quick so I can get some sleep."

He chuckles. "No promises on that front."

I grin widely and rip his jacket off, tossing it across the room. He tugs his tunic up and over his head. It finds a place somewhere on the floor too. I pull at his belt as his lips explore the sensitive spots on my neck and chest. I close my eyes and groan at the intense and delicious sensations.

My fingers have lost their purpose, and he brushes them away, even while his lips continue their journey down to my stomach. His pants fall to his ankles, and then his fingers curl into the waist of my panties. He drags them below my knees.

His palms grip my thighs, and he lifts me up.

I wrap my legs around his waist and he carries me across the room to the bed. He sits and then guides me on to him. I throw my head back as he slides inside. "Fuck Rev," I say as he thrusts, pulls me in tighter with each of my thrusts.

"Shhh," he chides. "You don't want the whole palace to hear."

I moan again, with no attempt at heeding his suggestion. "Let them hear. All of them. I don't care who knows."

Rev pauses, hands clenching my thighs tighter. "God, why is that the biggest turn on?"

Without warning, I squeeze him tightly and flip so that I'm on my back and he's on me.

I grab his hips and dig my nails in as I tug him into me, harder. He groans this time as he obliges, pushing harder. My breaths grow louder.

"Rev," I say desperately. "You're mine."

"Caelynn," Rev warns, his voice low. He presses his nose into my neck, slowing his rhythm. "Fuck, I'm going to come too soon if you don't stop."

"Then, come."

He tenses but rocks into me, deeper.

"Not until you do," he says through clenched teeth.

I laugh. "Believe me, I won't be letting you off that easy. Come, and then I'll put you to work elsewhere."

His breathing is labored, his eyes clenched closed.

"Now, come," I demand.

Rev obeys. His body convulses against mine, bucking his hips wildly. I'm able to fully enjoy it as he comes undone against me, my own pleasure never pausing.

"Good," I say as he stills, breathing heavy against my neck. "Now, get on your knees."

Rev obeys that order too, with a glint of amusement in his eyes. On his knees, he needs no further instruction. His tongue strokes me, and I throw my head back. "My God," I whimper as he works me. His finger enters me playfully, and I squirm against the new rush of sensation.

I tense, pleasure building, and bite down on my fist.

"Your turn, Angel," he murmurs against me. His expert strokes elicit a new rush of intense bliss that crashes into me. Waves and waves of pleasure sweep me into oblivion as stars explode behind my eyes.

He drags out the rush of pleasure, and then as I still, he looks up at me and smiles. "Good girl."

"Mmmm," I say, body suddenly heavy.

Rev sweeps me into his arms and carries me to the bed. It creaks as he lays me on the stiff covers.

I can already barely keep my eyes open as he pulls the blankets up and settles in beside me. "Rev," I whisper as I curl against his chest. "I love you."

"I love you too, Angel." He kisses the top of my head.

"Are you going to leave tomorrow?"

He stills for a moment then pulls in a long breath. "Yes. I have a few things to take care of in the Luminescent Court. But I promise we'll see each other soon. It's not goodbye, okay?"

My heart aches, but I refuse to allow it to break. Not now. "Okay," I whisper. I close my eyes, my cheek resting against his warm chest. It's hard to breathe, thinking about Rev leaving me behind here. But it's necessary. I've always known it would be necessary.

"You were right," I say.

"About what?"

"That this is worth it. The pain of being apart from you— it's worth having this." I look up to find a teary-eyed Rev watching me too.

"We'll make this work, I promise. We will," he assures me.

I nod and then close my eyes against the rising heartache. I'm thankful, then, for my utter exhaustion because even pain and the fear of losing Rev cannot keep sleep from claiming me.

32

CAELYNN

A crowd of onlookers gather as we approach the newly restored portal. The stones glisten against the scattered sun peeking through the breaks in the dark leaves hanging above.

I am both eager and terrified. I hadn't wanted this moment to come because it means it is time for Rev to leave. To go his own way.

He doesn't belong here, and he certainly can't stay forever.

His fingers interlace with mine, and my lips flicker into what is almost—almost—a smile. But I can't make it complete the intended form.

"It's not the end," he assures me again.

I give him one small nod. He squeezes my hand. It is the end, though. Not the end of us, but the end of this part of our relationship. We won't see each other much after this. He won't sleep in my bed. He won't be there to hold me when I am upset. He won't be there to whisper comforting words in my ear when I am near spiraling.

It is the end.

It is simply also the beginning of something new. And I

suppose that's okay too. Because only weeks ago, I'd thought we could never be together at all. Maybe that would have been easier. Now that I know what it's like to have his arms around me—what it's like to feel his pure adoration—I don't know how to let it go.

"Today is a day of celebration," I tell the crowd and only barely manage not to allow my voice to crack. "This is the beginning of our healing. The beginning of our reconnection to the rest of the realm." It's ironic that this reconnection means the separation of Rev and me.

It is not the end.

"The Crackling Court will be remembered as the first court to welcome us back into the fold. Our healing will not be easy. It will not be fast. But we will return to our former strength. This is simply our first step."

The crowd roars, breaking into ground-shaking applause. Finally, my lips slip up into a smile.

This is my fate. I will rebuild this court, my home. "I will make sure the world remembers us."

I nod to the Crackling fae standing beside the portal waiting. The taller of the two stands straight. He holds up a dark stone—obsidian—and the crowd hushes. He places the final piece of the portal at the crown of the archway. One beat, that's all we have to wait before power crackles between the stones. I suck in a breath as the dark ripples begin flowing like water.

Applause begins again over the gasps of awe. Then, only a moment later, a form steps through the archway. King Raijin, the Crackling King, stands before, me smiling wide. "Queen Caelynn," he bows. "No crown?"

I smile. "Not yet."

He holds out his hand, waiting for me to grasps his forearm. "It is only a formality."

I return the gesture, firmly grasping his arm with mine. "I thank you again."

"It is my pleasure." His bright golden eyes flicker to Rev over my shoulder. And I know he means it. I do believe in Rai's sincerity. I simply also see his shrewdness. He knew exactly what he was doing when he decided to build this portal.

In only a matter of weeks, he has become an anchor alliance for Rev. He will certainly be in his confidence, and he has rightfully earned it.

Rai and Rev greet each other with a firm embrace and easy smiles. The crowd applauds again.

"Are you ready?" Rai asks. His words are gentle, and we both know what he really means.

"Not at all."

Rai squeezes his arm.

"It is not the end," Rev says for a third time.

I step up to Rev. "It's for the better," I whisper.

He shakes his head. "No. It is necessary, but it is not for the better."

I take in a long breath.

"Will you stay at my court for a while?" Rai asks Rev casually. "The High Court construction is near complete, but I'd welcome you. And you, Caelynn. Any time."

"I have matters to deal with at home," Rev answers. "Then, I will travel to the High Court, but I do thank you for the offer."

I want to ask him what he must do back at home. I was too tired to ask him last night, and today was another day of rushing about, meeting newly hired guards and cleaners, and, of course, fueling the fountain. But now, my heart is tight, and I can't manage to ask the question. It doesn't matter, at the end of the day. His affairs are not mine. Not anymore.

"I will send you many messages," he promises.

I chuckle as Rev pulls me into his arms. No one present could mistake this embrace for a polite affection. Rev squeezes me, fingers digging into my back. "I don't want to let go," he whispers, his voice shaking.

"I know." I blink back tears, refusing to let go. We stand there for several moments. Will this be the last time we allow this kind of public affection? When will he hold me like this again? Ever?

I shake my head from those thoughts because I will not be able to hold back the tsunami of pain threatening to release in my chest. "I love you," I whisper.

He freezes. His face presses into the crook of my neck. "God, please don't make me let go."

I chuckle, tears welling. Shit. I can't hold it in much longer.

"I love you too, Caelynn. You will be in my thoughts every moment. And that is not an exaggeration."

Finally, he releases me, and I stumble back. My bottom lip trembles as I look up to the black leaves of the shadow maple. I am home. This is the love I can focus on. The one I can keep.

"We will fight together. Soon." He nods sharply, his own silver eyes dim and rimmed with red. We are still waiting for the next move. We've been surprised the Night Bringer has not yet reacted to my taking the throne. I'm just waiting for that bomb to drop.

"It is not over," Rev says firmly.

One last look, letting my love for him show clearly, and a smile, despite my cracking heart. That's all we have left.

Then, Rev turns and marches through the portal, leaving the Shadow Court, and me, behind.

33

REV

I fall to my knees the moment I'm through the portal, and I'm barely able to hold back sobs as the pain of her absence hits me. But though we are gone from the Shadow Court, there are still onlookers. Crackling Court soldiers stare at me, shocked and confused.

Rai squats beside me, but he doesn't speak. He lets me mourn these first few moments without her. I don't know how long I stay there, but eventually I lift my head and give Rai a pathetic, bitter laugh.

"I have a bottle of scotch with your name on it," he finally says, smacking my back. "Come on."

I resist the groan. As much as scotch isn't my favorite drink, the pain and burn may be more welcome than usual today. Rai keeps his arm slung over my shoulder as we walk down the hill toward Black Lake. A rushing sound catches my attention, and I stop, watching the usually silent waters slosh.

"Did something change?" I ask.

Rai frowns. "It's been a tad more active these last two

days. Still no tides, no disruptions. Just a gentle shifting of the waters."

I purse my lips. "Keep me updated on any changes."

"We've increased security all around."

I nod. "I'll send a message to the queen to send over some High Court guards to help. It's important we know the moment anything changes here."

Rai nods and guides me down a path the other direction toward his capital city. I'd planned to head to the Luminescent Court tonight to meet with my father, but... Rai is probably right that spending a night drinking away my sorrows first may be exactly what I need. Tomorrow, I will face the Luminescent King.

34

REV

The moment the High Court carriage bumps through the portal, there are gasps of awe.

I hadn't announced I was heading home, so they are unprepared, but one look at the gold carriage, and the Luminescent Court soldiers leap into action. One sprints back toward the palace, the other three run toward us. There are also half a dozen High Court guards marching behind us.

I spent a full day moping in the Crackling Court, chatting with Raijin. It was necessary to leave Caelynn in the Shadow Court, but it still hurts to be apart from her. To know that our relationship will never be the same.

Rai's wife was suspiciously absent, and I suspect it was for my benefit. They were right, too. As much as I'd never ask her to stay away, seeing Rai with her would have taken me out. I'm happy they're happy, but I'm miserable that I am miserable.

Today, though, I woke up determined. There is hope. It's far in the distance, but there are things I can do to solidify the future I want. The future I must know is possible or the next several decades will be torture. I honestly don't know if I'll survive it without a tangible path to being with Caelynn again.

In the Luminescent Court, the High Court portal is only a few hundred feet from the palace steps. But the other ruling court portals are farther out, closer to the rest of the city.

Since we passed through the Crackling Court portal, we're half a mile away from the palace gates and closer to the townspeople. And just as I expected, there are shouts and a pattering of footsteps as people rush to witness my return.

It's only the second time I've been back to my homelands since I was named High Heir, and it wasn't well known that I returned at all the last time. This time, the people will know.

The more interest I can stir, the better.

The carriage continues forward at a snail's pace, and by the time we reach the wrought iron gates into the palace grounds, there are a few hundred people lining the street behind me.

I open the windows and wave at the smiling fae who shout back. There is laughter and eager waving. A few bold souls rush up to the carriage and reach for me, but they are knocked back by High Court guards.

"Rev!" the crowd chants over and over.

These people don't know me, but they love me.

This kind of attention has always felt strange, but today it serves a purpose. I intend to use the people's devotion as leverage against my father.

Palace guards swarm the gates, carefully guiding the carriage through, and within only a few moments, we're safely inside. The carriage picks up speed, bouncing down the paved pathway until it halts right at the white stairs leading up to the palace.

I climb out without waiting for my personal guards to open it and I march up the glistening steps. With a loud crack, the massive doors part at the center and begin the slow drawl out, but I slip through as soon as I'm able to fit.

High Court guards and Luminescent Court guards follow behind me as I continue my purposeful march. The Luminescent King nor any advisors have met me yet, which means I'm right on time.

Down a long corridor, I stop in front of a shining silver-painted door. "Open it," I order to the closest Luminescent guard. With shaking fingers, the guard fits his brass key into the slot and turns it slowly until the door unlatches with a soft click.

I throw open the doors to the meeting chambers, ensuring they slam back against the wall.

I remember the time Caelynn did nearly this exact thing —barged into a public meeting, causing my father to nearly lose his shit. Still one of my favorite memories.

The thought allows my lips to quirk up into an arrogant smirk just as I meet my father's harsh stare.

He's sitting on his makeshift throne on a platform before several advisors, with my two half-brothers on each side of him.

"Reveln," my father's voice is low, full of undisguised venom, "we were not expecting you."

"Were you not?" I ask, tilting my head innocently. My snide smirk has not faded. I'm not as good at this as Caelynn. I cannot hide my pleasure at their discomfort.

When no one responds, I take the opportunity to pull a chair over and sit next to Arlan, the eldest of my brothers. Well, I suppose technically we share no blood at all, but no one outside of our family knows that bit of tricky truth.

My father is not my father by blood, and my two brothers, who were not conceived in an official union with the queen, are not considered true heirs. They can be *named* heirs but only as a backup plan when there are no true heirs. Ironically, I am a bastard as much as they are. My father is simply too proud to publicly admit that his wife had an affair.

And without that knowledge, the people would riot if the king were to replace me in the line of succession. It makes sense why he'd constantly tried to present me as weak and stupid to the public, so he'd have ammunition in case he ever had to strip my title.

From the day Reahgan died, he's been plotting to undermine and replace me. But I've bested him at every turn. Now that I'm High Heir, he cannot undo the High Queen's choice.

He hates me more now than he ever has—which is saying a lot. I've learned to enjoy it, to be honest. It feels good to shed the shame of a father who doesn't appreciate or care for me. And now, I relish the moments I can make him as uncomfortable as he has made me my entire life.

But, after my fun, I have a plan that will relieve it. Sadly. It is in the best interest of everyone.

The chair I choose is cool metal, not nearly as luxurious as the rest of the royal family, but I don't mind. I flop down and set my ankle over my knee in a much too casual position. The king openly glares at me.

I only smile.

"So, what matters are we discussing today?"

Arlan's brow lifts, but his features remained schooled. My eldest half-brother is nearly seventy-five years older than me, and we've never exactly been *friends*. Reahgan was in a true rivalry with him, and I was always on Reahgan's side.

Bastards, generally, are treated well but not given the same education as an heir would. Arlan and Brannon, both, were an exception. Often, they were given more attention than me.

At the time, that bothered me to no end. Now, it makes all the sense in the world.

My father has expected Arlan to take his throne for the last decade.

Cairo, one of the king's oldest advisors clears his throat. "We were discussing the shadow rebels involvement in—"

My father lifts a hand to stop him. "Of course, having the High Heir in our meeting is a pleasure," he pauses to give me a stare of veiled rage, "but these are not High Court matters."

The advisors grow still as death.

I let the silence linger, holding my father's stare. Brannon shifts awkwardly.

"These are Luminescent Court matters," I say.

The king doesn't speak.

"And I am the Luminescent Heir. Becoming High Heir does not change that." Not technically. But it is common knowledge that the High King cannot also govern an individual court during their reign. A steward takes control for those one hundred years. Occasionally, the previous ruler would continue their reign, but more often the successor takes control.

"Arlan is being prepared to take the throne now that you will be otherwise committed for the next century." He says it like it's an inconvenience, like being the High Heir is somehow bad for our court.

"That's wonderful," I say. One of the advisors lets out a relieved breath. "Arlan will make a wonderful steward."

The Luminescent King clenches his jaw and finally breaks eye contact.

"You can deal with your personal grudges and small court matters on your own," I say evenly, even though I'm itching to know what my father's plans for 'dealing with the Shadow Court rebels' are, "so long as you don't retaliate. That would then become High Court matters."

The king sneers. "If they attack us as they attacked the Crystal Court—"

"The conflict is already being dealt with. Any rebels will be punished accordingly. We needn't resort to war."

"You think because you put that bitch on the throne—"

My metal chair clangs to the ground as I stand rapidly. "Do not call her that, father."

"Do not call me that, Reveln."

A bitter laugh bubbles up in my throat. "Oh, are we being open about that sticky bit of truth now?"

Cairo retrieves my chair quickly and quietly, placing it just behind me.

"Thank you," I say kindly. He gives me a small smile. That smile is an impressive rebellion if I'm honest.

My heart is still hammering, but I take my seat again.

"What have you really come for, Reveln?" Arlan asks.

"I'd like to arrange a parade in my honor," I say.

The room stills once again. The advisors exchange uncomfortable glances, trying desperately to read the room.

"Is that a joke?" the king asks.

"No. It is customary for the home court of the High Heir to celebrate in some manner. As a show of support. The tension between us is no secret to those in this room, but the citizens have no clue. And it would be strange to skip this important step."

The king narrows his eyes. It is not direct anger but rather the examining of an opponent. "The townspeople held a celebration in your honor just last week. We provided food and drink. It was a merry time for all."

I resist an eye roll. "That's wonderful. However, did the palace plan it? Did anyone from the royal family attend?"

I wait, continuing the staring contest with the king.

"We do not need another event," he says firmly.

"What if I give something in exchange?" I smile. "I'd like to make a deal."

35

CAELYNN

My body is heavy with exhaustion, and my stomach is tight with anxiety. All I really want is to close my eyes and let the world fade away for hours and hours.

I lay down on the lumpy bed, the smell of dust still lingering in the air.

Yesterday, the Whisperwood Queen—Emberly, as she tells me to address her now—moved me to the royal wing on the other side of the palace. With the increase in magic, this section was deemed hospitable again. It is safer for a ruler in this part of the palace, and it's supposedly more luxurious.

For now, it simply seems dirtier.

I don't know what it will take to freshen up this place entirely. It's been hundreds of years since this portion of the palace housed anyone but phantoms. Now, even those are gone.

"You are allowed to rest," the book purrs against my chest.

"There's no rest for the wicked," I mumble.

I swear I can feel the book roll its hypothetical eyes. *"You are not wicked."*

"Sure I am." My voice is so soft it practically disappears

into the room. "I will do whatever it takes to win this chess game. Cheat, kill, steal. Anything."

"*Die?*"

"I have no problem dying."

"*Do you want to?*"

I frown, my heavy eyes closing by their own fruition. "Do I want to what?"

"*Die.*"

My eyes fly back open, stomach twisting. "No," I whisper. I don't want to die. I want to see what my court could become. I don't want to abandon them. Especially not now that I've seen what will happen if I disappear. The work I've done for the last week has given them back some strength, but it would all disappear quickly if I was to leave. There is no one else.

No others that could take on this burden.

There is no other hope for the Shadow Court. It's only me.

I also don't want to leave Rev. I know we'll be apart—I know we can't ever really be together—but I want those scattered moments of happiness.

"I want to live," I say more to myself than anything. But the book still purrs in pleasure.

"*Good,*" it says. "*You have much to live for. I'm glad you're finally beginning to see that.*"

With my luck, it will be just in time to lose my life for good. Like fate didn't want to take away my life until I truly knew what I was losing. I sigh. It doesn't matter. I want to live, and I will fight for the chance to do just that.

"*Are you going to rest?*"

"No," I say, even as my eyes drift shut again. "Give me an update."

"*Luscious is meeting with the rebels tonight.*"

I breathe in through my nose. "Does Drake have any influence or connection to this meeting?"

"*Drake has had no direct influence on the rebels since the attack.*"

Well, that's good news. "What is their mindset? Do they feel content with the changes in the court?"

"*Some. Not all. They do not intend to halt their activities, however. Some believe you are planted by the High Court to appease the Shadow fae only enough to stop uprising, but not enough to change course. They think you are in the pocket of the High Court.*"

"Of course they do." I suppose it doesn't surprise me, though, after I showed up with the High Prince. They'd either suspect our relationship or they'd think I'm loyal to the High Courts.

"*Those rumors have been perpetuated by Drake's inside men.*"

I groan. My body aches. I squirm, seeking a more comfortable position.

"*You could take a sleeping draft. Or pain-reducing herbs.*"

I shake my head.

"*You are a stubborn fae.*"

I shrug. All I really want, honestly, are Rev's arms around me. His warm chest to lie back on. His comforting and supportive words in my ear.

Tears sting my eyes, but I keep them closed. I'm so tired. So in need of comfort. But I will rise above those needs. Because those are things I cannot have.

Rev is mine, but he is far from me, and that will be true for the rest of my life.

"Do you think that me taking the shadow throne was part of the Night Bringer's plan?"

"*What makes you think that?*"

I shrug. "I'm tired and distracted; that seems to work in

his favor. And the fact that he has not made any big moves makes me think this is how he wants it. Maybe he planned for me to take the throne so I'd give all of my magic away, leaving me drained so that when he acts, I won't have the strength to fight back."

"*Caelynn, this battle is not about your strength. You will not win by your power. You will win by your determination, resilience, intelligence, and your allies.*"

"Allies," I repeat. "I've pushed away all of my allies."

The spell book sighs. "*If there is one thing that the Night Ancients could be pleased about, it is your separation from your allies. But they have not abandoned you. All you must do is ask for help if you need it. Do not be too stubborn for that, Caelynn. The Night Ancients want to dismantle your hope. They want you weighed down by heartache and loneliness. But you have the power to ensure that doesn't happen. He told you his plan. He wants to destroy you from the inside. Take away the things that bring you comfort. Take away the things that bring you hope.*"

I frown. "He will want to crush the Shadow Court, right?"

"*What better way to dishearten you, than to perpetuate distrust in your own people? Right now, you have enough allies to defend your court if he were to make a move against it. The best way to destroy the Shadow Court will be through the rebels.*"

I sigh. I can understand that. But the threats hanging over my head have me anxious. "And what plans are the rebels making?"

"*Drake has a line of spies that have reached those trusted by the rebels. He is feeding them information. The High Court is still seeking those responsible for the Crystal Court attacks, and keeping under the radar is the rebel's current plan of action. They are discussing how to utilize the gemstones they acquired. They are also planning to discuss you.*"

I roll my eyes behind my closed lids.

"Perhaps it's time I met these rebels."

Tameria, Octavia, Luscious, and the Whisperwood Queen—Emberly—sit in chairs facing me, in the same meeting room as every past meeting. The fire flickers weakly behind me. The walls are shinier than before, and in this one small room one can almost see what this place used to be.

Emberly and her nephews have spent a lot of time organizing the new staff and reopening sections of the palace. We now have a full wing in the east—where my rooms are—as well as two massive halls for dining and entertaining—in case the opportunity should ever arise.

The magic I've continued to flow into the fountain is spreading, seeping deeper into the stone of the Shadow palace.

They also tell me the farmers in the areas closest to the capital are experiencing impressive fall crops and there is increase in trade in the area. Those reports make me feel better. I know drinking from the well will help those fae individually, but part of me feels guilty for so much of the new magic going to restoring the palace. The queen tells me it's necessary, though. We must be able to put on a strong and established front if we are to have any hope of facilitating strong marriages with other courts.

I want to give more, but I heed Rev's warnings not to overextend myself.

My body is stiff and heavy at all times, though. Every time I begin to refuel, I give it all away again. Over and over. My eyes are heavy, and I find myself wanting to sleep between every visit to the well, but I can't. There's so much to do.

I think that's why the queen and her nephews have been

working so hard to get things in order for this new normal—to stop me from doing it all myself. It's helpful because I've never overseen anything before, let alone a palace full of staff or an entire kingdom. To learn all of that while also giving all my spare energy to the fountain... would be impossible.

The queen's older nephew begins our meeting, talking about the sections of the palace where the magical blocks have been removed and the areas that have been deemed livable. There are several others that will remain closed off while we work on rebuilding the magical structures throughout the kingdom. They only plan to have a quarter of the palace fully functioning and open for use until further notice. Which I don't mind. This place is massive, and we certainly don't need all of it. It's much more important to get the citizens the aid they need.

"There is still much to be done," Octavia says. "And much to discuss. Your relationship with the High Prince not the least of these."

I blink and shift my gaze to her. "Excuse me?"

The room quiets.

"What about my relationship with Rev?" I ask firmly.

"He loves you," the Whisperwood Queen says gently. "And yet he remains the High Prince." Her dark eyes are soft. Pity. It's pity she wears. "However, this isn't a conversation we must have yet." She sends a glare at Octavia, whose eyebrows rise. She doesn't look at all sorry.

"We've spoken about the need for strong marriages in our court," Luscious says, a bite to his tone, "and you are not exempt from that."

I release a sharp breath.

"I don't know what my intentions are regarding my future partner." It's as honest as I can be without outright declaring I'd never touch another male and they'll have to get over it.

Though, I admit only to myself the only reason that is true is because I haven't allowed myself to dwell on it. It makes sense I'd need a partner, someone to rule with, a father to a future heir. But the thought of being with anyone besides Rev is abhorrent, and I know that will never change.

Rev and I are not publicly linked, but our souls are bonded in a permanent way. Open relationships are common among fae but uncommon in both rulers and in fated mates. For me, there is only Rev. There will only ever be Rev.

But I know he'll also be pressured to marry.

"My rule will never be a typical one," I tell them. "And my relationship is not up for debate. I understand what is at stake and will fight for this court in every possible way—it just may not be in a way you or the other advisors like."

Luscious purses his lips but holds his tongue.

The table is quiet again. My advisors push their food on their plates but no longer talk.

"Do we have any other court members?" I ask, mostly to shift the topic anywhere but on my relationships. And it's something I've been thinking about. We're rebuilding the power of this palace, but we won't be able to do the same to smaller structures around the kingdom like the one my father owned. A count living in a shack in a small village. Are there others like that?

"A few," Octavia says. "Some have openly declared they want nothing to do with the royal family. Most of those don't understand the full extent of what happened all those years ago. They feel betrayed and neglected by the Shadow Court."

"Was my father one of those? Who wanted nothing to do with it?"

Emberly nods. "Your family has stayed away from politics for a few generations."

"And the other families?"

"Two in the mountains near the Crumbling Court. One living north near the Glistening Court."

"And the wanderer," Tameria adds.

"Wanderer?"

She nods. "He's a cousin of mine, but he has no living direct family. He lives in the Whisperwood. Alone."

I nod. "Invite them all."

"They don't want to come here," Luscious says. "They've denounced us..."

"Invite them."

"It's unlikely they'll even respond," the queen says more gently.

"That's fine. They'll be invited and welcomed if they change their mind. Rebuilding is about more than magic. I won't punish anyone for how they reacted during trying times."

"What about dissenters? Those who've integrated into other courts?"

I pull in a long breath. "To be honest, if those who've entered other courts want to come back, it would help us more than hurt. Besides, as you've said, many were forced into foreign marriages. I'd welcome those women and families back with welcome arms. We are not in a position to be vindictive or hold grudges. But we can take each situation as it comes."

"I agree." Emberly gives a soft smile.

"Is this meeting done?" Luscious asks, his eyes lidded. He's annoyed with me, but I can't muster the energy to care. "I have places to be."

"Do you?" I ask sweetly.

"Yes." His jaw ticks.

"Where?"

He frowns. "I am meeting friends. I don't see how 'where' would matter."

I cross my arms. "What friends?"

His jaw clenches. "You've threatened to kick me out of your council and have now deigned to invite those who have been disloyal to our court back without second thought. Now, you question me like a thief? What do you think I'm going to do? Plot to assassinate you? Or is it your lover you worry for?"

Anger wells in my chest like a burning fire. I stand slowly, glaring at this fae that is supposed to be an ally. Now clearly an enemy.

Panting, I clench my hands into tight fists. "No, I'm more concerned for the Crystal Court," I say in a smooth tone, despite my anger. My eyes do not hide my rage, though, and his eyes do not hide his fear.

His eyes flare, but his lips remain still. Good.

"Go to your meeting," I say, eyes pinned to his. *I'll meet you there.*

He pauses for only one moment before fleeing from the room.

36
REV

"Arlan will take the Luminescent Court throne when I am crowned High King, and he will never be asked to rescind it. That is my offer."

For the first time in my life, my father looks shocked. *Not father,* I remind myself. He has never truly been my father, not even in heart. I wished and prayed and fought for him to love me, but never once was he proud or caring. That won't change. That's one dream I know I will never achieve. But I can impress him. I can absolve some of his hatred and give him something he deeply—perhaps desperately—desires. He doesn't deserve it, and it almost pains me to do it, but a good politician puts aside petty disputes to make necessary deals.

This is necessary.

"You are saying," the King of the Luminescent Court pauses, eyeing me suspiciously, "that you will rescind your right to my throne... for a parade."

I snort. "Not exactly. I want an alliance. I want open support from the Luminescent Court. I do not want to be High King and be opposed at every turn by my own kingdom."

My father considers me. Arlan's eyes are wide, his expression softer than I've ever seen it. He looks... hopeful.

Arlan speaks, his voice deep and measured. "I do not intend to oppose you as High King." He clasps his hands together. A nervous habit. "I am surprised, though, that you would not want to become king of our court."

"Since the day my brother died, my goal has not been to rule this court. It has been to earn respect and become the High King of the realm. After one hundred years as High King, I don't see why I'd need to rule again."

"This also means your children will have no claim to the throne." Arlan leans back, his gaze scrutinizing.

I bite the inside of my lip, then I nod. "I believe that makes the most sense, given the circumstances."

The Luminescent Court King leans forward. He's shocked once again, but his expression cools quickly. "I know what this is about."

My eyebrows rise, but I keep my expression schooled. "Do tell."

"If you make that Shadow witch the High Queen, I swear—"

I hold up my hand. "Caelynn will not be publicly linked to me while I am High King."

He narrows his eyes. "Then, you intend to join her court after your rule?" His tone is calmer, but there is still clear disdain.

I nod.

The room remains utterly quiet for several more moments. "You expect us to align with the Shadow Court? You expect the people to simply forget her indiscretion as you marry the shade bitch that killed your brother? My heir. My son!"

I press my lips together tightly, working to control my

reaction. This time, I will let his insults pass. "I understand why that is uncomfortable for you. I don't ever expect you or the people of this court to love Caelynn or be happy when I leave behind this court for hers. But this is a fair agreement, and you know it. The Luminescent Court will have a High King. I will work for and with this court. And you will have your rightful king and future heirs."

"You ask for little in return," Arlan responds. "It's a fair deal."

The king's lip curls in disgust. "I hate you. I have always hated you."

"I know." I lean back in my chair. "But this gets us both what we most want. Sacrifices must be made in any negotiation. I don't ask for your love and acceptance. I only ask—do you agree to my terms?"

The king takes in a long deep breath and then releases it slowly. "Let us prepare a parade for the new High Heir."

37

CAELYNN

I slip the spell book into the new shiny black leather bag Emberly gifted me, and I sling it over my shoulder. My clothes are casual but all in black, as usual. I'm ready for my night of sleuthing.

"Luscious is leaving the palace now."

I nod as I pace in my room in front of the open window leading out to a courtyard of overgrown shadow maples. The mountains rise over the back of the castle, looming in their powerful way. The mountain range has its own form of natural magic. It's not quite as impressive as the Whisperwood, but I suppose I'm partial. There are shadow sprites and phantoms in those mountains too, maybe I'd love it just as much.

"How much longer should I wait?" I ask the book.

"The others are gathering already. You could leave at any time, but your magic is low. You don't want to overuse it. I suggest waiting to limit your time in shadow."

"You're an all-knowing spell book, not a mother hen."

"What good is infinite knowledge if I can't use it to order people around?"

I chuckle. Truth is, I'm quite happy that it adds in its thoughts. It makes me feel much less alone. I don't have anyone to bounce ideas off now, and I've come to realize how lonely ruling this court is going to be.

I will develop relationships over time, I know. There will be friends whom I can trust. But I will never have a full partner by my side.

Movement in the trees outside my window catches my attention. Shadows twist and dance. Only a Shadow fae could notice the small variances in shade.

"Are those phantoms?"

"*Yes.*"

I watch the swirling shadows move through the trees for a few minutes, dancing to their silent music. "Have they been out there the whole time?"

"*No,*" the book whispers. "*They have returned due to the resurgence of magic.*"

"I did that."

"*Yes.*"

From what I can tell there are only two or three, but they sway and swirl. One of their forms grows into something massive. It blows something from its mouth, like a dragon breathing fire, and then it shrinks back into a tiny form and skitters away, like it's embarrassed of its performance.

"What are they doing?"

"*Playing,*" the book answers. "*They are testing the magic here. There isn't much for them yet, but it will grow daily.*"

"Remind me tomorrow to go visit them."

"*You're making a difference here.*"

I smile, still watching the shifting shadows bounce through the trees. "I know. Thank you."

The phantoms fade away, as does the excitement. I spin

back to the large, shadowed room and the loneliness hits hard, like it has so many times before.

"Any updates on the Night Bringer?" I ask as I begin to pace. More distraction. I need more.

"He is moving and scheming as usual, but he is good at keeping his intentions unvoiced. The Night Terror has groups of wraiths settling in various places around the realm. It seems they are trying to cover up any connection between the Whirling Court and the wraiths at present. The Night Bringer has also made contact the nomad in the Twisted Forest."

My stomach churns. "And?"

"I do not know where the nomad stands on the conflict; he has made no definitive promises and has not changed his usual behavior. But even if he does side with the Night Ancients, it will not change our plans."

"We can't become complacent," I mutter. "We should act before they do."

"Act how? The only course of action we have is to rouse the Lady of the Lake."

Sleep weighs on my mind as we talk through all of the same things we've talked about for days. I consistently need the reminder that we are waging a war the people around me do not see. He is still there, waiting for the moment to strike.

"But Reveln does not want to rouse her without permission from his ally in the Crackling Court."

I sigh. "I know. I made that promise too—that I'd at least tell him before I do anything. But what are we waiting for?"

"It doesn't hurt to strengthen your court before we force the battle to commence."

I purse my lips. "I just want it to be over, one way or another."

"I understand. You are feeling a lot of pressure."

I nod and shift my gaze out the dark window to the courtyard beyond. The leaves of the overgrown shadow maples rustle serenely.

"Where is Raven?" I whisper, expecting the answer to be that he doesn't know. Not in the fae world. Outside of our reach. But instead, the book is quiet.

Another silent moment passes, and I sit up quickly. My vision peppers black with the quick movement. "Where is Raven?" I repeat more forcefully. It's been several days since I've asked the question. During my days in the Frost Court, I asked multiple times per day, and the answer was always the same. Eventually, I stopped asking.

"*She is with Blane.*"

"Where?"

Another pause, and I am ready to wring the book's neck. "*In the Glistening Forest, currently.*"

My breath catches, stomach clenching. Is this good news? Or bad? "What is she doing? Is she okay? How long has she been in the fae realm?"

The book again delays in responding, but before I can react, it finally speaks. "*She is currently well and not in direct danger. She has been in the fae realm for three days.*"

Three days. I blink. She's been here for three days and he hasn't told me about it.

"What are they doing here?"

"*They are seeking to uncover Drake's plans.*"

I release a trembling breath.

"Drake's plans," I repeat. My breaths come out much faster. "They don't know Drake's plans?"

"*They know very little.*"

"What... what are their intentions then? Are they not working with Drake?"

"*They are not working with Drake or the Night Bringer.*"

My eyebrows furrow, and I frown down at the leather

tome sitting on a table by the window. My heart pounds rapidly, all thoughts of sleep gone from my mind.

"Were they ever working with them?" I ask slowly.

Another pause. Anger stirs in my belly. Anger and pain so deep I bend over, panting. "You've been withholding information from me," I say. Irrational rage. That same loneliness hits me, except this time, I'm overwhelmed by it. The spell book is not my friend.

"*No*," the book says in a careful tone. "*I always give you the information you ask for.*"

"You..." My mind spins, taking all this in. The book knew I was desperately seeking information about Raven. Yet, it didn't tell me when she reentered the realm. It knew that Blane was not working with Drake and did not ever bother to correct my assumptions that Drake's brother was his ally.

"Is Raven in danger with Blane? Is she being held against her will?"

"*No.*"

My knees buckle. Raven is...I shake my head. Raven is okay, and not being held against her will. This is good news. It is... but, my already broken heart splinters further. I close my eyes.

"Why didn't you tell me?" I whisper. But I don't wait for an answer. I don't even want one.

Maybe I shouldn't have trusted an inanimate object so fully. Maybe I should have realized the ancient spelled to give information to its owner is not my friend or ally.

Maybe I'm an idiot to feel this blindsided.

Tears well in my eyes. My heart aches so desperately for Rev's comfort once again.

But I'm alone.

Always, always alone.

I wrap my familiar shadows around my body as I slip out the window and shadow walk to the dark pathway beyond. Our soldiers are still new, and there aren't enough to cover every exit. I ignore the ache from my shattered heart as I slip from the palace walls and into the dark city.

I debated leaving the spell book behind after the realization that it's been keeping information from me. My hands still tremble at the thought.

But frustratingly, I realize I need it.

I need the book to figure out where the rebels are inside this complex city. And it will be extremely helpful to be able to weed out who is who and what each has done.

So, I will use the advantages I have, but I won't let my heart get involved a second time. I don't trust the spell book, except with information I know it is spelled to give.

It takes little effort to slip from my own palace without being noticed. I run, shadows covering me entirely, through the dark pathway and down into the city below, following the directions the book gives step by step.

The city is dark and silent, even once I reach the rows of small buildings. Only a few glowing lights are visible down the narrow streets. Not much night life, at least not in this part of the city.

The city is silent, at first, but soon the sounds of shouting and laughter and clinking drinks float through the air. *"There are three active taverns down this street. The last has a basement where the rebels meet weekly."*

I let my shadows fall as I approach the glowing shop. The windows are smudged, one of the panes cracked. The sign reading 'Whisper Wing' is crooked. Inside, there are wooden tables and chairs, all painted black. The smells of vomit, sweat, and beer slam into me the moment I'm through the door.

"Can I help you?" a deep-voiced bartender asks.

I smirk. "No."

"Then, scram."

"Certainly." I pull shadows around me again and disappear right in the middle of the room. I watch the barkeep, a tall but thin male with long-pointed ears and a black apron. His brows furrow, but after a long pause, he shrugs and goes about his business. If he recognized me, he didn't show it. If he cares that someone is using magic to hide from sight in his bar, it's not enough to react.

"*Take the hall to the right.*"

I follow the book's continued instructions and enter the narrow hall with faded black pain. I pause when the wood creaks beneath my boots. Keeping my weight even, I inch forward carefully. Soon, indistinguishable voices sound down the hall. Inching forward just a bit more and I can make out the words.

"She is not queen yet," someone else adds.

"She will be," a gravelly male voice says. Luscious, I recognize.

I continue until I am standing in the doorway just before a storage room. There are mead barrels and crates stacked in the corners. The light is a dim yellow, leaving much of the room still in shadow.

"Unless we stop it," someone says.

"There is no stopping it," Luscious says. "She is the last Shadowspell."

The room hushes.

"Truly the last?"

Luscious nods gravelly. "The wraith confirmed it. With

the news of her father's death, there is only her and deserters who have adopted other elements."

Wraith?

A female standing in the back of the room with crossed arms takes a step forward. "We always have the option of bringing those fae back and reclaiming the bloodline for the Shadow realm."

"Those are the royals who have betrayed us. You'd make them the ruler over us all?"

I frown. I hadn't considered that. Are there those of the Shadowspell line remaining? Just with other elements controlling their magic?

Maybe this game would never end.

"But the magic would be weakened, perhaps irreversibly so," Luscious says with a heavy sigh. "And it would take time. It is not a feasible choice."

The female quirks an eyebrow. "I'm only saying, we always have another option. We don't even need a Shadowspell. We only need a powerful Shadow fae to refuel the magic."

"We don't have any of those either," Luscious says. "We can explore those more desperate options if it comes to that. But for now, we will stick with Caelynn and see what can be done."

"Is she to be trusted, though? I've heard rumors of her role in the High Court."

"I don't yet know," Luscious says slowly. "She is certainly close to the new High Prince. I will admit, it seemed that he is more smitten with her than the other way around. But she holds her emotions behind a shield, so it is hard to say. It is possible she is controlled entirely by the High Court. It is also possible she is loyal to the Shadow Court, with the High Court in her pocket."

"You think she could control the High Prince?"

"She did seem to have a strong hold on him. But he left recently. It all remains to be seen."

"So, what will we do until then?"

"We'll find something on her," the female in the back says. "A secret she doesn't want anyone to know."

Luscious purses his lips. "The girl certainly has demons— literal and non. We could find something to hold over her and go from there." He nods sharply like that's the end of the conversation. "The Crystal Court attack was a success," he says, continuing the meeting, apparently.

"Are we to plan another?" a voice asks in the small crowd sitting among the mead barrels.

"No, not yet. The courts are angry with us. It won't be safe to act so soon after the last." Luscious crosses his arms and leans back in his chair. His expression is smug and confident. Distinctive from the indifferent annoyance he carries in meetings with me. He likes his power. "I believe that is why they planted our new queen."

"To root us out? You must be very careful, Luscious."

"I will be. She doesn't trust me, but she will not find out about this group. I will ensure it."

I quirk a brow and allow a smile to spread across my face. I resist the urge to show myself here and now.

"Rumors of her return are everywhere," a wrinkled fae male says. "They say she's the queen who was promised. They say she's the savior of the Shadow Court."

"She has brought us ruling court allies. People are talking about us returning to the High Court's favor," the standing female says.

Luscious shakes his head. "We will not allow it."

I blink back my surprise. *He doesn't want those things?*

The group slams their hands on the tables three times. *They agree?*

"We will not forgive their crimes without payment!"

"We will make them suffer as we have suffered!"

My heart sinks. *Oh, hell no.*

"What of our spies in the Whirling Court?" the female asks, hands on her hips.

"Our allies have been quiet since the Crystal attack. They did mention a parade in the Luminescent Court that would be a tempting target."

The fae murmur in agreement. Excited chatter expands through the room.

My stomach sinks, anxiety rising. These are certainly the people who celebrated the death of the last High Prince. The people who called me a hero for that terrible act.

My magic reacts to the anger building in my chest. The ground beneath my feet trembles, and the chattering settles into silence.

I take in a long breath and settle my anger, keeping my magic tight. My shadows curl tightly around my body, ready to spring into action. A snake coiled and ready to strike.

Luscious frowns, but when the shaking ends, he ignores it. "For now, we go along with her plans, and I will test her. See where her loyalties truly lie. A queen with control of the High King would be quite an asset."

"And if she is loyal to him?"

"Then, we will kill him."

My magic strikes without thought. Shadows streak from around my body and snatch Luscious by the throat. I stand and let my shielding magic fall. The small crowd scrambles away from me as I march toward a wide-eyed Luscious being strangled by my magic.

"Threaten him again," I say. Luscious gurgles in response

as my shadows constrict. "And you will see exactly how powerful I am." I clench my jaw. I desire his death. To show them who I can be—

The male that would dare conspire to control me and kill my mate? *I want him dead.*

I curl my lip, and I let him see the hatred in my eyes before I finally have my shadows release him. His body falls into a heap on the ground. *I control you*, I tell my magic.

"No one will touch Reveln." I turn to face the group. "No one, will touch another High Court ruler without *my* permission."

"We do not bow to you!" a male calls from the back of the room, even as he cowers behind three others.

"I am your queen," I say firmly. Luscious squirms at my feet. He pushes away, holding his neck and sucking in gasping breaths. "You will bow or you desert your court."

"She is a spy!"

"She's loyal to the High Court!"

I hold my chin up. "You know nothing about me."

The standing female takes a step closer to me into the light. She has thin brown hair pulled back into a ponytail, and her clothes are near rags. Her shoulders are back, and her eyes are dim, with remnants of fear, but she feigns her confidence which takes bravery enough. "We know that you attacked your countrymen in defense of a ruler from another court." She nods to Luscious still cowering at my feet. "A court that has taunted and shamed us. A court that has stolen our women and what little pride we have left."

"He's still alive," I comment casually, shifting my boot so that it nudges Luscious's leg. He scoots ever farther from me. "He is lucky I let him live."

"You'd kill your own people to defend a prince from another court?" she asks, like it only proves her point. I pull in a long breath, wondering if debating or negotiating with these people will even do any good. Perhaps I should have them all arrested. Or kill them here and now.

My magic purrs.

I understand their rage, though. The pain and fear in their eyes. They are seeking some way to take control over their circumstances. Some outlet for their anger. So, maybe it's pointless, but I will try anyway.

"Do you truly believe in such generalizations? That anyone from the Shadow Court must be innocent and anyone from the Luminescent Court must be guilty? I do not. I believe in individuals. I believe in actions deciding guilt, not blood. I understand your anger more than you know. I understand your thirst for vengeance. I remember feeling those exact things as an adolescent. I wanted the ruling courts to fear me. I wanted them to see how strong we can be."

"But that has changed?" the female asks, eyebrow quirking.

"In some ways, yes. In others, no. I believe in the Shadow Court, and I fully intend to show the ruling courts how powerful we can be. But I don't intend to use violence to do it."

"You are no Shadowspell." Luscious spits at my boots. "Your ancestor, were he here, would shun you. Punish you."

A few people in the crowd chuckle. "I'd pay to see that," someone says under their breath.

I narrow my eyes as I turn to face the male at my feet. He said 'ancestor.' Singular. And they did mention wraiths before. "Which ancestor?" I ask calmly. "Is that the wraith you spoke of?"

Luscious curls a lip. "The wraith is Darren Shadowspell, your last great ancestor. And he would have been disgusted to see you as his heir."

A soft sort of joy swells in my chest, but also rabid amusement.

I snort at first, but it rises into a true laugh, full and throaty. "You knew him," I finally get out. "You knew Darren in wraith form?"

Luscious frowns. It makes sense. I knew Darren was working with the Whisperwood Queen before the trials. And he would so be the type to participate in rebellion.

I remember his words when he first approached me in the human world to convince me to enter the trials. *There are those in our court who consider you a hero.*

I peer down at the pathetic male at my feet. Darren was terrible in some ways too. He would doom the whole world to save his court, but in the end, he found affection and empathy. Perhaps these fae could too.

"We really should have had this conversation over drinks, Luscious. It would have been so much more enjoyable."

"What are you talking about?"

I rock back on my heels casually. "You must not have seen your wraith for weeks, now, huh? At least three."

The female frowns. "Do you know what became of him?"

"Didn't he help the Crystal Court sacking?" someone asks from the back of the room.

My eyebrows rise. "No. But that explains a few things. Darren had nothing to do with the wraith attack on the Crystal Court. Your wraith friend was gone by then, and he will not be back."

The female frowns. "He is dead?"

"No, but he is gone from this world all the same."

No one speaks for a long beat.

"What are you talking about?" Luscious asks, finally rising to his feet and dusting the dirt from his slacks.

"Darren guided me through the Schorchedlands, all the

while attempting to convince me to turn back and abandon the spell book and Rev. But we grew close in those final days, and he finally agreed to be a true ally to me. He saved Rev, the fae you spoke of killing, even though he believed it would end his legacy for good. He found his redemption in the end when he chose love over his revenge, over the power in his beloved court."

Luscious and the female exchange glances, but I don't particularly care what they're trying to communicate.

"I will follow his legacy as I understand it, not as you do. I loved him. And believe me, I would give anything to have him guiding me through this too. I fully intend to fulfill his legacy —not by punishing the ruling courts but by killing the beings that put us in this situation to begin with. I am not happy with how our court has been treated over the years. There are certainly some in the ruling courts that are guilty of wrong doings, but so long as those courts are willing to reverse course and stop oppressing us, I don't need revenge. Not on other fae."

"On who then?" the female asks, eyes narrowed, considering.

"The being that trapped me as an adolescent and tried to trick me into slavery. I would have been his true puppet if I had followed his plans. If I had been foolish enough to trust him. When I killed Reahgan, it was not out of anger against the High Courts. It was to save myself from that fate."

"The Night Bringer," the female standing says in a whisper.

I nod. "And I have spent every moment since," I speak now through clenched teeth, "trying to get free from that monster. That is what I work toward now. I'm going to kill the Night Bringer."

38

CAELYNN

"You can't kill those beings. It's impossible. Fighting against those creatures is what ruined our court to begin with."

I shake my head. "There were repercussions to that battle. But I have been face-to-face with both of those monsters. I know who my true villain is. It is not the Ruling Courts. It is not Reveln or the High Queen."

The females's eyes remain unkind.

"The High Court is not innocent, but we will anger them plenty when we prove them wrong with our power and worth. We can, and we will. Our enemy is the Night Bringer, the Night Terror, and anyone who would align themselves with them. That reminds me—if anyone in this room has made a deal with those beasts," I lean forward, eyes intent and cruel, "run now."

Several fae pull in audible breaths, but no one moves.

"*None directly,*" the book answers my unasked question.

"Good." I nod. "Another line I will draw now—Drake of the Whirling Court has bargained with the Night Bringer. He is their ally, making him my enemy. Anyone who is working with the Prince of the Whirling Court is by extension the

Shadow Court's enemy. I will not condemn every Whirling Court fae, but I do not trust them. Not now. You mentioned having spies in that court. Who are they?"

"We are not giving you any information," the female says, crossing her arms.

I quirk a brow. "I can find out on my own if you wish."

She wrinkles her nose. "Go ahead and try."

My lips curl into a smug smirk.

"Gareth Humminger. He is a Shadow fae living over the border. Drake has several lines of spies feeding him information and gaining influence on the shadow rebel's actions."

"Darren, your wraith leader, did not have anything to do with the wraith attack on the Crystal Court. Prince Drake of the Whirling Court did. He knew of your attack through your friend Gareth."

The female's mouth drops open in shock.

"And believe me," I continue, "Drake did not add to your attack to do you a favor. He did so to increase fear in the ruling courts. He will do it again, and soon. Only this time, on a court that will have no problem retaliating. Do you know what will happen when a court at full power attacks these lands? You called me disloyal, but I see loyalty a bit different from you, obviously. I do not wish to see my people slaughtered, something it seems you are all too willing to accept in your irrational anger. There are several courts who would be happy to demolish the entire Shadow Court. One more large scale attack and that's where we could be."

The room remains still as my words sink in. Is it a reality they'd truly never considered?

"And your plan," the female says slowly, "is to kill immortal beings instead?"

"Yes."

"It's impossible."

"It is not. I know exactly how to destroy them for good."

"I don't believe you."

"That's fine. You don't have to. I am used to being under-estimated." I smile. "I am not here to ask for help but to give you a warning. I am stronger and smarter than you think. I will dismantle anyone that undermines me or my court. That includes you. I suggest you send a message to your friend Gareth that someone in his confidence has betrayed him by giving information to his enemies. And I highly suggest you do not harm anyone or anything in courts you deem enemies. Next time, there will be no forgiveness for your crimes. You will stand trial before me. And I will know what you have done. I have no problem executing a citizen of my own court to save the rest of the kingdom. You will not get out of punishment."

39

REV

I stop before the High Court portal, watching the soft rippling magic.

The queen sent me a message this afternoon that I am to return to the High Court today. I'd planned on heading back soon anyway, but now that I'm standing on the edge of the magic that will take me there, my stomach squirms with anxiety.

Memories flash through my mind of that awful night. Fae falling through the glass flooring. Blood splattering as stone slams into fleeing fae's heads. Bodies peppering the trembling ground.

Traumatic memories aren't the only things bothering me, though. It's that now, I'll be stepping into that role without her.

Taking my place as High Heir while she is gone feels wrong somehow.

And then, there's the fact that I know the Light Ancient is there watching. He's resting below the palace. A powerful being that hates my mate.

But this is something I must do. And so, I take that heavy

step through the archway. Magic washes over my body, and when I open my eyes, I am standing before the High Court palace.

Pristine. The castle and grounds look perfect, not a stone out of place. Gold and white stone lines the pathways, with not a pebble out of place. As if it never happened. As if only a week ago, dozens of fae didn't meet their end here. I pull in a long breath, my chest tight.

Then, I march forward, pulling on the mask I learned from Caelynn and pretending that my mind isn't throbbing with horrific images. I hold my head high, and I face the future I chose for myself.

My heart hammers in my chest, blood pumping so fast I can feel it in my limbs.

The princeling is back.

I suck in a breath at the sound of the ancient powerful voice, but I'm honestly not sure if it is real. There is no tremble in the earth along with the power. Only within my own body. Maybe I'm just hallucinating.

"Oh good, you're here."

I blink and realize I'm standing in the dining hall. The walls look the same as before, covered in the same golden and red tapestries. The chandelier appears exactly as before, with its stretching flames over every prong.

The High Queen sits at the head of the table as usual, staring over maps and letters spread out in front of her.

I wordlessly take a seat to her right.

"Caelynn is settled?" she asks without looking up.

"Yes," I say, mouth dry.

"Good." She looks up for the first time since I entered the

room, her amber eyes focusing on me. "It's for the best." Her smile is reassuring, but it only causes my gut to clench even harder.

Where is your shade witch mate? the voice echoes through my mind

I bite the inside of my mouth and force a nod.

"Reigning without a partner will be a challenge, but you are more than capable, Reveln."

"Thank you," I say, voice still too quiet. My chest still tight. But I do mean the words. Her confidence in me is encouraging.

"The council will be meeting later this afternoon. There have been a few events we must discuss."

"Events?"

The queen nods. "More wraith attacks. Two fae deaths in the Twisted Forest last night and an attack on the Whirling Court palace."

My stomach drops. "What... will be done?" I ask carefully.

"We are completing our investigation on the rebels. Three have been arrested and interrogated, they are awaiting trial. And on the wraiths, we have traced the attacks to wraiths residing in the Cave of Mysteries."

My heart pounds, mind spinning. The pieces all align. An attack on the Whirling Court, wraiths inside the shadowlands... Drake is planning to attack the Shadow Court. He is building his own justifications.

"The Whirling Court, what has been their response?"

"They are reasonably increasing their defense."

"Defense. You mean they are assembling an army."

"I have spoken with the King Tommin. They will attack no one without clear cause. We do not have a cause if we do not know who orchestrated the attacks."

"Drake did," I mumble.

"Excuse me? Do you really still believe that narrative, Reveln? I know you do not trust Drake, you believe him in bed with the monsters you fight, but do you really think he'd attack his own court?"

"He would if it gives him justification to attack the Shadow Court."

The queen shakes her head. "You concern me, Reveln. You do not think clearly when it comes to her."

I stand, chest heaving. "No. I think very clearly. The Night Bringer sent Caelynn a message telling her he would destroy everything she loves. An hour later, we learned of the rebel attack and Kari's injury. He can't attack Caelynn outright, so he's looking for ways to take away everything she cares for. Including the Shadow Court. He will vilify her court using the rebels—a real issue, I admit, but one we could handle. He will use that threat to justify the destruction of her entire court. It makes all the sense in the world."

The queen takes a long breath through her nose. "Sit, Reveln."

I obey, but my face is still hot, my heart still pounding.

She taps her forefinger on the table for a full minute, staring at the chandelier of flickering flame. "You believe the Night Bringer is behind all of the wraith attacks."

I nod.

"Did you know that the shadow rebels have been known to work with wraiths in the past?"

I frown.

She sighs. "The Whirling Court is not acting on anything yet. We have a council meeting tomorrow to discuss this. Take time to consider how you will approach the issue with the council, and get a firm grip on your feelings."

I nod, forcing long breaths.

"In better news, after the meeting, we are planning a

small gathering to celebrate the reopening of the palace. It will be only council members and their loved ones. We are in several delicate situations, so please be considerate and careful in your actions, but you may invite Caelynn."

A flickering of hope grows in my chest. Caelynn. I can see Caelynn tomorrow.

Give me a sacrifice, princeling.

I blink rapidly. "Thank you," I whisper.

The queen nods, and I rush to send off a message to Caelynn.

40

CAELYNN

I love you.

I frown at the scrawled words on the worn pages of the spell book in Rev's handwriting. Again, the phantoms are outside, dancing and performing. A few have even braved close to my window a time or two. They've shown me a warrior killing a massive beast. A female being crowned queen. And two lovers dancing.

Though, most of the time, they're bouncing through the trees with the shadow sprites. Those moments where they give me a show, I know, are meant for me, to give me strength.

"That's from Rev?" I ask the book, voice soft. I haven't spoken to the spell book since last night. And part of me wonders if he's only using a message from Rev as a way to force me to stop my cold shoulder.

"Yes," the book says softly. *"There is more if you'd like to read it."*

I grip the open book and carry it to my lumpy bed. "All right," I concede.

I miss you more than you could even imagine. I wish I

was better at poetry or something so I could express what I feel now, being apart from you, but I can't. Though I'm not very good at expressing my emotions through written word, I do have some good news to share. And bad, but I'll start with the good. You're probably aware of the bad already anyway.

I am back in the High Court as of an hour ago. The queen has informed me that there will be a gathering tomorrow to celebrate the rebuilding of the palace. It will consist of only council members and their loved ones. The queen suggested I invite you.

Please, for the love of everything holy, come. I need you here. I need to hold you again. I need to know that, though we're apart, there is hope for us. Because if I don't get that reassurance, and soon, I will implode.

I chuckle, tears welling in my eyes.

Please send your response as soon as possible so I can relax knowing I will see you tomorrow.

On to the bad news. I assume you are aware of the wraith attacks. One of them on the Whirling Court palace. The Whirling Court is said to be building its "defense" in response, which I worry means they are building an army. I wanted you to know where it seems the next attack will come from. We will do whatever we must to protect you.

Please respond soon. I love you.

My stomach clenches at the thought of war against my court, now, while we're still so vulnerable. There's little I can do to protect us on my own, though.

I suck in a few breaths. The High Court. Tomorrow.

"I'm surprised you'd even show me the whole message," I say, slamming the book shut. "You won't want me going to the High Court, will you? You can't trust me to be near the ancient you dislike."

The spell book sighs, pages fluttering. "*I am sorry for withholding information from you. It was wrong,*" the book says, its voice quiet. "*I am still your ally. Your friend.*"

I shake my head. My heart clenches again, the pang of betrayal still fresh. "Why? Why did you do it?"

"*I feared you'd use the truth behind their actions as fuel to approach the Light Ancient.*"

I bite the inside of my lip so hard I taste blood. "Why does that matter so much to you?"

"*You will die if you approach him.*"

"You don't know that!"

"*I am confident that once he realizes I am the one behind your knowledge—*" the book cuts off.

I narrow my eyes as the spell book, now sitting haphazardly against the window frame where I slammed it in my anger. It is a living being, with hopes and fears and memories and trauma.

"*Would you like an update on Raven? I can tell you everything I left out before.*"

I narrow my eyes at him. He's using her as a distraction now. Unfortunately, it's going to work.

My chest tightens. I cross my arms, willing my face to remain impassive.

"Blane went to find her at her school on his brother's orders, but he did not want to be involved in his brother's plans. So he agreed, but when it was time to turn Raven in to Drake, he hid her instead. They are friends, the three of them. They have been hiding together ever since.*"

My heart clenches. "I really wish you'd have told me that sooner."

"*I know. I am sorry.*"

"Now? What are they doing now?"

"*She and her allies are heading toward the Black Lake.*"

I blink at the use of the word allies. Raven is with her *allies*. I sit up straighter. "Why?"

"*They believe Drake or his allies are planning to approach the Lady.*"

I press my eyes closed, fingers pinching the bridge of my nose. If Drake or the Night Ancients get the Lady of the lake on their side... we'll be out of options.

41

REV

I wring my hands anxiously as the council members arrive one by one. The queen and I greet them at the front walk, and I do my best to remain emotionless.

Caelynn responded last night. She'll be here in the afternoon, after the council meeting. Soon. I'll see her soon. I'll have her in my arms soon.

I smile and embrace Rajin as he approaches, a beautiful redheaded female on his arm. Her smile is kind, her eyes the color of storm clouds. "Prince Reveln. It has been too long," she says, though it's only been a few days. I incline my head in greeting.

Alia was a countess from the Glistening Court, and though we were never close, we certainly ran in the same circles for a while. Even as Rai and his mate pass by us and enter the palace arm in arm, I watch how he clings to her. How she leans into him. How his eyes shine when he smiles at her.

My mate will be here soon.

But it will never be the same.

Will you bring me my sacrifice, Reveln?

I clench my jaw against the whispering words of the ancient inside my mind. I wonder if I'm going insane or if it's real. Honestly, either could be true. I'm still terrified of this place. I still see the blank stares of dead fae staring at me from the rubble in the courtyard and on misshapen bodies on the palace steps.

"Rev?"

I blink, only to realize Kari and Ty stand before me, looking rather concerned. "Sorry," I mumble and then wrap my arms around Tyadin quickly.

He chuckles and returns the embrace. "Where did you go just now?"

I shake my head and decline to answer that one. I'm not sure how anyone would take it if I was to admit I am hearing voices now.

"I hear Caelynn has claimed her throne," Kari says.

"And that King Raijin was the first to build a portal in her court," Ty says, wiggling his eyebrows.

"Don't remind me," she groans. "Don't worry, I have my own surprise planned for her coronation. When will it be, by the way?"

I ignore the pit in my stomach and allow myself to focus on the now. On my friend supporting the love of my life. "We haven't planned it. The Whisperwood queen wanted to make it this week, but Caelynn wants to focus on our... other issues first."

Kari's smile fades.

"I'm almost surprised you're still here, wearing silver and gold," Ty jokes.

"Black would look good on you." Kari winks. "I think I'd look rather good in gold." She stares up at the palace admiringly.

I sigh but give no response. Because there isn't one to give. They're teasing me, I know, but it still hurts.

"We'll see you inside," Kari says suddenly, perhaps reading that their jokes didn't go over as intended. Then, she pulls Ty away and toward the palace gates.

They're right; I would look good in black. And sometimes, I wish I was brave enough to walk away from all of this to live out a destiny beside Caelynn.

42
CAELYNN

The Crackling Court is quiet when I step through the portal.

The other ruling court portals quietly shimmer in a circle all around me. The trees rustle in the breeze.

The world feels so peaceful. The sky is a pretty blue, no clouds in sight. The wind rustles the leaves of the forest around me. The waters of the lake are as glassy and still as before.

But the sounds of wildlife I heard the last time I was here are noticeably absent.

"*He is here.*"

"Where?" I whisper.

"*In the tree line west of the lake. He's expecting you.*"

I frown and step toward the hill leading down to the dark lake. My chest is tight, but I force myself to take in deep breaths, in through my nose out through my mouth. I'm done waiting. Done playing this chess match.

I'd like to ask the spell book how it knows the Night Bringer is waiting for me. He doesn't know intentions. Is he guessing, or did the Night Bringer say it? To whom? Was it another message? But I don't want to converse with it more than necessary. I'm already salty I need him at all. But I'm not stubborn enough to lose this battle by ignoring one of my largest assets—even if I'm pissed at it.

"I'm going to see you soon," I whisper to no one.

The ground trembles beneath my feet in a rumbling of distant laughter.

"Are they going to wake her now?" I ask the book, my voice quiet, heart throbbing.

"*They made an attempt a few hours ago.. She did not respond favorably.*"

I swallow. That's good news, I suppose. "But they're trying again? Now?"

"*That's what they say.*"

That's what they say. As in, he doesn't necessarily believe that. But I hate taking opinions from a being already proven untrustworthy. They say they're planning to wake the ancient beneath Black Lake, right now. "And you still think I should do *nothing*?" I bite out, watching the still waters in the distance.

"*You are not strong enough to stop them, Caelynn.*"

I curl a lip, anger simmering in my chest. Frustration crawls down my back, every muscle tense. I refuse to stay idle. I've done it for too long. I trusted a stupid book, and it was holding back information about people I *love*.

The spell book sighs. "I think you should go talk to Reveln and Raijin. Tell them we must act now. I think the Night Bringer is taunting you. He wants to push you to approach—" he cuts off suddenly.

"What?" My heart dips.

"*Raven is here. They're going to board a ship, bound for the center of the lake.*"

I don't wait for further explanation. I run.

I'm at the edge of the lake in only moments, but then I stop, panting. The water is still, and I don't see any ships, except the few docked a few feet away. "How far are they?"

"Miles. They began on the other side of the lake."

"Hey!" someone shouts. I turn to see two guards running toward me. High Court guards. "You are not permitted to be here," they shout.

I pull in a long breath and wait for them to reach me. Rai increased security on the lake, I knew, but High Court guards?

My lips spread into a sweet smile. "Sorry, I was just admiring the lake on my way to the High Court." I tilt my head innocently.

The guards' gazes drop to my silky blouse and crystal necklace.

One of them nods. "Best be on your way then."

My stomach twists. I can't leave Raven out there. I can't let the Night Bringer wake the ancient beneath these waters.

"I saw a ship out there," I tell them. "No one is supposed to be on the water right now, are they?"

The guards frown, exchange glances, and then turn back to me. "We'll take care of it."

I give them another sweet smile. "Thank you. I'll head back to the portals then." I spin on my heel and march back up the hill I'd run down. I make sure to walk quickly but not rushed. "Are they watching?"

"No."

Shadows pull at my body, wrapping around me. I heave a relieved sigh at the comforting pressure. Using shadows requires magic I've been saving for the fountain, but even though they require energy I have little of, they are a comfort I've missed. Like the warm embrace of a parent.

The Night Bringer once used them against me. Corrupted them, made my own shadows carve me up from the inside the way he did. That thought sends another wave of anger through me.

I'm going to kill them.

I run back down the hill and onto the dock, shadows still veiling me from sight, and I slip onto the ship the guards are preparing to take out to sea.

"This is a bad idea, Caelynn."

I don't respond because the guards cannot know I am on board. These are not regular Crackling Court guards, and they are very likely trained at spotting Shadow fae using shadows to hide, which means I must be especially diligent. I slip over the railing at the bow of the ship and then climb up the mast to the sails just as they open them wide. The wind tugs at the white cloth and pulls the ship forward. I lurch but manage to hold on tightly to the beam.

There are two water fae at the bow, consistently pushing water behind us, causing the ship to move quite a bit quicker than my last trip out on the lake.

I force my heart to settle, breathing evenly as we sail out toward my monster.

"You are so determined that I don't approach the Light King," I whisper to the book at my back, "then we better stop the Night Bringer from getting this ancient on his side or I will have no choice."

The book rumbles against me but says nothing. We both know it's too late to turn back now anyway.

Shouting below catches my attention, and I look down to see the two guards pointing up at the mast—at me. My stomach sinks. They see me.

But then, a shrill laughter rings out over the surface of the lake and the ship rocks violently. I grasp desperately at the mast to stop from hurtling down to the deck.

The guards yell again, only this time, they're pointing out over the surface of the water, where a massive glowing wave is rising and heading straight for us.

43
REV

Finally, we're able to enter the palace and begin the meeting while the loved ones remain in the great hall, mingling. Caelynn has yet to arrive, but I'm not particularly surprised by that. She wouldn't want to wait in a room full of fae who mistrust her until the council meeting ends.

The meeting room is full of casual chattering when the queen and I enter. All of the ruling kings and queens of the realm stand as we approach, and all sit as the High Queen takes her place at the head of the table.

"Tommin, please update us on your court after the attack," the queen says, jumping right into business.

The Whirling Court King nods. His hair is golden but shorter than Drake's. His cheek bones are just as sharp and his eyes a gentle golden color. "We are faring well. The southern wing of the palace took on serious damage, but the only injuries were healed within hours. The wraiths have not been seen since."

The queen nods.

"We have not uncovered the source of the attack,

although I worry we all already know. In response, we are increasing guard in every area of the kingdom."

"Who do you suspect?" Rai asks casually, his hands folded in front of him.

The Whirling King blinks. "The same group that orchestrated the *last* wraith attack only days ago," he says tightly.

"Do we know who orchestrated the wraith attack on the Crystal Court?" Rai asks innocently, glancing at the queen and the Crystal Court Queen.

The Crystal Queen shakes her head.

"Oh, come on, Rai," the Glistening King jumps in. "It occurred in perfect unison with a shadow rebel attack. It does not take a genius to—"

"Jump to conclusions?"

The Whirling Court King's eyes flare. "We are not—"

"Nothing wrong with building a defense, Tommin." Rai waves his hand. "I believe we will all begin doing the same after this meeting if we haven't already. However, I wonder at you implying blame without evidence."

"I do not believe in coincidences, Rai—"

"Of course not," I say quickly, sending an appreciative glance to Rai. "There is obviously something deeper happening in our realm. And as King Rai has stated, building a defense is not outside the realm of reason. All we ask is that you not act on your assumptions, as strong as you believe them to be, without cause."

The room stills.

"I agree," the Crystal Queen nods in my direction. "Though there is evidence to suggest the shadow rebels have interacted with wraiths in the past, there is also a case to be made that it is in the best interest of our greater enemies for us to turn against the Shadow Court."

The Whirling King rolls his eyes.

"So, it's settled," the High Queen says with her chin high. "We continue our investigations. Every court will begin doing what they believe necessary to protect their kingdoms from inter-court conflicts and greater enemies alike."

There is a murmuring of uneasy agreement from the group. The queen gives me a soft smile and some of the tension in my chest eases. I didn't have to do much at all. My allies did it for me. I am beginning to think I will owe Raijin more than I can repay.

"We've noticed High Court guards spending disproportionate amount of time at the Crackling Court," the Whirling King says casually. "Tell me, is that part of your building a defense, Raijin."

Rai leans back in his chair, arms crossed. "The increased guards have been there for Reveln. The same as the increase in the Frost Court while he and the queen spent time there during their displacement."

"And around Black Lake?" the Whirling King adds with a flick of his brow.

Rai leans forward, his expression darkening. "How would you know of anything regarding Black Lake, Tommin? You have paid no visits. Where is this information coming from?"

King Tommin doesn't respond. Rai lifts his chin.

"Don't think we haven't noticed you growing so chummy with the new High Heir," the Flicker Court King says, his tone is misleadingly casual. His eyes tell a different story. "Taking advantage of a young ruler is unseemly, Raijin."

Rai merely flicks a golden eyebrow. "Befriending a young ruler, however, is not. I don't know what you think you've seen, Midea, that has been inappropriate, but then again your idea of friendship is seducing young fae and forcing them into servitude, so I do suppose I understand where you'd become confused."

The Flicker King hisses, revealing his elongated canines. Rai merely smiles.

"I have no slaves."

"No, only a throng of males ready to *serve* you at a moment's notice."

A few of the rulers chuckle quietly.

"They are quite happy with their roles and able to leave any time they wish." His sharpened red nails dig into the mahogany table.

Rai smiles again. "Reveln and I are simply friends. Do not make it into some political scheme."

"It's always political, Rai," the Glistening King murmurs solemnly.

"Then, perhaps you should befriend the heir too."

"I hear all it takes is insulting his Shadow fae ally," the Flicker King says, his tone much more jovial than moments before. "What was it you called her? The shadow bitch?"

"Ahh, if that's all it took, then Reveln's father would be his best-mate," the Twisted Queen adds.

Chuckles resound through the room, and I shift awkwardly. One part amused, one part horrified at the turn in conversation.

"No, I believe it was the scotch that did it," Rai says with another wink as he takes a sip of his golden liquid.

"Have I mentioned I hate scotch," I say with a groan.

There's a pause, eyes of all colors turning to me in surprise, and then laughter breaks out. Rai, the Flicker King, the Glistening King, and several others are all near tears in their laughter.

I sit there awkwardly as they laugh at our expense. My stomach is still in knots over the events taking place in the courts. But maybe this kind of conversation is usual for the council. They are a group of prideful rulers, after all.

Rai settles, sniffing. "If you want the truth, it turns out it's shared vulnerabilities that creates friends."

I smile, muscles easing into a more relaxed state. "And when vulnerabilities are shared," I add, "and not used against you."

Rai nods, a small smile on his lips. "Trust."

"Trust is earned," the Whirling Court king says as he stands, eyes pinned to mine. "And you have not earned my trust, Heir."

44

CAELYNN

The fae on the main deck scream as the massive wave rises over the ship, but then it simply... stops. The massive tsunami remains suspended, water cascading down the crest gently.

Glowing white eyes open, staring straight at us.

"What is that?" someone yells.

"Move!" another hollers. "Get us out of here."

My heart pounds as the Lady of the Lake stares directly at my spot in the sails. She blinks.

"Hello, Rose," I whisper.

The figure flinches, and then head and shoulders rise above the surface, towering over our little ship, still covered in a layer of flowing water.

"Who dares to wake me?" The waves quake with her power.

My breath catches.

The ship rocks suddenly, tipping. I squeal, fingers digging into the mast to keep from falling into the waters below. The entire ship quakes, rattling intensely. The ancient twists her neck, turning her back as our ship rights itself splashing in the waters just under her massive form.

"Move!" someone shouts below. The water fae struggle to shift the waters away from the ancient. Especially because now, she is not alone.

A massive black silhouette stands behind the female in the water.

"I woke you," a deep echoing voice sends a rush of panic through my body, and for that moment, I can't breathe. Can't think. "Hello Rose, I see you've met my pet."

The female ancient stands at her full height, water finally draining down completely so that her naked body is visible. She looks more fae than any of the other ancients I've met. Her body is curved like a fae, her limbs the same proportions and her skin a soft pink.

"She is yours?"

"Yes. Please do not harm her. I intend to make her existence miserable before her end." The void of shadow turns toward another small ship beside him. I can only make out their white sails rocking in raging waves, but I know exactly who it is. "Starting with this." His voice full of cruel amusement.

The Night Bringer swings a fist toward the ship where Raven stands helplessly.

Stomach in my throat, I leap without thinking. Magic pulls at me, but I force it into submission, shadow leaping three times until my body crashes onto the deck of the small ship.

All I see as my body crumbles to the ground are the glistening black claws of my worst nightmare streaking toward me.

45
REV

The queen dismissed the council meeting quickly, deeming it a success. Her proud smile as I left the room was a rare encouragement.

Even so, it did little to relieve my anxiety.

Drake has influence on the Whirling Court, we've always known that. But we never knew exactly where his father, the true ruler of the court, stood. Today, we learned much, and the news was not good.

Of course, we don't know if the king is aware of the Night Bringer's influence on his son, but he is clearly against Caelynn, and the rest doesn't matter so much.

"I've heard rumors that the Shadow Queen will be in attendance." I spin to find Rai smirking at me, his mate on his arm.

"Have you seen her?"

"Not yet."

My heart clenches. "Thank you," I tell Rai. "For your support in the meeting. I'm going to be far in your debt before long, I think."

He chuckles. "There is no debt among friends. Even if... your position was to change. I'd continue to support you."

My eyebrows rise. My gaze shifts to Alia, her red curls cascading over her shoulder down to her dark blue dress.

"I've heard a lot about you and Caelynn," she says sweetly. "I'm looking forward to our friendship growing."

I nod politely just as a melody begins soaring through the air, bright and jovial.

"Can we dance?" Alia looks up at Rai with her stormy eyes full of love and happiness.

There's no gift like giving your mate happiness.

"Anything for you, darling." He gives me one last smile. "Good luck."

I pull in a nervous breath as Rai sweeps his mate out into the middle of the newly sealed glass floor. Down below are crashing waves that I refused to even glance toward because it causes unpleasant memories to flash through my mind. I remember that red dress fluttering down. I remember that fae's screams.

Will your mate be next?

I shake my head, ignoring the voice, still honestly unsure if it's real or in my mind.

Though the gathering is small, several couples now populate the dance floor. They laugh and twirl in circles, holding each other close. The Flicker King holds tightly to his current male partner. The Frost Queen spins around with her mate. And the Luminescent King even holds my mother.

My mother who abandoned her mate, my real father, to continue her comfortable life as a queen.

My heart clenches.

I catch a flash of blond hair through the small crowd, and my heart leaps. Hands in my pockets, I casually cross the room. Eyes follow me as I push through the small crowd, but I am not approached or badgered the way I usually am during a full populated ball. There are very few available females here, which is a relief.

I pay no mind to the fae I pass, my eyes only for the beautiful blond fae in black slacks and a silky black blouse. No one, not even the queen can stop me from claiming her while she's within reach.

Everything I desire is here but not for long. The closer I get, though, the more I notice the wrinkles in her clothing, the strangled knots in her hair. Is her hair wet?

She'll be heading back to her new home, thousands of miles from here, in only a few hours. I don't care what she looks like. Whatever is wrong, I can fix once she's in my arms.

Caelynn remains in the light, sipping a bubbling drink beside Kari and Ty. Kari gives me an almost indiscernible nod and steps away from Caelynn, passing through the crowd to chat with another council member.

Caelynn sucks in a breath as I step up to her. My fingers glide over her hip, her smooth silk blouse rippling under my fingers. Caelynn lets out a shuddering breath as I spin her so that her back is against my chest.

"I've missed you," I whisper against her hair.

"Rev," she rasps, and the sound of her name on my lips ignites something inside of me. "They'll see," she says breathlessly.

I press my nose into the crook of her neck. "Let them," I growl. My hand glides down her back until I find the hem. She gasps as my fingers find bare skin.

"Rev," she warns.

"I don't care what they see. I don't care what they know. You're mine."

She shivers at my words and lays her head back. One glance to the queen's platform tells me she has noticed and is not happy. But I don't care. There are some things not worth sacrificing, even for a dream come true.

I almost give her a rebellious glare—but in the next blink, the room is gone.

Magic sucks at my body, and then Caelynn and I are both in darkness. She's still pressed against me, drink in her hand. Where did she take us? Honestly, I don't even care. My hand, still on the searing skin of her midriff, presses downward. Caelynn gasps. She pushes back against me in the sweetest way.

"Caelynn," I groan against her ear.

I push her forward until her hands are pressed against a wall. Her drink crashes to the ground, splashing at the hem of my pants.

"Where did you take us?" I murmur with a laugh, but I'm too distracted by what my fingers find next.

Caelynn moans. Gentle swipes with my fingers cause her to clench the wall tight and writhe against my touch. My lips are on her shoulder, teeth grazing ever so slightly.

"This is what we can have, Cae," I whisper to her. "This never has to stop."

I spin her to face me. Even in the darkness I can see her flushed cheeks, the shining desire in her golden eyes.

Her lips crash into mine, and I moan at that first taste of her. It's only been days. Days since I've had her in my arms, and yet it feels like an eternity.

How will I do this? How can I survive being parted from her for weeks at a time?

I pull back, panting, and press my forehead to hers. "I love you," I tell her.

Her smile is small, her eyes dim.

"You're still tired?" I ask, just now noticing that her hair is tangled and damp Her blouse is wrinkled and torn at the hem.

"I have news." Her voice is hoarse. I step back, eyes examining her closer.

"Did something happen?" I ask. There's slight decolorization around her neck. My stomach sinks. "What happened?"

The fear in her eyes causes my blood to turn cold.

"The Night Bringer woke the Lady at the Lake."

46

CAELYNN

Rev's hands on my skin felt so incredibly good that I didn't have the will to stop him. I melted into his touch, his kisses, and for those moments, I could pretend that everything wasn't crashing down around us.

And it was worth it.

But now, now I have to face reality.

"He wanted me to be there. He wanted me to see it," I whisper, trying to keep my voice calm and steady. "He wanted me to watch as he destroyed Raven too."

Rev's palm is on my cheek suddenly. "Are you okay?"

I nod. "I saw it coming. I was faster than he expected, and I shadow leaped onto Raven's ship before he could smash it to bits."

Rev frowns, his brow furrowing.

"He couldn't destroy the ship while I was on it—the bargain."

Rev swallows and then pulls me against him.

"His fist stopped before it hit the ship, but the waves crashed against it anyway, and the female ancient, Rose, flicked us away. I don't know if it was to help us or out of annoyance, but a wave carried us all the way back to shore and smashed the ship against the bank. Raven was okay, but kind of out of it. She said her friends would take care of her."

Rev frowns. "You left her and came straight here?"

I nod. "She… they're her friends, Rev. The spell book conveniently left that part out."

"What?"

"It's complicated. But apparently Blane has been keeping Raven away from his brother for her protection. That's why they've been hiding in the human realm. Blane and Aurora promised to take her somewhere safe now. I told them I'd find them again soon."

"That's… that's insane."

"I know."

Rev pulls in a long breath. "What now?" he whispers.

"Now, they have the ancient of the lake, and we only have one choice."

"No," Rev says firmly, his voice shaking. "We… shit, Cae. The Ancient King has been talking to me. Sending me messages."

I pause. "What kind of messages?"

"Threats, sometimes. Taunts. He says… he says he requires a sacrifice."

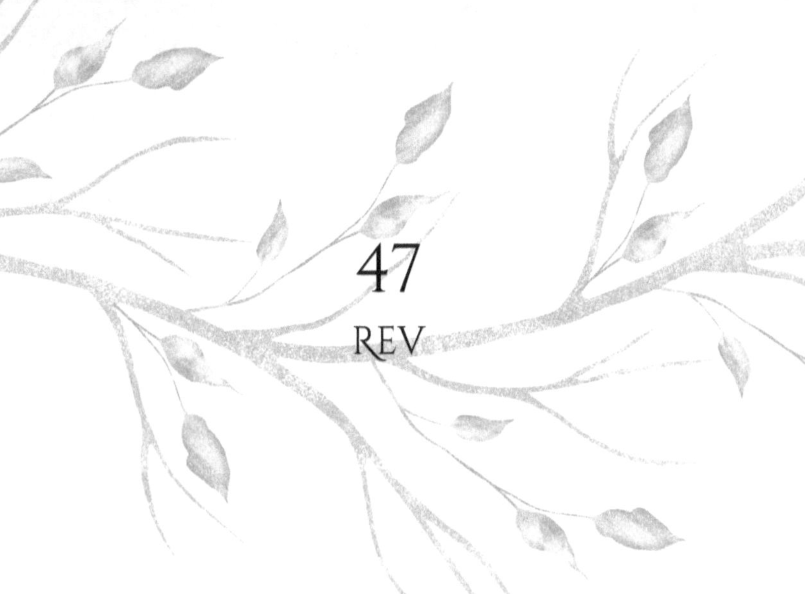

47
REV

"Look at me," I say, heart pounding. God, just moments before we were blissful. Now... now, I wonder if this will be the last moment I have with her. She's going to go. I can see it in her eyes. She's going to approach the King of Light, and it's going to kill her.

I require a sacrifice.

"Do not go without me."

Her beautiful golden eyes fill with tears, but somehow the color remains. "I'm not afraid to die, Rev."

Those words carve through me like a knife, splitting my heart in two. "Maybe not," I croak. "But it would destroy *me*."

Caelynn closes her eyes and shakes her head. "What if... what if this was always my destiny?" she whispers. "I shouldn't have ever taken the bargain. I should have died then and there. I should have taken the pain, accepted it. Instead, I brought that evil into this world. I gave it life."

"No!" I say. "You are wrong, Caelynn. You are not at fault for their evil."

Her eyes meet mine again, dimmer this time. She doesn't believe me. I pull in a long breath, determination filling me.

"Listen. I need you to wait for me. I'm going to talk to Rai and the queen. Then, we'll decide. There's no rush. If we go, we go together." I hold her upper arms tightly, willing her to believe me. *Agree.*

Her breath shudders, confusion and indecision raging in her eyes. But finally, she nods.

48

CAELYNN

The moment I step out of the storage closet with Rev, the power of the Light King sparks deep below the High Court. Like static electricity, thick and pulsing. There's a pull low in my belly that's eerily familiar. A wordless beckoning. Offering me everything I've ever desired.

Magic squirms in my veins, shifting away from the call even while my body longs to follow it.

I've felt this before, this pull.

I was naïve and hopeful, then. Not so much any longer. I know what this kind of temptation leads to, what it costs.

"*He's already decided you are unworthy,*" the book whispers in my ear. "*He doesn't believe in your cause.*"

I have the power you need to crush your enemies, Caelynn of the Shadow Court. I shiver as his voice rumbles through me. Rev's right—he's taunting us.

The Light King thinks I am just another power-hungry fae. He thinks I want to use him for my personal revenge.

Rev and I step back into the great hall. The music still plays, the couples still dance joyously. The High Queen still glares in my direction.

"We're going to have to convince him," I say to myself as much as anyone. The Light King thinks he knows who we are. But he is wrong. We will prove that our cause is worthy. Without him, the world will be devastated by the very monsters that betrayed him millennia ago.

Rev marches toward the High Queen's perch. Kari glances my way, her expression wary. I didn't tell her what was going on, but she is perceptive enough to know something is happening. She frowns over my shoulder.

"Convince who?"

I spin, surprised by the sudden voice behind me. Most definitely not the spell book.

I suck in a breath as I come face-to-face with Drake. His eyes are bright yellow now. Unnatural. Has no one else noticed the difference? His shoulders are back, one eyebrow quirked, adding to his cocky grin.

How had I ever been his ally? Disgust swells in my chest.

"Would you like to dance?" he asks casually. "Or were you saving that for your *mate*?"

He says the word mate like it's an insult.

Drake slowly steps around me, a predator cornering its prey. Good thing I am not prey.

"You see, if you were mine," he continues in his smooth, melodic voice, "I wouldn't let some old hag keep you from me. I wouldn't abandon you to your far away court without doing a damn thing to help."

My nose flares, but I know his game. I am not fooled.

"If you were mine, I'd give you the world," he says. "And I could too. Rev will never be High King, you know. I will. Because I am not afraid of change. Not afraid of powers so much bigger than myself. I embrace the wave crashing down on the world. And because of that, I will come out on top."

I roll my eyes. "Is that what this is all about? You're still pressed you lost the Trial of Thorns and your chance to be High King? And now, you're grasping for any way to retain the power you lost out of your own *weakness*."

Drake growls, and a gust of wind crashes into me, knocking me off balance. Gentle hands steady me, though. "Something wrong?" Raijin's voice says smoothly from over my shoulder.

"Just some good old-fashioned goading," I say, wiping my pants casually. "You know how it is with rivals." I smirk at Drake.

"Rev holds you back, Caelynn," Drake says with a smug smile.

"You're okay?" Rai asks.

I nod, still not taking my eyes from Drake. Rai watches us both closely as he departs.

"I know your game, Drake. I can play it too."

His yellow eyes narrow. He thinks I mean his sharp words and mental games—and he's right; I can do that too. I know what hurts him as much as he knows what hurts me. But I have something else in mind.

"The difference, Caelynn of the Shadow Court, is you don't realize that you've already lost."

I curl my lip and spin to find Rev kneeling beside the queen, whispering in her ear. My stomach churns. Rev will try to stop me. The spell book will try to stop me.

But I refuse to allow their fear to hold me back from killing the monster that still haunts me.

"We'll see about that," I tell Drake, even as anxiety curls low in my belly.

49

CAELYNN

I watch Drake stroll across the ballroom while couples still twirl with smiles on their faces. *You've already lost.*

He turns, looks straight at me and winks.

My stomach drops. What's to stop Drake from approaching the Light King himself? It wouldn't take much to convince the ancient to kill me. I spin to the platform where the queen sits stoically, staring out at the dancing figures. Rev is no longer with her.

I frown, heart hammering. Where is he? I can't wait any longer.

Breath shudders from my lungs, and I make a snap decision. Maybe it's the wrong one. Maybe I'm being as foolish as I was back then. But I can't do nothing. I'm so tired of playing these games while my enemies continue getting the upper hand. If Drake convinces the Light King to trust him, all of my happiness will slip from my fingers like sand.

I follow Drake.

50

REV

I stop, staring at the little ball of light inside the cavern, far beneath the banquet hall.

While Caelynn spoke with Drake, I slipped down the corridor, following the Light King's call. She's going to come down here soon. But if I can get there first, maybe I can get ahead of the punishment.

I don't have a spell book to guide me, but it doesn't seem that I need it. The Light King is waiting for me.

The pulsing magic guided me down the stairs toward the dungeons, where Caelynn was kept, and into a cavern covered in crystals. A light flickers over the shallow water, and I step forward.

"I've been waiting for you, Reveln."

"You've been waiting for the chance to kill my mate," I growl.

The shallow water trembles with his harsh laughter. "You believe I desire fae deaths."

"Do you not?"

"I have rage. I thirst for any way to alleviate my pain. And for a Shadow fae so eager to give her life for her cause..."

My blood runs cold. Panic fills my limbs until my chest is heaving and mind is spinning.

"Is that what you fear most, Reveln, the High Prince? Your mate's death?"

"Yes," I admit.

"She is coming now," the king says quietly. "She will offer me her life. Would you like to watch?"

My stomach drops, but before I can react, my muscles freeze and I am trapped. A hand of light shifts me to the side, behind him. Fast footsteps echo through the cavern, and then she's there. Caelynn. Her eyes shine with determination, her jaw set.

I watch as Caelynn speaks to the ancient. She doesn't even know I'm here.

"I require a sacrifice," the king purrs.

"I said no matter the cost," she says through gritted teeth.

No! I cry out inside my mind, but I cannot form the words. *Don't let her. Please.*

A massive wave of white glowing power rises up over her. I scream and beg and plead inside my mind, but I can only watch helplessly.

51

CAELYNN

Come, he purrs. *Come claim the power you seek.*

I close my eyes, heart racing, stomach in knots. This is it. This is what I must do, or everything will have been for nothing. If I don't kill them, defeat them—he'll win. My heart and soul and body will be *theirs.*

There's nothing worse than knowing you've done the bidding of something evil.

They can't win. I won't let them.

The beckoning of the Light King pauses. I can feel his curiosity, his surprise like a spark in the air around me. His power dominates this place.

I pass the irons doors of my once prison, but I refuse to look at them. Twice I've been put behind those bars but never again. Today, I will live or die—free.

There is no sign of Drake down here. "*He is tricking you,*" the book hisses, but can I even trust it? "*He did not come down to the Light King.*"

Anxiety curls in my gut, a constant ache these last few hours.

The king's magic purrs, welcoming me as I follow it, but

the tune has changed. Has he somehow already realized that his assumptions about me aren't entirely true? I seek his power, yes, but not for myself.

Past the prisons and their stale sewage smell, I find the hot spring Kari brought me to a while back, except it appears to have been drained. Now, only a few inches of water sit at the bottom of the massive stone basin. Colorful crystal still lines the ceiling, but most of the water and all of the warmth are absent. A tiny white light flutters in the center of the room.

"Come," the voice calls, this time aloud, with the power I've felt from previous ancients. Rumbling the very core of the planet.

"*Caelynn*," the book hisses. I consider dropping the bag and moving on without it because despite my fear, my mind is made up. I'm going in. I'm going to talk to the Ancient of Light. I'm going to figure out what I must do to gain his aid because I'm done playing these games.

It's the only way to win this fight.

The sound of crashing waves greets me as I take my first step into the shallow frigid water of the once hot spring, and then all at once, I am blinded by white light. Searing pain shoots through my eyes. I whimper and cover them, but it's a pointless endeavor.

I am fully exposed and blind. And that is exactly how the Ancient King wants it.

"I wasn't sure you were ever going to come." The voice reverberates through the open area. I know we were just standing in a cavern, in the empty pool of stone, but now I can see nothing. For all I know, we're in a different world. There is only light, the sound of distant waves, and his voice.

"Everyone that cares for me feared you'd kill me the moment I approached you."

"I considered that," he admits. The water trembles at my feet.

I swallow. "But I knew I would make it here eventually."

"Did you?" His voice pitches high with amusement.

I try to force my eyes open, but it's too bright. I wince and cover them again. It doesn't stop the burning pain clawing into my head, but I hold my eyes tightly all the same.

"You are my only chance to defeat an enemy much greater than myself. An enemy that has trapped and tortured me and will continue to do that and worse to those ruling this realm if left unchecked."

"You think yourself noble," he says. It's not a question. "Yet, I have heard many rumblings through this palace since my awakening. You are hated by many."

"Most," I admit. "Most fae in this realm hate me for my past deeds, and I don't blame them. But that doesn't mean that my motives now are not pure. There is much the realm doesn't know. Most don't know about the monsters stalking them."

"Monsters?"

I bite my lip, eyes still pressed closed, and take another tentative step forward. Cool waves clang into my shins, chilling me and knocking me off balance. "They're like you," I tell him, "but I'm hoping you have more empathy. From the stories I've heard, you would not be befitting of the term beast, or monster, or nightmare, as I've always called my enemy."

"Your enemy." The king breathes, like the swish of waves.

"He's an ancient."

The water stills at my feet. "How did you, child of the fae, become the enemy of an ancient?" His voice is low. He is dubious but curious.

"When I was an adolescent, I... I made a mistake. I

disobeyed my parents and ran away into a set of tunnels where I believed I would find my freedom. Instead, I found him. The Night Bringer."

"Night Bringer," the king's powerful voice repeats slowly, tasting the word.

"Do you recognize the name?"

Water washing over my feet is his only response.

"He trapped me. Tortured me. And forced me into a bargain."

The sound of a clicking tongue makes me pause. "You cannot be forced into a bargain."

"No," I whisper. "But you can be coerced into one. I was given a choice—live a long life full of agonizing pain—pain he ensured I felt plenty of before my decision—or agree to the bargain." The hair on my arms stands up straight as I recount my worst moments. The decision that haunts me, even now. The pain and fear that brought me to make it. "He had me in his grasp," I say, voice growing quieter and quieter. My breath quivers. "This was my only way out. Sometimes, I hate myself for making that choice. But I did, I agreed to kill one fae I'd never met to earn my freedom."

"You killed an innocent fae to spare yourself."

"I agreed to those terms, yes. But what happened… was more complicated. I was given instructions on who to kill, but he was never named. I was misled. I was told to kill the youngest heir of the Luminescent Court king. I went to a ball and met Rev, the youngest Luminescent Court Prince. And if I had killed the fae prince the Night Bringer led me to believe was the target, not only would I have killed an innocent—my fated mate—but I would have failed the bargain and become this monster's eternal slave. Because Rev is not truly the Luminescent King's heir. He is not his son. The game would have ended there, and I would have freed the Night Bringer and his mate without any ability to protest. But when I met Rev, I couldn't do it. Instead, I stalled, and by luck or sheer stubbornness, I uncovered the twist in his bargain, and I instead killed another. The true target of the bargain."

The water at my feet freezes, stilling.

"Reahgan, Rev's brother. He was not innocent. He was not good. And I do not regret his death."

The water rushes again, rising to my knees, growing in power. "You mean to tell me, child, that you have come here to convince me to give you my aid by telling me the story of how you killed your mate's brother to save your own skin?"

"No," I whisper. Breath trembles from my lungs and refuses to return. "The story I'm telling isn't about me. It's about the enemy I am requesting that you help me defeat. I have never believed myself to be a hero. And you might think my story makes me a terrible person; I don't think I could disagree with you. But Reveln knows all of it, yet he still loves me. Still chooses me. I don't always understand why, but it has to mean something, right?"

The king does not respond.

"But the monster that put me in that position to begin with—the monster that plotted to enslave me and use me for his own evil—he must be dealt with, no matter the cost."

"I require a sacrifice," the king growls.

"I said no matter the cost," I say through gritted teeth.

The water retreats quickly, sucking at my feet. I nearly lose my balance.

"And you want me to kill this monster for you?"

"This monster is a common enemy," I tell him. "I don't know what name you knew him as before. But he was once the ancient of the Shadow realm."

A growl reverberates from the still retreating waters.

"He and his mate were among those responsible for the

conflict that led to your slumber." My bag trembles on my back, as if terror has taken over the spell book.

The Light King's growl turns into the deafening roar of a colossal wave rising over me. I cower before the power that's ready to end me here and now. And I wonder, if it will all be for nothing. If I fell into the same damn trap as when I was a child. Tears sting my eyes as I think about Rev.

It will destroy me. I curl into a ball, shaking as my end finally greets me.

52

REV

I am surrounded by blinding light, and Caelynn is no longer visible. I don't see the wave pummel her. I don't hear the crash or her screams. There is simply nothing.

"She is not worthy of death," I say, realizing that my body is mobile again, but I am trapped inside this bubble of light.

"You are all worthy of death," he hisses.

"If that is the kind of king you want to be, then be our judge and kill us all."

The water stills. "That is not the kind of king I was. But now, I am no king at all."

"And whose choice was that?"

The room fills with such aching silence, my own breathing stills. Waiting.

"You are a brave being to speak to me this way."

"You have the life of my mate in your hands. I have very little else to lose. I will do what I must to save her."

"Her? The fae that killed your brother? You would risk so much to save her?"

"Yes," I answer quickly. "I'd risk it all."

"Why?"

I press my lips together, considering how to best respond. I'd say that I love her, but it won't make a difference to him. "You say she is deserving of death, but I disagree. I have seen her strength, her loyalty, her honor, her compassion. She has faced more pain and fear than any being ever should. And when I put myself in her position—I don't know that I could have done what she did. I would have been too cowardly. If it had been me, the Night Bringer would have already won and this game would be over. But because of Caelynn's strength, even sometimes the strength to do terrible things in the name of justice, we have a chance."

"So, if I were to test her, you believe she would pass?"

I pause. "Test?"

"Yes, a test."

I blink rapidly. She is so strong, stubborn but strong. "Yes," I whisper. "If you need her to prove it again—well, it hurts me to think she must suffer another time, but I know she will succeed. I know it in my very soul. So, fine. Test her if you must. She will surprise you, the way she has surprised me."

"You think so very highly of this Shadow fae."

"I do."

"Would you pass too, High Prince? If I were to give you a test as well?"

"Yes," I say, not even stopping to consider the details. "Test me too."

The King of Light smiles.

53

CAELYNN

The blow never comes. The roar of rushing water settles into a simmer.

"My mate was the Queen of the Shadow realm. Like you," the Light King says.

I press my trembling lips together tightly, still half cowering before the stillness. I can't see anything in the blinding light, and I assume he's holding the wave towering over me, deciding when and how to destroy me.

"But you knew that," he whispers.

"Yes," I rasp.

"How?" he demands.

The spell book trembles against my back. This is what the book has feared these last few days. This moment.

"A lot has happened in the years you've been slumbering," I tell the ancient. "Most of the ancients are gone for good but there are several still around. You. The Night Bringer and Night Terror, who are actively seeking to regain their power over the world and reign over the fae as gods. There was an ancient slumbering beneath the Black Lake. This afternoon, she was awakened and has joined my enemies. There is the nomad, an ancient living in wolf form in the Twisted Forest. And one other." I pause.

"Who?"

I take a deep breath and pull the bag from my back. I hold it against my chest for a long moment and then reveal the leather tome. "This book holds the soul of an ancient. His power, along with a spell, allows the book to see all. It knows everything that has happened."

"Who?" The waters tremble at the sound of his voice.

"His name was Taliesin."

A curse releases from the Ancient King's rumbling voice. "How is it only my enemies have survived all these years?"

My stomach sinks. His words solidify my guess.

Why the spell book was so against facing the Light Ancient. Why he is so fearful now.

He was one of the ancients that betrayed him.

"As I said, a lot has changed in the last ten thousand years. Several hundred years ago, the Night Bringer and his mate began their crusade to take control of the world. They began by assassinating any remaining ancients that they believed would stand against them. Some, they deemed not a threat and they were left alone.

"But rumor has it, they were too afraid to attack you, even in your slumber."

"*They didn't attack me and my sister,*" the book quietly explains the part he left out before, "*because they thought we'd remain on their side.*"

"But they did not account for changes of heart," I continue. "Two of the fae that betrayed you, worked against the Night Bringer and Night Terror thousands of years later. Along with my ancestor, Darren Shadowspell, they fought to trap the Night Bringer and his mate forever. To achieve this, both willingly imprisoned their own souls. One became this spell book, the other, the walls that could imprison them inside the Schorchedlands. The spirit inside this spell book was once your enemy but has since redeemed himself by working to defeat the Night Bringer. He sacrificed his own soul to do it."

The ground trembles, and my breath hitches.

"We have a common enemy. Help me defeat them, and then take whatever you want."

"I do not give my aid freely, child. Common enemy or not, you must be tested."

I release a long breath. Water continues washing out toward the source of the light, tugging at the sole of my boots. I hold my ground. "Then, test me, and let's get this over with."

I've been through the Trials and the Schorchedlands. I can manage one more test.

"You believe yourself strong," the king says, his voice shifting around me. My breathing quickens as my mind flashes to the last time I was this close to one of these creatures.

An ancient. A being with so much power no fae could even pretend to stand against them. I remember what it felt like to be utterly helpless.

To tremble and beg to be let go, for the pain to end.

To dwell in my own desperate fear and have it used against me.

I swallow, and though my heart still quakes, I remind myself that I am not that girl any longer. And this time, I am here by my own free will. I was not trapped or lured. This is my destiny, and if I must withstand literal torture, this time I will do it willingly. Because my eyes are wide open.

I know how and why I am here. I know what lies on the other side of the pain.

"*Thank you for defending me,*" the spell book whispers in my ear.

"I don't know why you were so terrified. What could he do to you?"

"*I did not fear my death, Caelynn. I feared yours. That you, and the rest of the fae realm, would pay because of my past guilt. I feared facing what I'd done. He was once a friend, whom I betrayed.*"

I swallow. "I know that feeling."

"*You are strong, Caelynn. You are brave and intelligent and caring. If the Light King does not see it, then he is an utter fool.*"

The ground trembles as the Light King laughs.

54
CAELYNN

"Fight. Win." Those are my only instructions for my first test. The blinding light around me falls away into nothing. Total blackness covers every inch. And then, a blindfold is wrapped over my eyes. I can't see anything at all. Wonderful.

My ears begin buzzing too.

"Hello?" I call. I can't even hear my own voice.

All right, this is going to be an interesting fight.

No sound. No sight.

My heart rate picks up.

I crouch, preparing for an attack. Do I move forward? Do I move backward? How do I fight if I can't see or hear?

I can't even hear my own breathing, even though I'm near gasping in anticipation. "Where? What do I fight?" My voice dies at end of my lips.

"You'll know," comes a whisper. Well, I can hear him at least.

"Thank you for the detailed instructions," I hiss. Then, I take a tiny step forward. My mind whips over all the possible things I'd have to fight. What would the Ancient King want to test me on? What would he need me to prove before he declares himself my ally?

His mate was a Shadow fae who betrayed him. He sees her in me. Will he need me to prove loyalty and sincerity? Honesty? Compassion?

Or would this Ancient King still value cunning and ruthlessness?

I remember that he was the king that always wanted fae to rule themselves. He was benevolent. It seems likely he'd remain the same, but ten thousand years is a long time, even when sleeping.

He'll need me to prove that my end game is not power.

The blow comes so quickly, so powerfully, it knocks me immediately off my feet. My head slams into the hard ground, sending a ricochet of pain through me. Water splashes up over my head. I leap to my feet, shaking off the discomfort, but the frigid water leaves me dripping and shivering. I judge the distance of my unknown foe based on where the hit came from.

It felt like a baseball bat, which is not exactly helpful. I go entirely still, crouching low, and I wait.

"I don't want to hurt you," I tell my foe. My words die in the void. But I speak just in case they can hear and understand me. It's a far stretch, but you never know.

The water at my feet shifts. I can't hear it, or see it, but it crests just a tad higher over the arch of my foot. And that's how I know the second blow is coming.

I duck and sidestep. The water splashing to my shins tells me it worked. My foe leaped past me. Maybe even fell in the process. I could leap at them; I could probably even shove my dagger into their heart if I got lucky.

But I still don't know what I'm facing. Maybe they have a long sword. Maybe it's a damn scorpion with a spike waiting to impale me. The options are limitless. I will not jump into this until I'm able to better judge the situation.

I wait a second time, focusing on the water. This time, they wait too.

When my attacker still doesn't move, I take the opportunity to make my first move. I shift to the left, and then to the right. I don't know if they can see me, but my best guess says they can't. So, I want to confuse the few context clues they can get from my movements.

I twist, moving in toward the pulsing warmth of the nearby body, and pull my sword back then slam the hilt down, where I'm guessing I will find a head.

I find only open air, and then a blade slices across my forearm.

I shriek and dive away. I grip the wound as warm blood drips down to the water below. It's shallow, but it stings and is already slick with blood. My foe anticipated my move too well. Maybe they can see better than I'd thought. The water rustling from my own movements leaves me vulnerable, and I can't tell if they are coming for me. I twist away just in case, and the sharp movement of air tells me I only barely missed having my throat split open.

I leap at my attacker, knowing that if they missed me, they'll be off balance. This might be my only chance. I can't disarm them or knock them unconscious without seeing or hearing them. So, my only choice is to aim to kill.

I don't know what this is supposed to be testing, but either way, I'm going to lose if I'm killed in the process.

I send my blade flying down at the foe I can't see. A clang reverberates through my blade hand—they deflected. Then, a warm, callused hand is wrapped around my upper arm. They'd been going for my throat, I think.

I slice at the arm, and they retreat.

My heart hammers.

I'm definitely fighting a fae—male. A good fighter. They either can't hear me, or they don't care when I said I didn't want to hurt them.

My lips begin trembling as a new, unexplainable anxiety crawls in my bones. Something is wrong. Something... I don't know what.

I swallow. Am I more injured than I'd realized?

A splash of water on my shins tells me my attacker is coming again, and I quickly measure out their trajectory. I duck and then shove my blade up—and sink it into warm flesh. My stomach drops again.

The body shudders and leaps backward, falling to the ground. I'm honestly not sure where I hit. Maybe shoulder. Stomach. I may have hit a major organ, but based on the resistance, I don't think so.

The ground shakes slightly with the fall of his body. Water rushes over my feet. I wait.

Nausea rises in my throat as warmth fills the air around me in a flash. The tingle of magic zaps near me. I flinch, but no magical blow comes.

Light magic.

Healing magic.

Am I fighting the Light Ancient himself?

My breathing quickens. No. No, I'm not fighting the Light King. My blade shakes in my trembling fingers. "Rev," I whisper. The realization hits me like a truck.

The hair on my arms stands up, and my mind begins to race. I cut him deep, hurt him. My heart pounding.

He's okay, I tell myself. He healed himself.

But now what? I'm fighting Rev, and he doesn't know it's me, and there is no way for me to tell him.

Rev charges again; this time, his footfalls are so hard the

ground vibrates. I drop my blade and then dodge. "Rev!" I call to him. "Rev!" I scream as loudly as I can.

I grip his wrist, but he rips it from my hand before I can do more. How do I signal to him it's me? How do I stop this?

"Rev, please," I whisper.

55
REV

That bastard king put me in an impossible fight. Blindfolded and deaf. I utter curse after curse at the asshole as I heal my wounds from my unknown opponent.

What is the point of this? He's just taunting me.

My anger only increases as my opponent lands hit after hit. They sliced my shoulder wide open, and I was only able to do a surface healing on it. It stings like a mother now, and it has me weakened. But I will not give up.

I will win this.

This time, when I swing, my super speedy opponent dodges and somehow curls behind me. A small hand wraps around my blade wrist and twists violently. I feel a snap, and streaks of pain shoot up my arm.

My blade falls to the water.

Damn it!

Without missing a beat, I swing my fist back and land a shattering blow to their head. The splash and ground quaking tells me they fell, hard. I leap on top of them, knowing without my weapon, I'm at a disadvantage—even more than before.

The slight body wriggles beneath me, but I manage to pin their legs between mine. I struggle with their hands, trying to get a grip. Instead, I find their throat. Small, so small.

A female, maybe?

She's screaming, I can feel the reverberation beneath my hands. Screaming desperately as I squeeze her throat with both hands. Her hips buck, and then she shoves the base of her palm between my arms and straight into my nose. I don't need my ears to hear the crack as my head whips back. I curse as she uses the opportunity to shove me off. Blood pours down my front, and I seethe.

Before I'm even able to stand up right the female fighter flies at me, slamming me onto the ground back first. She's screaming still, those small vibrations tingling into my chest. She's too small to pin me entirely though, and I spin her around so that she's below me.

But she twists, snaping both arms out, and then she jerks in toward me. I wince, almost expecting her to bite me but instead feel the hard press of lips against mine.

My mind freezes for only an instant, and then my body reacts. I roll off of her and pause. I'm on my feet, panting, mind spinning. What the hell is happening?

My limbs are trembling now as I touch my lips gently. She kissed me.

Kissed me. I'm fighting a female. Is she blindfolded too? Is she deaf too?

What if...

Oh God.

I fall to my knees. I've been fighting Caelynn. The whole damn time.

I curse again, only this time, it's not to the Ancient King. It's to me. How much of an idiot am I? How did I not realize?

The water ripples gently as she approaches. Then, her

fingers intertwine in my hair. I lay my head against her belly, panting desperately. "I'm sorry," I whisper. Can she even hear me? I don't know.

She leans over, pulling my chin up and presses her lips to mine again, and this time, I feel such warmth and love and devotion in the kiss. How did I not know? How did it take me so long?

Her fingers gently pull at my blindfold, and it falls away easily. I blink rapidly. It's still dark and shadowed, but I can see her form now. She's wearing a blindfold too.

I reach up and pull the cloth off of her, revealing red, tear-streaked eyes.

"Are you okay?" I ask, my voice finally audible.

She nods, her eyes still sad but full of such beautiful adoration. "Are you?"

Light flickers in my palm, and I run it over my broken nose.

"Sorry about that," she says with a small smile.

"I did worse," I say, reaching up to touch the bloody mat of hair on the side of her head. I wince as I remember that cracking feeling as my fist hit her skull. I heal her head quickly, without much thought at all.

"Well, I broke your nose after I knew it was you."

I chuckle through a shiver. "I didn't give you much choice." I reach up to the bruises forming on her neck. My stomach sinks again. Shit. I hurt her. I'm not supposed to ever hurt her.

She pushes my hand away. "Keep your magic. I don't know what else we'll need here."

"Congratulations, contenders," a voice booms through the darkness dramatically.

I sneer at the unseen king.

"You've completed your first task. Prepare for the next."

56

CAELYNN

I roll my eyes at the Light Ancient's dramatic announcement.

"He's enjoying this too much," Rev mutters. I release an amused breath from my nose.

Then, I step closer to Rev. If he's mad at me for coming down here without him, he doesn't show it. When he looks at me, all I see is love. I touch his chest gently and try to soak up this moment, along with all the rest.

As much as I'm tired of fighting, I kind of like fighting alongside him. "I'll miss this," I tell him, and then my cheeks warm at the admission.

He licks his lips. "It's not exactly the most romantic of moments," he says, but his lips curl up into a small smile. "I did just smash your head in and nearly choke you to death."

I roll my eyes. Obviously, this was an extreme circumstance. "And I stabbed you in the shoulder." His thumb runs over the ragged hole below his collar bone. "Besides, some girls like choking."

Rev's eyes flare, and then he coughs.

Blinding white light rises quickly, extinguishing the darkness. I squint from the flaring light. "Ow."

"Well, are you ready or not?" the king roars over us. I still can't see where he is, but I stop trying to tell quickly. My eyes are already in pain.

"No," Rev says. And then, he reaches behind my neck and pulls me into him. His lips crash into mine in an incredible, adoring kiss. "I love you," he whispers as he pulls back. "We do this together. Okay?"

I'm breathless as he releases me, but I smile up at him. "We're ready," I tell the king. I'm ready to fight anything.

"Test number two, tell each other your deepest fear. Be honest. I will know if you are lying."

I frown. What kind of test is this?

Honesty. It was one of the things I'd mentally listed as something he'd likely test. He wants to know how truthful we'll be when it comes to revealing something vulnerable... even with someone we trust. My stomach sinks as I consider what kind of fears I harbor in my soul.

Rev sees me as strong, but he doesn't really know how much darkness is inside. My palms are sweating already. "You go first," I whisper.

Rev blinks. "Me?"

I nod quickly. Our romantic moment long forgotten.

Rev frowns. "Is there a trick?"

I press my lips together. "I don't think so. He's testing our honesty and willingness to be vulnerable. He sees inside of us somehow. He knows the answer, maybe even better than we do."

"I fear losing you," he admits, "but I'm guessing the answer isn't quite so literal."

I nod slowly. "It's... something deeper. More personal."

Rev sucks in a long breath as he considers. "I think mine will go back to my father," Rev whispers. "And Reahgan."

I swallow and turn my gaze away, cheeks red.

"Reahgan was my father's favorite. He was the perfect son. Powerful, poised, intelligent, and charming. He was beloved. I was... none of those things, really."

I frown as I return my gaze to Rev. He is all of those things... but I don't say that because this is his time to delve deep. To sift through those feelings to uncover the fear the king wants him to reveal.

"I was quick to fear. I was too compassionate for my father's liking. He called me dumb so often I believed him. I was shy before my brother's death. Introverted."

"And after his death?"

Rev purses his lips. "I changed a lot. I grew hard and angry. I didn't care what people thought so long as they saw me as powerful. Important. So, the shyness fell away easily. Charm, I developed over time. It's not my greatest skill, but I'm capable. I worked most at my power. I became the best fighter in the room, better than any of my trainers. I honed my magic. I proved myself in every possible way because I knew I had to be better than Reahgan or I'd always be considered a failure. Not just by my father but by everyone. And I'd shame him, my brother who should have ruled. I... tried to become him. Replace him."

I resist the urge to take his hand.

"Even now, I... feel a desperate need to prove myself. To be powerful and important and intelligent and charming and everything the entire realm expects to see. I work so hard at it because I'm terrified they'll see the truth. They'll see that I'm not made for this. I'm not the right king. I'm not the right son. I'm an imposter. A fraud. I'm not as strong as I pretend to be. I'm not as powerful as they all think."

I blink. "Inadequacy," I whisper the word he's searching for. Rev feels inadequate at all times, and he's desperately trying to cover it up.

"Is that terrible?"

"No!" I say quickly. "No, it makes all the sense in the world. You've tried to replace your brother, and you never felt worthy. But you don't have to replace him, Rev. You don't have to be him. You are important and strong and powerful because of who *you* are. Not because of the position you were thrust into. You're not his son. You're not supposed to be. You can stop trying to force yourself to fit a mold that was never meant for you."

His lips part as he stares at me.

"And to be honest... I was kind of afraid your fear would have been about me."

"You?" he whispers. His warm fingers intertwine with mine.

"I thought you might... be ashamed that I am your mate. That I'm just another thing that doesn't fit the vision you and the world had for your life, and now you've got to fight for even this." I squeeze his fingers tighter.

"No," he says, voice hoarse. "Cae, you're the only thing I'm certain of anymore. The only anger or fear I feel regarding you is that the world doesn't understand you. That even you don't see how incredible you are. They'd love you, adore you, if they saw you how I do. I am so fucking proud that you are my mate. I mean that with all of my heart."

Tears well in my eyes, and I swallow down a sob. It feels so good to hear that, to know he doesn't resent being connected to me in a way he can't control. But my heart sinks again because I don't know if he'll still feel that way if he knew my true fear.

I don't know if he'll still see me the same.

"I'm afraid I'm irrevocably bad," I whisper.

Rev stills, but he doesn't respond. He watches me closely, his silver eyes dimming.

"When I was a child, I was bold and stubborn and arrogant. I thought I knew best. I remember thinking that I wanted the world to pay for how they treated the Shadow Court. I wanted them to see that not only are we not weak but that they... should fear us. Part of me wonders if my life had gone differently, would I have joined the rebellion? I was like that. Angry and determined. And I... well, it was those thoughts and feelings that the Night Bringer fed off. He told me I was like him. And I... don't think he was wrong." My voice is trembling now.

"N—" Rev begins, but I hold up my hand, cutting him off. I shake my head quickly, unable to form words. Tears slip down my cheeks. I have to get this out. I have to...

Rev's jaw is set, fear and pain so clear in his eyes now. He wants to prove me wrong. He wants this pain to end, but he can't stop these fears by telling me to stop feeling them. They are here, and not only do I have to live with them, deal with them, but this is my challenge. I must express this or I will fail my test.

"I was power hungry. I was vindictive. And even though when it really came down to it, I didn't *want* to cause pain, I didn't *want* to be bad, the potential was all there. He showed me that; he showed me what I could become if I let myself. And I spent every day after fighting it. I knew when I killed Reahgan that there was no going back. That I was soiled forever. I was shamed. My hands were dirty in a way that could never be undone. But it's more than the stain of Reahgan's death."

I pause, the next words catching in my throat. I take a few deep breaths then force them out quickly. "The Night Bringer's soul is in mine. They're intertwined. I couldn't... I can't tell the difference anymore. It's seeded so deeply in my soul I don't know if I could even become good if I tried. I... I'm terrified that he'll slowly suck the life from who I am and I won't even notice. And not like in the Schorchedlands where my soul died and his consciousness took over. I mean, I'd still be here, in control, but we'd be one and the same. What if... what if that already happened and I didn't know it? What if..." I shake my head, a sob catching in my throat. "That darkness is there all the time. I feel it crawling, carving, digging. What if I am bad?"

"No," Rev says firmly this time. He scootches in and curls his arms around me. "No, Caelynn. You're wrong, and I'll tell you why."

I lay my head against his chest, and he squeezes me tighter as I sniff against his blood-stained tunic.

"You've lived with that monster's soul inside of you for a decade."

I shiver against his warmth.

"But that's doesn't make you weak or bad. That is something that happened to you. And the fact that you are who you are now, despite what has happened to you—despite harboring a piece of true darkness inside—makes you so fucking strong, and I'm shocked you don't see that."

I focus on each word intently. I want to believe him. I want to believe in me.

"If what you fear was true, Cae, you wouldn't have saved me during the Trials. You wouldn't have shied away from the glory your court showered on you during them. You wouldn't have sacrificed for me, over and over and over again. You continue to fight so hard to resist the Night Bringer's plans. You would have died in the Schorchedlands if it had been up to you. Do you think any of those things could be even remotely true if he had any control over you in the slightest? If his soul had any influence on you, you wouldn't be this compassionate, caring, and wonderful female. I know it with every ounce of my being."

I'm trembling now, cocooned in Rev's arms. I squeeze him tightly as a sob escapes my lips.

"You, Caelynn of the Shadow Court, are so bright and so strong that even an ancient power cannot control you. You are deserving of legends, Caelynn."

I bark out a bitter laugh through my tears. "You almost had me there," I joke. "But you went a bit too far with that one."

"It's true," he whispers against my hair. "I adore you more deeply than I could have ever imagined caring for anyone. You are beyond incredible, Caelynn. And I mean it when I say I am proud that you are my mate. That fate would match you with me makes me feel more confident in myself. Because if fate thinks I could be worthy of this incredible fae, then I must be more than I think too."

Okay, yeah, now I'm crying.

The waters beneath us seem to give a deep sigh, pulling in and out like gentle waves washing over the beach. "You have passed the second trial," the king declares softly. "And now, here is your final test."

57

CAELYNN

"Here is your final test, Caelynn of the Shadow Court. If you agree to these terms, I will be your champion. I will fight against your monster."

I swallow and stand up straight, shoulders back. "What are your terms?"

"I require a sacrifice."

I suck in a breath.

"You offered me anything. Told me you didn't care what happens to you. I require you to prove it. Promise me that you will freely offer me your life if I kill your monsters."

"No!" Rev yells immediately.

I simply close my eyes. A wave of bone-deep sadness washes over me, but it's followed by acceptance. I am not angry, not afraid. I feel only... defeat. "Okay."

"No!" Rev grabs my upper arm forcing me to face him. "No, you can't do this. I won't let you. We can find another way. If this asshole won't help us, we'll... we'll fight together and we'll find a way."

I nod, meeting his stare with a lackluster expression. "We'd fight," I whisper. " And we'd lose."

"No," he whispers, his voice breaking. "No, I refuse to believe that."

"I can't let us lose this fight. I would rather give my life here and now and know it can be done."

His trembling fingers grip my chin. "No. Please Caelynn look at me."

I see his dark eyes, the tears streaming from them, but I look no further. I can't. I can't bear to witness his pain.

I know without a doubt that I cannot live while those beasts do. And while Rev believes there is a way, I know there isn't. This is it. This is the way. And if this is what the King of Light requires, I'll give it.

A growl reverberates through the ground, and I step away from Rev. He reaches for me, but a solid wall of light blasts from the floor straight up into the sky.

"Caelynn!" he roars from the other side. He slams himself into the wall. His fists pounding so fiercely I feel each thud in my chest. He cries and roars and screams.

My gut twists violently as I turn my back on my mate to face a fate I expected for years. A fate that would have once been so easy to accept, welcome even. I suppose it's not really a worthy sacrifice if it doesn't cause pain.

And this is painful. So excruciating that for a moment, I can't move. Every muscle clenches so hard my thighs begin cramping. My arms. My stomach. Debilitating pain ricochets through my chest. And I cry out, expressing the agony I feel inside and out. Like my very soul is ripping.

"Come," the king says softly. "Leave him behind and we will complete your mission before I end you."

Eyes closed, I lift my face to the sky.

It will destroy me.

The pain is still intense everywhere, but my mind begins

to clear. This pain is awful, but Rev's... his is worse. Can I really do that to him? Is that really right?

My stomach clenches again, and I remember the first test. My intuition told me what I was doing was wrong long before I realized. It knew I was hurting something precious to me.

And I feel that same thing now.

This... this isn't right.

I take in a long breath and the cramping pain releases.

I turn back to face Rev. I can't see him behind the wall of light, but I can hear his helpless cries, his fist pounding against magic he is no match for.

"Not like this," I whisper.

I thought... I thought removing myself from everyone I cared about would make this easier. I thought it would keep them safer but... I can hear and feel Rev's agony.

I step up to his prison and place my hand on the wall of light.

"What are you doing?" The king sounds vaguely curious but mostly annoyed.

"Drop the wall," I say. "Please."

"He'll stop you from doing what you must," he says calmly. "Have you changed your mind? Do you refuse my final requirement?"

"No. I will give my life if that's what you require. But not like this." I press my palm harder against the burning light. "Drop the wall."

The king gives an exaggerated sigh, and then the wall of light drops and so does Rev. He falls to his knees, water splashing. His body sags, shoulders slumped. I drop with him, pulling him into my arms.

"I'm sorry," I cry. "I'm sorry, I'm sorry. I won't leave you like that. I won't. I'm sorry."

Realization seems to dawn on his expression, and he

desperately claws at me, pulling me in tight, fingers clenching against my clothing and skin and frigid water soaks us. He stands, lifting me against him. I wrap my legs around his waist.

We stay like this, clinging to each other for what feels like an eternity. Our final eternity together. I sniff back my tears.

His breathing evens out after a few moments. "What's happening?" he whispers.

I pause. My next words will hurt him, and I don't know if I'm ready to let go of this last moment with him. Finally, I gather my strength. "I'm still going to offer my life in exchange for his help."

His chest quakes. "No, please," he begs. "I can't... I can't just let you do that."

I swallow tightly. "Leaving you like that was wrong, I could feel it. So, maybe," I lean back to look him in the eye, "maybe I need to explain to you why I have to do this."

He drops down to his knees, and I curl up on his lap. His eyes are red, but he nods, ready to listen.

"What lies on the other side of the pain, Caelynn?" The Light King's voice whispers in the stillness, in the breath between moments.

I pause. "What?"

"Though my heart still quakes, I remind myself that I am not that girl any longer." The king's slow and steady voice reverberates through the air. I blink. Those are my words... No. My thoughts. "And this time," he continues, "I am here by my own free will. I was not trapped or lured. This is my destiny, and if I must withstand literal torture, this time I will do it willingly. Because my eyes are wide open. I know what lies on the other side of the pain."

I swallow.

"What lies on the other side of the pain, Caelynn?" he asks again.

Revenge. That's what I'd been thinking.

But... but instead, when I open my mouth to respond a new word rushes in.

"Freedom," I whisper, echoing the thought.

That's what this was always about. Tears well in my eyes as understanding dawns. I've been so focused on justice and punishment for my tormentors, but that's not really what I'm seeking. That's not really what I need.

That's not the real reason I must do this.

I sniff. "From the moment the Night Bringer gripped me in his claws, I've been living in the reality that he forced me into. I've been trapped. Every moment of every day." The words flow from my mouth quickly, easily. A gift of clarity to help me express my needs to my mate so that he can understand why I must do this.

"In the pain and the shame, the suffocating hatred of every person I ever cared for, I've been trapped in my own failure."

I close my eyes, lips trembling.

"I entered the Trials to earn my freedom from banishment, but also to earn just a little bit of freedom from my own shame. I gained so much more by the end. I gained hope. You... you gave me hope, Rev."

Rev stares at me, eyes wide.

"Even when I was drowning in my own darkness—when *his* infection was spreading—your light was growing. And that light is what saved me from that terrible fate. Despite your own pain and anger, you chose me in a way no one ever has."

His eyes search mine, seeking to understand.

"But even despite all of that," I tell him, my voice hoarse, "I am still not free."

"Caelynn," he whispers.

"I have so much more to fight for. I have joy and purpose and love and friendship, but I am still trapped. I *need* the Night Bringer to be defeated. I don't care how or at what cost. Because I will never be free while his soul continues to exist in this world."

Rev swallows. He shakes his head slowly, but his eyes soften in understanding.

We sit in stillness for a long while, just holding each other. "Okay," he finally whispers. "We'll do this together then."

"What?"

"If you feel you have to do this, I understand. But I won't let you do it alone." He turns to the sky. "You will take us both. Or neither."

The light pulses with a soft chuckle. "I require no lives, children. You have passed your final test."

58

REV

"What?" Caelynn says.

"You asshole! Why would you do that?"

"I did not say I would take her life. Only that she must offer it."

"So... So, you only needed me to be willing?" She asks dubiously.

"The test was never about you giving your life. I knew from the moment you stepped into my presence you were willing to die for your cause."

"Then, what was the test?"

"Leaving your mate behind to do it."

I blink rapidly. He parted us. Imprisoned me and told her to leave me behind. She thought that was her test. But she refused. She came back to me.

"Offering your life or not, if you were willing to abandon your mate, you are not the kind of fae I would align with. Your choice is not the issue. Just like my mate should have spoken up about her beliefs and needs before or during our final council." The king's voice dips low, sadness seeping into the sound. "It doesn't matter if you disagree. You should always communicate and compromise. I wish my mate had learned that lesson. Maybe she was right that I wouldn't have listened. That is my own fault. But... well, you chose correctly, Caelynn. I would be proud to have you as a mate also. And I am proud to have you two as allies."

59

CAELYNN

Rev calls an emergency council meeting, which was quite easy considering all the council members were still in the palace. A few of them have had a bit too much to drink, but this is still a better option than announcing our plans to the entire ballroom.

"What is happening, Zanterleisha?" the Luminescent King asks, eyes hooded.

"We're going into battle," Rev announces from his seat beside the queen.

Everyone in the room freezes. I approach the table, my black blouse now ripped, one of the strips flowing behind me.

All of the ruling kings and queens from the entire realm turn their attention to me.

"Against whom?" the Whirling King asks, teeth exposed in an ugly grimace.

"The Night Ancients."

"What do you mean?" High Queen stands, her red nails gleaming as she grips the edge of the table.

"We have the weapon we need."

"What weapon?" she asks, leaning forward. Her eyes narrow in on me. "Tell me you did the forbidden and I will—"

"Do what you must, Zanterleisha," Rev says, arms crossed. "Caelynn and I will do what we must."

My brows furrow. I hadn't realized the queen had forbidden him from approaching the Light King. Is that what they were talking about while Drake antagonized me?

The other kings and queens glance at each other, confusion clear in their expression.

"We don't require your help," Rev says. "We will finish this war with or without you."

Kari marches from the edge of the room. She's only occasionally allowed in council meetings as an apprentice to her mother. I suspect today was not one of those days. "I will stand with you. In whichever way you need. Even if it means defending the Shadow Court."

Gasps resound through the room.

Rai stands as well. "As will I."

"You side with the Shadow Court in a war against my kingdom?" the Whirling Court King asks.

"I am not against any court. But I will defend the Shadow Court if it is attacked."

"They have attacked my court!" the king yells.

"And your son has allied with the Night Ancients." I cross my arms.

The Whirling King's eyes grow so wide I worry they'll pop from his head. "You believe her falsities? Her lies?" He is now speaking directly to Rev.

"I believe in my mate, yes."

A hush falls over the room, and Rev responds by snaking an arm around my waist. My heart hammers.

"There have been many rumors about Caelynn," he says calmly, silver eyes bright. "Much speculation about our relationship. Hear the truth straight from my lips: Caelynn of the Shadow Court is my fated mate. I love her. I choose her. I will no longer keep it secret. She is mine."

"Reveln," the High Queen says through clenched teeth.

Rev holds his chin high. My heart throbs in my chest. What is he doing?

The High Queen's harsh eyes turn to me now. "Caelynn, we made a deal."

My lips part, but I don't know how to react. He's only spoken truth.

A silver swirl on Rev's forearm appears. The bond mark glows brightly in the dimly lit room.

"You would break a vow with the High Queen?" she shrieks. "I will declare the bargain broken. You know the punishment."

I examine Rev's expression, confused and scared. But he is utterly confident.

"What bargain, Zanterleisha?" the Frost Court Queen asks quietly.

His right arm remains curled against me and his left slips casually into his pocket. "Ahh but what were the terms of that bargain, your Majesty?"

The High Queen frowns. "That you not marry or bond *publicly* to Caelynn. Which you are threatening to do here and now. You may have broken the bargain already by revealing your bond to the entire council. I don't know that you want to test the magic and risk finding out the hard way."

"You've missed an important piece. *While I am High King.*"

My stomach sinks, and I release a shuddering breath.

"You—" she studders.

"You thought you had me. You held the thing I'd wanted more than anything else in your hand and you used it to control Caelynn and me. But things change. I've come to realize that this dream—to be the High King of the realm—was only a response to what happened to my brother. I sought to prove myself to a father who hated me. I sought to hold up my brother's legacy. But I'm not even sure he was deserving of the legacy to begin with. And I never accounted for finding a mate as brave and strong and incredible as Caelynn. A mate with a destiny more important than even mine. Someone else can take my place as High Heir. Choose another High Ruler. There are many who would take the role and do it justice. But there is only one person in the entire realm that can give me true happiness. Only one person in the entire realm that can destroy a set of monsters that have been plaguing our world for millennia. Only one person that can rebuild a crumbling court that was never deserving of its punishment. Those are causes I am happy to sacrifice my once-dream for."

My wide eyes meet Rev's soft and unconcerned gaze. He means it. He really, truly believes the words coming from his lips.

"I will not be High King."

60

REV

Caelynn's shocked expression is almost comical.

"Rev," she whispers. "You don't have to..."

"No," Zanterleisha says. "No, you will not dismiss me like this. The courts. We..." She marches forward, panic filling her eyes. "We will discuss this. We can—"

"No," I say, not bothering to look away from Caelynn. My mate. My love. My fate.

"I will revoke the bargain. Allow you to marry her." The queen's eyes are frantic. Pain and fear clear in her expression. I almost pity her.

I hold up my hand. "I'm sorry," I say. "But you were right when you said the realm is not ready to accept Caelynn. They would not accept her at my side in the High Court. And neither of us would be willing to abandon the Shadow Court, which needs her—requires her. As far as I see it, I only have two options. I can live apart from my mate, keeping our relationship a secret. Or I can join her in the Shadow Court. I choose the latter."

"Rev," Caelynn whispers, squeezing my hand gently, "you don't have to make this decision now."

"I have never been more sure of anything in my life," I tell Caelynn. "I don't know what will happen in the next few days, but if we manage to outlive those creatures, I want nothing more than to be the husband to the Shadow Queen."

Caelynn releases a sharp breath. She blinks rapidly. "That's not exactly how I'd expected to be proposed to."

I chuckle. "It's not a proposal. Not yet. I will give you the mated jewelry you deserve once this war is won. I will shout to the world that you are mine."

Caelynn covers her mouth with her palm, fingers shaking. "I don't understand."

"I want you more than I want the realm," I say. "It's an easy choice, to be honest."

She closes her eyes.

Finally, I turn my attention back to the gawking kings and queens. "Raijin, I understand if this changes your stance on defending the Shadow Court."

Rai frowns. "It changes nothing. I'm proud of you, Reveln. And I am beginning to see what you do." He takes in a long breath. "I will defend the Shadow Court."

"You are all insane," my father says.

"I quite agree," Zanterleisha says. "This is ludicrous."

Caelynn turns to meet her stare. "The Ancient King has agreed to fight for us. We are going now to deal with the Night Ancients. During that time, my court will be vulnerable. Anyone willing to defend my court during the battle, I will be beyond grateful. But we are going now. And when the dust settles, we can talk again."

I nod sharply. The High Queen's hatred sears into my back as I pull Caelynn away and we march together toward our new destiny. "I will not change my mind," I whisper to Caelynn.

She nods, but I get the feeling she doesn't entirely believe me. She has always had a hard time believing that she is deserving of happiness. But if we can survive this, I will ensure she is the happiest fae that ever lived.

61

CAELYNN

We march down the front steps of the High Court just as the ground begins to quake. The palace rattles and sways.

"What is happening?" The High Queen says, looking out at the waters of the source sea. The waves rise and toss, building into a massive wave.

"That's our ally," I say.

The rumbling increases until the pebbles at our feet are leaping. The castle behind us sways.

"You did," she says. "You raised that beast that destroyed the High Court. You fool!" She marches down toward us, finger pointed and glowing red along with her eyes. "I wouldn't want you as a High King, Reveln. You will be nothing, you selfish, moronic fae, wooed by a helpless girl who thinks herself important."

Rev whips his head in her direction, and before I can even blink, his hand flies up, sending a jolt of white light right at the High Queen of all the fae. The light settles right over her mouth, sealing it shut.

"I will no longer tolerate anyone insulting my mate,

including you. I am no longer your problem. I am glad you agree it's for the best."

The High Queen stands there, red eyes glowing, her mouth sealed shut by white light. She has the power to crush him here and now but she remains unmoving. Her guards are equally as stunned.

I pull Rev by the arm quickly and rush from the palace toward the newly reconstructed portal bay.

"Where are we going?" Rev leans in close. Nothing worse than making a dramatic exit and then having to stop to ask directions.

"They are still in the Crackling Court; we can head them off there."

"I will meet you there," the powerful voice of the Light King reverberates over the island.

A bright light rises from the crashing waves beyond until his massive bright white form is towering over the palace.

The council stands, mouths ajar, at the top of the palace steps. I pull Rev through the Crackling Court portal before the High Queen decides to act on Rev's treasonous response. Magic shocks our senses as we step through into the pine forest clearing.

"We should talk to Raijin," I tell Rev. Down the hill, the glistening dark waters of Black Lake can be seen in the distance. "If this battle happens at Black Lake..."

Rev curses under his breath.

Three figures join us through the portal. Rai, Kari, and Ty.

"We're coming with you," Kari says breathlessly. "You can't change our minds."

I shake my head. "Like hell I can't—"

Rev pulls me in close. "We may need help."

"And they may get killed!"

"Then, we'll get killed," Kari says. "We're willing to fight with you, risk and all."

I glance down at her full ballgown. She's going to fight in that?

"You're not the only one who can risk your life for a good cause, Cae." Tyadin crosses his arms.

"On this note, we did have to speak with you Rai," Rev says. "The ancients are currently at Black Lake."

Rai's eyebrows rise. "You are going fight this battle right next to my court?" His nostrils flare.

"Sorry," I say. "If we get the chance to shift the battle away, we will. In the meantime, do what you can to protect your people."

"Kari and Ty, you can help Rai protect his city," Rev instructs.

"Let's go, before it begins," Rai says, his voice tense.

Kari nods, but she turns and wraps her arms around me. "You are so brave, Caelynn. You did this. You're going to rid the world of those monsters for good."

Ty piles onto our hug before Kari can let go, wrapping his thick arms around the both of us. Rev laughs and joins in, hugging the other side of us. I hold onto my friends tightly.

"No matter what happens, I'm so glad I met you all."

"Family no matter what," Ty answers.

Tears well in my eyes, and I don't bother to hide them even once they let go. "I love you all," I tell them.

"Us too, Cae. We'll see you again soon."

Ty slaps Rev's upper arm. "I'm proud of you." He winks. Ty hesitates again, but Kari pulls him down the path toward the capital of the Crackling Court.

I release a breath. "Come on then, let's kick some monster ass."

62

CAELYNN

My chest is so tight it's hard to breathe as we slowly walk down the hill to Black Lake, quietly watching the glassy waters. I'm almost surprised when we reach the edge of the lake and there has still been no change. No monsters prowling toward us. No magical explosions. No death.

Nothing.

My breathing is labored as we stand there, waiting for something to happen. Are they even still here? Did we miss our chance?

"We're going to do this," Rev whispers, echoing my own thoughts. "We're going to kill them."

"Together."

He nods, eyes blazing.

Another quiet moment passes. I'd like to be able to appreciate it, our last moment of peace, but I can't. My anticipation is too strong.

"Are you afraid, my monster?" I say loudly to the quiet waters.

Rev quirks a brow. I shrug.

The ground rumbles with his sadistic laughter. The breath freezes in my lungs. Rev squeezes my hand tightly.

A shadow forms over the surface of the lake like a massive void. A black hole, ready to consume everything.

"Have you come to die, my pet? I did tell you I wouldn't oblige, didn't I?"

"We're not here to die," I tell him. "We're here to end you. For good."

The Night Bringer pauses. The massive void pulses with breath, but I can see no relatable characteristic. He has no eyes. No mouth. Not even any arms, though I know he has appendages. I've seen his claws. I've felt them through my body.

"How do you intend to achieve that?" the Night Bringer asks, his voice unsure for the first time since I've known him.

"Like this." The voice is quieter than I expected, but his first blow is not. Blinding white like slams into the black void.

The world seems to explode with them. A wave crashes against the bank, smashing the dirt into bits, sending Rev and me flying. Sharp pain flashes over my limbs as I land on gravel. I sit up to find Rev ten feet away. He rubs his head and stares out at the ancient powers battling only a few hundred feet away.

The Ancient King takes the form of a fae with white glowing skin, and he wrestles with the black void. Blinding white light and pure unending darkness.

The ground continues shaking with each hit and twist and roar.

This is it, I think. *This is the moment my nightmare dies for good.*

Another form rises from the dark waters. The female with pink skin leaps at the Light King, baring sharp fangs and claws. Her eyes still glow, but this time bright yellow. She slams the Light Ancient into the waters, sending a tsunami our way.

"Caelynn!" Rev screams as the hundred-foot wave careens our way.

I cover my head just as Rev wraps his arms around me. The water barrels down at us. With a cry I send out my magic, covering us with shadow. Rev does the same with his light, and just as the water crashes down on us, we are surrounded by an orb of light and shadow.

The world is gone entirely. There is only me, Rev, and our magic weaving together to protect us. I almost don't want to release it. I want to live in this orb, where Rev and I can be free and together in true peace.

But these moments never last nearly long enough. It's only a flash of peace in the chaos. My power is too weak, and it slips from my grasp before I'm ready. Rev and I cling to each other as we fall into cold water.

The water is deep, even here where there was just solid ground beneath us. Tree tops stick out from the settling waters that cover the land for miles. We tread water near the closest cluster of trees.

"What do we do?" Rev asks. The ancients are farther out now, their clashing shakes the waters and the trees, making it hard to hear anything else.

A fourth form appears in the fray. A massive, monstrous tree, with a dozen red eyes in a circle. The Night Terror. The tree's limbs are sharp as blades, and they swipe toward the King of Light. He roars in his rage, sending blasts of his blinding light at all three of his foes.

"Can he beat all three?" I ask the spell book.

"*I don't know.*"

My stomach sinks.

I grab Rev's forearms and pull him toward the closest tree

trunk. The water is already pulling back toward the lake, and we really don't want to be any closer to the warring titans.

My fingers dig into the thick bark, and I pull myself up on the nearest branch. The needles of the pine sting, but I ignore the pain and embrace the discomfort. Rev winces, breathing through clenched teeth, but he joins me on the branch just feet from the sediment-filled water.

A ground-shattering scream tears through the air, and my blood runs cold. I twist to see one of the Night Terror's branches breaking through the Light King's chest and reaching out the other side. My eyes widen, watching in horror at what has to be a killing blow.

The Light King rears back in writhing pain.

"We will not bow to mortal rulers!" the Night Terror screeches.

Rev's arms reach around my waist and pulls me in close as we watch the horrific scene. Our only hope is moments from being torn apart.

Like an atom bomb detonated, the world explodes in light, with only a high pitch ringing to accompany it. I hold on tight to Reveln, pressing my eyes close as the power slams into us.

We fall from the tree, grasping, desperately trying to keep a hold of each other if only to die in each other's arms.

63

REV

Caelynn is ripped from my arms by the force of the waters. My back stings, my mind is overwhelmed by the rush of chaos. I still can't see anything but bright light.

There are more unnatural screams and screeches in the distance, but it's impossible to tell what's happening. All I know is that my body was frozen the moment I saw her beady eyes and talon branches.

The Night Terror is the stuff of all my nightmares. Caelynn is most terrified of the Night Bringer, the shadowy void, but it was the female monster that tortured me in the Schorchedlands, and my body has not forgotten.

I kick back to the surface, but my vision is still peppered by white spots, eyes unable to refocus on the world around us. I can hear nothing but the high-pitched ringing.

I pant, spinning around, desperately searching for Caelynn in the turmoil.

Another scream pierces the air, and I turn back toward the ancients. I blink rapidly, trying to clear the remnants of shock from my vision. At first, all I can see is a massive head flying through the air. My eyes widen, heart freezing mid-beat.

Glowing red liquid flows from the decapitated head.

Then, I see the body of a giant female fall limp out in the middle of the lake. My heart resumes it's beating. The Lady of the Lake has met her end.

Not bad news, I tell myself. *Not bad news.*

The Light Ancient and the Night Ancients clash again, and I watch helpless, barely able to focus on treading water. "You will die today," the Light King yells as he slams into the shadowy void again and again. "Just as you should have died all those years ago."

The Night Bringer doesn't respond. Doesn't speak. And I can't tell if he's dying--if he's losing—or if the Light King simply cannot hit him hard enough to hurt him.

"You will not win," a familiar voice, full of venom and power, says from so much closer than I'd expected. My heart stops again as I realize the Night Terror is here, beside me.

No, is all I can think as something rips me from the water, imprisoning me. Nails like claws piercing me in a hundred places at once.

"Rev!" Caelynn screams, but I can't tell from where. I can't tell much of anything anymore. Pain explodes over every inch of my body. So quickly. Too quickly, I succumb to the darkness.

64

CAELYNN

My whole world comes to a screeching halt as Rev is taken by the massive wolf. The Night Terror stands beside the giant black canine, laughing.

I'd swam helpless, unable to see or hear anything, for far too long. And by the time my sight returned, he was gone. Limp in the monstrous creature's jaws. The Nomad joined the fight after all.

"Rev!" I scream in a world-shattering plea.

Except, it's not world shattering. I am nothing. Not strong enough to fight this battle. Not strong enough to even survive witnessing it. No one listens to my cries, my pleas. No one hears me.

I try anyway. I swim toward the beast crushing my mate. I can feel his pain streaking through my body like a distant echo. He will die. Rev will die if I don't stop it. If someone doesn't stop it.

"No, no, no," I'm crying now, screaming. Begging anyone or anything to listen. He can't die. Not him. Not Rev.

"Take me," I groan. "Please take me instead."

Booming laughter shakes me to my very core. I would

know the Night Bringer's voice anywhere. The sound has haunted me every day for a decade. Every night, I hear his bitter laughter. How gleeful it made him to rip my soul to shreds.

"I told you, my pet," his sadistic voice reverberates through the dozens of yards between us, "I would make you beg for me to end you."

I whimper.

"But I will not oblige."

I continue, desperately clawing through the rippling waters, rushing back toward the center of the lake. "Rev," I whisper, knowing my pleas will remain unheard. Unheeded. No one cares.

"I care, child."

I blink, turning to the Ancient of Light towering over the beast and the Night Terror. There is a massive hole in his stomach flowing with flickering liquid, like his own light is fading, but he still looks so strong.

Another blast of light streaks toward the wolfish beast and the Night Terror. There is a roaring snarl, a piercing scream, and cataclysm of exploding power.

I am thrown back, but this time, despite my blindness and the paralyzing fear, I scramble back toward Rev without even a pause. "*Keep going,*" the spell book coaches me. "*Forward. You're going the right way.*"

I follow his quiet encouragement, the water rushing out and pulling me even faster. Soon, it's shallow enough I can wade my way forward. My vision slowly returns, and I follow the tiny flare of our mating bond barely pulsing with life.

"Rev," I whisper again, but there is no taunting laughter left. No preternatural screams or world-shattering clashes. There is the gentle rush of water and my cries.

Nothing else.

Finally, I see Rev's form lying limp in the water, only inches deep now. I turn him over, so he is face up, then I freeze. He's pale. His lips blue.

I can't move for what feels like an eternity.

Hands shaking, finally I press my palms to his chest. There are large puncture marks over much of his body, his silver and gold tunic ripped to shreds. His chest does not rise.

He's not breathing.

Blinking back my desperate tears, I claw at his chest. "No, no, no, no."

"Child," a deep yet soft voice says. Uncomfortable warmth hits my back, white light streaking down at me.

"Save him," I beg. "You can save him, right? You said you cared. I heard you. You..."

"I am able to bring him back," the king says, and I blink, thinking I didn't hear him correctly.

"Then, do it!" I yell.

"You must first understand the repercussions. I can bring him back, but it will require much of my magic. Magic I will not get back."

"Please, please," I chant. I look around as my vision finally clears completely. A massive, warped tree lies on its side, twisted and deformed. The Night Terror. Beside her is the wolfish beast. Both dead.

"I killed three of the four ancients in that battle, but the Night Bringer fled."

Fled. The Night Bringer fled. He's alive and not here.

"If I bring your mate back from beyond, I will no longer have the ability to defeat him."

"No," I whisper. I can be free from my monster, or I can save my mate. "You cannot force me to make that choice."

"I'm very sorry, Caelynn. But there is no other option."

I shake my head, tears blurring my vision, and I pull Rev's

limp body into my arms, holding the cold skin of his cheek against my chest. I scream into the sky.

I know everything that is precious to you. And I will take it away bit by bit.

"He was right," I whimper, rocking Rev's lifeless body back and forth.

I could choose to save Rev here and now. I could bring him back and heal his broken body. But to what end? The Night Bringer would remain. He would continue to hunt us both. He would destroy my court and my friends. And he would find a way to kill us both.

Saving Rev would leave the entire realm in darkness.

Not saving Rev will leave me in darkness.

65

CAELYNN

He was going to leave the High Court for me.

We were going to be together, for real. Forever.

I can picture that life so clearly. He would have proposed in a stupidly elaborate way. Got down on one knee and presented a ring of glowing lumi-stone. The sprites would have passed on the news to the whole kingdom, whispering their joyous celebration of our union.

We would have said our vows, publicly, in the Shadow palace while gargoyles looked down on us with their bright shining eyes. He would have held me through every trial being a ruler will inevitably bring. I would have woken in his arms every morning.

We'd have played hide and seek in the Shadow palace courtyard. We have danced before the Phantoms in the ballroom. We'd have made an entire wing of the palace our home. We'd have walked into the High Court, arm in arm, wearing matching crowns and smug smiles, not at all caring who hated us and who admired us.

He'd have kissed my belly, swollen with his child. The strongest Shadow heir in hundreds of years.

He was mine. He believed in me like no one else ever has. As I look at his eyes now, void of life, I realize that I lost. The Night Bringer won.

66

CAELYNN

Tears stream down my cheeks as I face this new reality.

But I can't let Rev go now. It's maybe the most selfish thing I've ever done, but—he did it for me. He doomed the world, to save my life. Now it's my turn to do the same.

"Save him."

"You're sure?" the Light King says, his voice empty of judgment.

"Caelynn?" someone calls in the distance, the voice is soft, feminine. I frown, looking over the mess of a battleground. Most of the water has retreated, flowing back into Black Lake but it left a mess of slippery muck over the surrounding miles.

Kari and Ty stop the moment they see us, lying in the mud. Kari's wide eyes stop on the Light King, his massive form still pulsing with a dull light. Ty is equally as stunned but then he clenches his jaw and marches closer. Kari is right on his heels.

"Is there another way?" I ask the spell book. "To defeat the Night Bringer. Is there a way?"

The spell book pauses.

"I need Rev. I need you to save him. I don't care what it costs. But I'm not going to give up."

"*There might be a way…*"

Kari gasps as she noticed Rev's body, still. Skin grey. Ty falls to his knees beside him. "No," he whispers.

"Do it now," I demand. Ty looks up at me, fear and confusion on his expression.

The Light King reaches down and touches his massive forefinger to my mate's chest.

67

REV

First, I am cold. An icy chill rushes through my limbs, and the darkness seeps into my very being.

Then, there is warmth. A gentle light that soars straight at me, growing brighter every moment. Soon, it covers the darkness.

The pressure, the weight, the burden—it's gone. Why was I so burdened before this moment? I can't remember. I can't even fathom. But I do know that this feels good.

I am surrounded by white light on every side. "Where am I?" I look down at my body. I'm naked. How the hell did I get naked?

Death is freedom, a whisper floats through my mind, and I blink rapidly.

"You have passed beyond," a voice in the distance tells me. The voice is gentle and feminine.

"Beyond," I repeat slowly. I twist back, trying to find the place I came from. "I died." My voice is hoarse.

"Yes."

My stomach sinks, but I struggle to grasp all of what that will mean. "My... my mate is not here."

"No."

The weight on my chest is back, and I can't breathe.

"Death is not the end, Reveln. It is only the beginning. There is much for you to find if you continue walking. A whole new world. All you must do is continue forward."

"No," I groan.

The bodiless voice grunts. "Yes, yes. Those who pass without their mates tend to have a harder time adjusting."

"Well, no shit. Only half of my soul is here," I say, panting. Hands on my knees, I try to force air through my lungs. My vision peppers with black. Can one pass out when they're already dead?

Do I even need to breathe here?

"No," the voice tells me.

I stand up straight, the urge to breathe suddenly gone.

"You will meet your mate again," the voice assures me. "This is not the end."

Flashes of memory appear in my mind's eye. "We were in a battle. What happened?"

There's a caress of darkness against my heart. I spin toward the tiny shadow in the distance and step toward it.

The right *death is freedom*

"Their battle is not ove—" the disembodied voice says softly but cuts off. "What are you doing?" she asks as I take another step toward the darkness. Shadows that are as familiar as my own soul pull me away from the voice and back toward the heaviness of life.

A sweeping shadow curls around my wrist and tugs. A smile spreads across my face. "I don't think my battle is done yet either."

68

REV

All of the weight and pain drop back into me at once, and I gasp as air rushes into my lungs.

Then, she is on me. Her arms are around my neck, her chest against mine. For one moment, all I feel is the absolute bliss of *Caelynn*, and I breathe it in. But then, I notice she's sobbing.

I return the embrace, wrapping her up in my arms and squeezing tighter than I probably should.

"Rev," she cries against my neck.

"I'm here," I tell her. "I'm here."

"You left me," she whimpers. "You were gone."

"Not by choice, Angel." I chuckle lightly. "I'm pretty sure I was in heaven."

Caelynn pulls back suddenly, her bloodshot eyes wide in shock.

"Don't worry, I'd rather be here any day." I pull her down to meet me for a sloppy kiss, but I don't care, any touch from her is perfect. "This is my heaven, Angel."

She chokes on a desperate laugh. I wipe the tears from her cheeks.

"What happened?" a deep voice whispers. A voice I've never heard so soft, so pained.

"Ty?" I ask, looking over Caelynn's shoulder. She leans back and reveals the dwarfish fae smiling through tear filled eyes, kneeling right next to me.

"I don't know what happened exactly," I say. "I feel awful." My whole body feels like it weighs a thousand pounds. My head is throbbing.

"What did… the afterlife feel like?" Kari whispers. I turn to her. She's standing a few feet away, arms wrapped tightly around her middle.

"Much better than this," I chuckle, trying to force my body up into sitting position.

"Facing death is the easy part," Caelynn whispers. "Facing life—that's the struggle."

I press my cheek against her chest. "Life might be hard, Angel. But it's so, so worth it."

"We should go," a low voice says. I blink, looking up to the being made up of pure light towering over us. My eyebrows shoot up. Right, the battle of ancient evils continues on.

"You brought me back?" I ask.

The Light King nods.

"Thank you, maybe you're not such an asshole after all."

The Light King chuckles.

"Where are we supposed to go?" I ask, as Caelynn helps pull me to my feet. My body feels heavy and strange, my legs wobbly, but the wounds beneath my ragged clothing are healed. "What happened?"

"Well, we have some things to discuss," Caelynn says slowly, sniffing back the rest of her tears.

"By giving you life," the ancient made of light says, "I released some of my magic that I cannot get back. Between that and my injuries…"

I frown.

"He doesn't have the power to kill the Night Bringer anymore," Caelynn explains.

My stomach twists. "Then, you shouldn't have brought me back," I say quickly. I shake my head trying to wrap it around the current situation. We can't win. The Night Bringer remains and not only can our current ally not win in a fight against him... there's no one else. No other ancients. They're all gone.

Caelynn grips my chin, forcing me to face her. I blink rapidly.

Her eyes are dark and determined. The severe Shadow fae I've come to expect her to be around others. Not me. It's the face of sheer determination and anger. The face of revenge.

"We have a plan."

"Okay," I say slowly. "What is it?"

"There's only one way we can beat the Night Bringer now, according to the spell book," Caelynn tells us. "We can't kill him—but we can trap him."

Kari's eyebrows rise. "Like your ancestor tried to do before?"

Caelynn nods. "But we're not going to the Schorched-lands where he'll have access to fae and magic."

"Then where?" I ask

"We have to go to the human realm."

Kari's eyes grow wide. "What?"

"The Night Bringer will lose power if he travels into another world and the spell will have a stronger hold on him. We can separate him permanently from the spell book, which would be required for him to break his curse. We can make sure he can never break free."

"How?" I ask.

"By destroying the link between our worlds."

69

CAELYNN

The Light King's zap of magic flashes through Rev and me and the world disappears. Power rips at my body and then all at once the world spins back into focus.

My boots land solidly into mossy ground. My mind spins, as we refocus on our new surroundings, twisting vines and a canopy of leaves. I cling tightly to Rev, and he holds me steady.

I refuse to let him go. I need to feel him with me at all times or I will fall into the maze of agonizing panic. Luckily, Rev is okay with this arrangement, and he hasn't even commented on how tightly I hold his hand.

"What the hell?" someone says. A voice I don't recognize.

Two fae scramble to their feet just feet down the path, weapons out. The male holds a long sword. The female' bow and arrow is pointed straight at Rev's chest. I shift in front of him.

Rev holds up one hand up. The other squeezes mine tightly.

"Caelynn?" a sweet voice breaks through the tense silence.

My eyes light up as I shift my gaze past the defensive fae to the human girl behind them. "Ray?" I whisper. And I cannot help the smile spreading across my face. I release Rev's hand for the first time, and I rush past the two fae, who relax quickly, and I throw my arms around Raven.

"You have no idea how worried I've been!" Raven cries into my shoulder.

"You?" I say, pulling back to look into her pretty brown eyes. "I thought you were—" I shake my head.

"I'm fine," she says bashfully.

"How?" I whisper, eyes darting around. "What happened to you?" I face the two fae behind me. Blane, with his yellow eyes and sharp cheek bones, his blond hair in a ponytail. So much like Drake.

Next to him is a dark-skinned female with bright green eyes.

"What about you?" Blane asks calmly. "What the hell happened to you?" His amber eyes flit down to my torn clothing.

"And more importantly, how in the world did you get here?" the female asks. "We're smack in the middle of the Twisted Forest."

We are surrounded by bright green foliage. The ground is worn dirt covered in patches of moss, but the trail is surrounded entirely by twisted vines that remind me of the Wicked Gates, and the trees rise up high into the sky, creating a canopy of green leaves.

This forest is legendary. No one can travel through it without a fae with the magic to control the plant life. Only a Twisted fae can traverse these paths.

"The book told us where to go. The Ancient King brought us here." I shrug.

"The what?" Raven asks.

I shake my head. "Long story."

"Well, tell it, and we'll tell you ours," Blane says with a confident smirk.

70

CAELYNN

The whole group sits in a tight circle around the small fire, and we begin to share our tales.

We tell Raven and her friends—Blane and Aurora—how we managed to kill three of the four ancients against us. There is only one left. And we no longer have the power to defeat him.

Raven explains how Blane came to her school and eventually—sort of—kidnapped her. My chest tightens as I watch them. Raven is sheepish as she explains the situation. Aurora twists her lips in a guilty expression. Blane shows no emotion at all.

"I was pissed," she says, her eyes cast to the ground. "But eventually, they learned to treat me like an equal, not something to herd and control." She shrugs.

I resist the urge to lecture the fae about treating people—even weaker people—with respect. I don't want to overstep on relationships I really know nothing about.

"And you decided it was a good idea to wake an ancient king without anyone knowing?" I quirk a brow at Blane. He's the one who completed the spell.

Blane purses his lips. "In hindsight..." He shakes his head. "We should have done it differently, but at the end of the day, how do you beat a monster?"

"Release a bigger monster," Aurora answers.

"And you did it," Raven says in awe. "You leashed the Ancient King of Light?"

"I leashed nothing," I say, breathing out through my nose. "But yes, we have the Ancient of Light on our side. He doesn't like being called a monster or a beast, and no one could ever leash him."

"He is an ally," Rev adds. "He will respect you so long as you respect him."

"But he is capable of squashing you like a bug if he wants to, so don't be a jerk." I cross my arms.

"Noted," Blane says. His arm hangs over his raised knee, his chin high. I watch him for a moment, unsure what to make of him. He looks so much like his brother, a fact that gets under my skin.

He has bright amber eyes full of cunning. He is proud and pretty and intelligent. All of the things I'd expect from a Whirling Court prince. All of the things that make me not trust him.

Is he truly an ally, or do I need to maneuver around him like I would Drake? Placate but watch at all times for the moment he will inevitably turn against us?

I shift my gaze away from Blane, if only because I don't want him to notice me watching him.

The ground rumbles beneath our feet in what sounds suspiciously like growls.

Kari frowns and stares down at the bouncing pebbles. "What is that?"

"There are tunnels below us," Ty says. "Are those the tunnels the Shadow Court used to attack the Twisted Court?"

My eyebrows rise. I'd forgotten the Twisted Court and the Shadow Court had history. This forest is renowned for being a fortress. No strangers can travel here, and there is only one major settlement in this court—smack in the middle of the forest. Only two courts have ever successfully waged battle against the Twisted Court.

The Flicker Court, who burned a quarter of the forest down several centuries ago. And the Shadow Court, who used tunnels to reach the city. Neither have been forgotten by the forest dwellers.

"It's been doing that for a week straight," Aurora answers. "It's been making the court really nervous, the rumbling."

"*Wraiths are gathered in the tunnels below,*" the spell book whispers.

"It's wraiths. Maybe they're just there to sow doubt against the Shadow Court. Or maybe the Night Bringer is planning something."

"He's hurt though, right?" Kari says.

"*He's licking his wounds. It should be safe for the night. Tomorrow... tomorrow, he may come for you.*"

"I don't know what he'll do. But I know the Night Bringer won't let this go."

"What do we do then?" Raven asks.

I shrug. "Find a place to stay for the night. He won't attack just yet."

Raven groans. "So, more camping out here?"

I snort at her complaint. Apparently, they've done this a lot.

"More camping," Blane says with a sharp nod.

"That sounds pleasant," Ty comments.

"*Move away from the mountains. Only camp in spots not above a tunnel.*"

I purse my lips and look up at the tree coverage. I hadn't

even noticed we were close to any mountains. The trees and vines are so thick all we can see is foliage and a few scattered spots of blue sky.

"Aurora, can you lead us away from the mountains? We'll find a place to camp in a few miles."

Aurora smiles, her green eyes lighting up.

The group packs up quickly, and once we're ready, Aurora approaches what looks like a wall of twisted vines blocking the path. The vines shift, curling away like slithering snakes, exposing another stretch of worn pathway.

Our group sets out down the winding, shadowed trail. Massive green wines wiggle and writhe just beyond the path, but nothing impedes the walkway.

The air grows heavier, the sounds of the forest louder. Bugs and birds chirping. Animals rustling in the leaves.

My fingers find Rev's again as we walk slowly through the forest. Periodically, the vines shift and move away to expose more worn path at Aurora's demand.

After an hour of slow walking with very little talking, Aurora stops.

"Is this good?" she asks. "The city is still a few days' trip north, but we should be far enough from the mountains by now. If we travel much farther tonight, we'll reach the marshes and the mists. They're not fun to camp in."

Kari and Ty exchange looks.

"There's a tunnel pretty far below." Ty shrugs.

"Tell her to keep going until you reach the moss trees. Rest there."

"We should keep going a bit longer," I say definitively.

Aurora narrows her eyes and looks down at the ground like she could somehow sense the tunnels.

Aurora leads us through the trail for another half hour. I keep my eyes out for the moss-covered trees, which turn out are obvious. The moss is a sage, a much lighter shade than the rest of the vines so everything lightens when we reach the spot the spell book instructed.

"Here," I announce. "By the moss trees."

"How about after this bend?" Aurora adds. "It's best to camp next to one of the walls."

"Sure."

We take Aurora's lead the last stretch until we find a block in the pathway, and we stop there.

"Good?" Aurora asks. I pause, hoping for input from the spell book, but of course he's silent now.

"Uhh sure?" I say.

Rev chuckles and drops his bag on the ground. "Here, it is."

Our group works quickly to set up a camp. Between Rev and Blane, there is a small fire flickering in a few minutes. We have several bedrolls and blankets set out.

"Want to do a check of the area?" Aurora asks, speaking directly to Raven.

Raven, the only human in the group.

I frown, but then Raven is no longer a pretty, young human girl. With a pop and zing of magic, she's soaring up into the thick tree cover in the form of a blackbird.

I gasp, watching her disappear quickly into the leaves above. "Did you do that?" I ask quietly to Aurora. Cause it sure didn't seem like Aurora or Blane used any magic at all. I'm not even sure transfiguration is an ability of plant fae. Maybe Whirling fae?

"No. That was all Raven." Aurora smiles.

My lips part. "What?"

Rev steps forward, his expression equally as perplexed. "She's human..."

"She is," Blane says matter-of-factly. "But somehow, she's

retained some of the magic from this realm." He shrugs one shoulder like this isn't a big deal.

"That doesn't make any sense," Rev whispers.

My eyes remain wide, but I look up at the canopy of leaves. "How soon will she come back?" I ask quietly.

Aurora shrugs. "Probably a few minutes. But she likes to fly, so maybe a bit longer."

"Thousands of humans have been to the fae realm and interacted with all kinds of magic. None have ever absorbed any. How—"

Blane sits beside a large tree, leaning back against the mossy side casually. "Honestly, you'd know more than we would. We know she somehow has magic, but it happened before us." He wiggles his finger at us. "That's all you guys."

Rev turns to me. "What—did you do anything particular with her? Magically, I mean."

I shake my head. "I turned her into a raven or owl pretty often during the Trials. She was a bird almost the entire maze challenge. She was off on her own a bit during that time, maybe something happened then? I don't know. Because then—"

"She died as a raven," he whispers.

Aurora whips her head toward Rev. "What?"

"During the final trial," he says slowly, "Brielle snapped her neck while she was still in bird form."

Everyone in the clearing stills.

"She was dead," I echo. "Lifeless." I don't even want to remember that moment. How incredibly awful it was to believe that my friend was dead because of me. I should have never brought Raven into the fae world. I should have... I don't know, done so many things, probably. And she died.

Rev, my barely ally, still an enemy in many ways, saw my pain, and he healed her. But he's right. She was dead.

"You brought her back to life," I whisper. "You gave her some of your magic."

71

REV

Less than a minute later, the little blackbird soars down from the treetops and seamlessly leaps back into human form. I stare wide eyed at Raven. An adolescent human girl. Her hair and eyes are a pretty brown, but dull. No sign of magic. No sign of anything *more*.

"What?" she asks innocently, eyes darting between all of us. We're all still watching her. Though, Blane still appears surprisingly at ease. He leans back against the mossy tree, shoulders relaxed.

"Good news," Blane says, "we've solved the mystery of how you have magic."

"We have?" Her voice squeaks.

"Is it even possible, though?" Aurora asks. "To bring someone back to life?"

"It is," Caelynn says quietly, frowning like she's focusing on something else. The spell book, maybe? "But a fae has never done it before..."

I shrug. "I know she was lifeless, but her soul was still present. I healed her, and she lived again after. I... don't know what I did. I just acted on instinct."

"And now Raven has magic," Blane says.

Raven shrugs, her eyes cast to the ground. "What do you think it means?"

Caelynn sniffs. "I don't know. Maybe nothing. You just have some of Rev's magic."

"It might fade over time, or you might keep it forever," Kari adds.

"Have you felt it getting weaker?" Aurora asks.

Raven twists her lips. "No. If anything, it's getting stronger."

Caelynn frowns.

"What all can you do?" I ask, and though my stomach is still in knots and my mind spins, I feign indifference as I take a seat across from Blane, the small fire flickering gently between us.

"Turn into a raven. I flew for a few hours once, but I was really tired after that. I haven't really tried much else."

"You threw a wraith back that one time," Aurora adds.

"And glowed in that tunnel," Blane says.

My eyebrows rise. "Was there a hue to the magic when you used it? Any color at all?"

Raven shrugs.

"When she was lit up, it was white or yellow," Aurora says, "but it was fairly dull, so I don't know."

"Well, that's pretty incredible, Ray," Cealynn says sweetly. "We... don't really know what it means at the end of the day, but it's pretty cool. And great that you have a way to defend yourself while you're here."

Raven nods sheepishly and takes a seat by Aurora's bag. Aurora reaches out and squeezes her thigh gently.

"The sun is just beginning to set," Raven says.

I look up to the treetops, but only a few spots of blue sky can be seen from here.

"I didn't see anything else out of the ordinary."

The group quiets down, taking a seat around the fire. Caelynn passes around pieces of bread we'd brought, and we settle in for a quiet dinner.

"What do we do now?" Blane asks. "We can't kill the Night Bringer, but he's not going to stop."

Caelynn sighs. "No. And he's going to come back for us. Soon."

"So?"

"So, tomorrow, we act."

"What do we do."

"We catch his attention, and then run," I say.

Raven frowns. "Run where?"

Caelynn smiles. "The human world."

"That's where we need your help."

72

CAELYNN

We only manage a few hours of rest before Rev and I become restless. The forest is dark, but the sounds of creeping creatures never settle. If anything, it grows louder.

Aurora, Raven, and Blane sleep side by side, and at one point, I notice Aurora and Raven's fingers interlacing in their sleep. I'd love to know what is happing with those three, but I don't want to be nosy or push something that's not yet settled.

I curl up on Rev's chest, and he kisses my head.

"I love you," he whispers against my hair.

"I love you too." I think again of that sweet future with Rev, by my side in the Shadow Court.

My heart aches to think that is a future I could have. I could have if...

I shake my head.

We lay there, listening to the sounds of this untamed forest and looking up at the rustling leaves high above. This forest is strong in magic, that much is obvious. I've only ever heard legends of it. I had never expected to experience it myself.

Are there other things I'll never get to experience?

In a few hours, we're going to face my nightmare again.

"What are you thinking about?" Rev whispers.

"What our lives will be like tomorrow." I nuzzle into his chest.

We can imprison the Night Bringer, but it's not only him. One of us will have to stay behind when we destroy the portals.

"*He's moving.*"

I pull in a breath. "We should wake them," I tell Rev. He sits up immediately, and before we're even across the clearing, Blane is jerking awake.

"What?" he whispers.

"We need to head out now," I tell him.

Blane blinks back his surprise, but then he nods, his eyes growing wide—his first show of real emotion.

"The Light King will create a sort of temporary portal for us. Just enter into the light."

As if on cue, a doorway of white light appears in the pathway before us.

Raven stirs, rubbing her eyes.

"I love you, Ray. We'll see you soon."

"Okay," Raven whispers, her brown eyes full of fear. I long to take her into my arms and erase all of that fear. But I know better than that now. Besides, it seems it's no longer my arms she desires.

Aurora pulls her in closer.

My lips curl into a content smile as I take Rev's hand and step into the door of light.

Burning, blinding light overwhelms our senses for only an instant, pulling at everything we are, and then throws us back together and drops us in a new world.

The next breath I take tastes like home. Shadow magic fills my lungs, and I shiver in delight.

But then, my vision comes into focus and the mouth of the Cave of Mysteries stands before us, like an open mouth waiting to consume us. I squeeze Rev's hand tighter.

"He is here."

My fingers tremble.

For this part of our mission, it is only Rev and me. Facing the spot of my shift in destiny. The place of my nightmare.

Inside the cave mouth is pitch black, rippling with ancient magic.

He is here. The Night Bringer.

I swallow down my fear. The memories of this place.

A set of red eyes blink before me, and I gasp, a scream lost in my throat. A low rumble of laughter causes the cave to tremble. That's when my panic swells into an intensity that could shatter my fragile body. A sharp blade pierces my flesh, straight through my torso. Warm blood rushes down my body.

Shaking, I stare down at a deep black talon sticking out through my stomach.

I shake my head from the image. My body is whole. My heart is strong. I am not that girl anymore.

"Hello, my pet," a voice purrs.

My hands curl into fists, eyes pressed closed against the wave of fear. Rev's hand is warm against my back, comforting me. I am not alone, this time.

My eyes flash open. I will greet my nightmare head-on. He will not win today.

"Have you come to beg me to end this game now? To leave your friends and court alone?" he growls. "Now that you've lost the power you need to kill me?"

"No," I whisper.

His laugh is more desperate than in the past. His mate is

gone. He's lost a lot of his edge too. "I'm proud of you, my pet, for overcoming your fear of me. It's cute that you think this is going to be enough to defeat me."

"My friends are out of your reach," I tell him defiantly. "You'll never get to them now."

"I will kill the Light Ancient once and for all," he growls low and fierce. "and then it will only be me. And I don't care where you run, I will find you. I will destroy everything you love."

"He's going somewhere you can't touch him too."

"I will turn all of the courts against you. Right now, you have allies defending your borders, but don't worry, my pet, I will dismantle that too."

"I believe you," I whisper. "But I won't be around to see it."

Rev and I, together, take one big step backward, into the door of light that has appeared right at that moment. The burning light sucks at us and drops us only a few miles away —at the portal to the human world.

We wait and listen to the rumbling anger of the Night Bringer. The ground shudders, trees wave, and birds take flight. "*Now.*"

Heart pounding, I step through the archway to the human world for the last time.

73

CAELYNN

Birds chirp joyously when we first enter the human world. The lack of magic is noticeable, even with sparkling sprites bouncing around here and there.

"Go home," I whisper to the sprites. "Leave this place or remain forever."

The little fluttering creatures pause, considering me. Then, they dart through the portal back home.

We are in a forest clearing, with moss-covered logs and rocks stacked in a circle.

"*I don't know what's happening in this world,*" the spell book tells me. "*I feel blind.*"

I nod. I'd expected that part. The spell book's all-knowing power stops with the portals. "You can still help us with the spell, right?"

"*Yes. That spell is ingrained in me, and my magic remains.*"

Rev pulls me against his chest as we wait again. Tremors rock through the portal behind us.

"He's coming," I whisper, my chest tight. This is part of the plan, I remind myself. Taunt the Night Bringer. Make him think we're fleeing and never coming back so he'll follow us where his magic is weakened.

Rev tugs me out of the way. The Night Bringer is still bound by the bargain. He cannot harm me or Rev.

But that's not what he's coming here for. He's come to kill the people I care for, that are currently taking a not-so-leisurely stroll through a deep tunnel in the Smokey Mountains.

A black hole shakes its way through the portal, and I gasp, stumbling back away from the Night Bringer, who now crawls with its gangly, talon-tipped limbs. He does not shift and pulse the way he did in the fae realm.

Now, I can see his gaunt face that looks almost like a man's—but not quite. His body is curved like a spider's but with only four limbs and multiple joints on each. I shiver at the monstrous beast that is the Night Bringer. His pitch-black eyes are so much like the void he was in the fae realm. Unending darkness.

"You didn't think I'd have the courage to come here, did you? But if you think I would let you go after what you did to my mate..."

I stumble back into Rev's chest.

"I will live up to my promise and tear it all away from you." He prowls forward. "I will tear Raven apart limb by limb. Slowly. And then, your Crystal Princess. Then, your ugly dwarf friend. Then, I will destroy the final ancient—the weak fool I failed to kill so long ago—and my reign will be unstoppable."

He smiles, exposing sharp fangs dripping in slime.

Then, the Night Bringer bounds away from us, sniffing the air. The group isn't very far from here. The path we chose is a mile into the mountain range, and they're hopefully a mile deep by now.

This cave was Raven and her friends' idea. They hid there once in the last few weeks.

We'd planned to send them to the deepest cavern we could find, but our time is also limited. We needed the Night Bringer to be able to follow the trail, so they couldn't go too deep. He needed to think the hunt was on his terms.

This is the best we can do.

I watch in terror as my nightmare monster chases after my friends. The bait.

I'm still shaking minutes later when Rev releases me. "We need to go," he says softly.

I nod and take his lead as we run, following the predetermined directions to the cave system in the mountains. For miles around, the ground shakes like a massive earthquake.

The Night Bringer might not be at full strength in this world, but he's still powerful. Still stronger than all of us.

We find the trail and sprint at full speed over the rocky terrain.

"You are a fool, Drake."

I pull to a stop in an instant. Harsh voices sound just around the next bend.

"And you are a coward."

Blane and Drake are here... where are the rest of my friends? The voices pause and then one of them—I honestly couldn't tell you which—begin to laugh. "Don't worry, Caelynn, you can come out."

My heart sinks. Rev gives me a look, but I take slow steps until the open path is revealed. Drake stands, one palm directed at his brother, one toward us.

My eyes flit past Blane, where the small cave mouth is set

low in the stones. How did Drake even get here? He must have followed his brother through the portal to the human world.

Drake's expression is fierce, eyes darting between us and his brother.

"What are you doing here, Drake?" I ask.

"You surprised me, Caelynn. I didn't think you had the ability to convince that king to side with you. Your manipulation skills are…" He kisses his fingertips then spreads them wide. Chef's kiss. I roll my eyes.

"Have you come to die with your last ally?" I ask him, popping a hip confidently.

"Do you think you can win, Caelynn? You have a few weak friends and an ancient on the brink of death on your side. He can't do anything to the Night Bringer without dying. Why would he die for you?"

My brows furrow. *He's a manipulator*, I remind myself.

"You're not getting past me, Drake," Blane says, crouching low.

"I don't need to get past you, brother." Drake winks over his shoulder. "I just need to stop these two from getting down there."

Blane blinks back shock. His eyes meet mine, terror on his face. He's right. And Drake knows exactly what we're doing. He knows that as long as Rev and I don't get down into the cave to complete the spell, we can't win.

Does that mean the Night Bringer knows too?

I don't wait another moment; I fling magic at Drake. He meets my shadows midair with a massive blow of his own. Swirling air and inky darkness clash.

Each of us with magic from the Night Bringer.

Drake pushes my magic aside, knocking me off balance. A blade of wind appears in his hand. He leaps at me, the blade slicing down at my face. I barely twist away from him. Rev sends a steak of light at Drake, but he easily outmaneuvers him.

He smiles. "I'm stronger than both of you now."

My heart hammers, panic constricting my chest. We can win. We can beat him—but not fast enough. Anger stirs in my belly, and I use it to my advantage. I pull at my shadows to rally for me, and darkness drops down from the sky, covering our surroundings with pitch blackness. I breathe it in, and then I strike.

I dive and slice at Drake. He deflects and dodges. My magic pushes and pulls desperately for any in. Any way to end this quickly. If I don't get down into the caves soon, my friends will be dead.

Drake still easily deflects. He matches each of my moves, dodging them all like he can see perfectly in the darkness. Was that a gift from the Night Bringer too?

I cry out in frustration.

"Rev, go!" I yell, suddenly realizing what needs to happen. Drake can't stop Rev from going down and fight me at the same time.

"No," Rev whispers. "Not without you."

"Go or we all die!"

I can't spare a moment to look at him. I slice and lunge at the still smiling Drake. "You can complete the spell without me."

I toss my backpack at his feet. He has the soul stone. He can use the book and complete the spell with the Light King without me.

Drake laughs at my desperation. I'm using too much of my magic anyway. It's going to have to be Rev.

Rev grabs the bag and begins toward the cave. I swing my blade of shadows at Drake again and again.

But then, Drake stills, his eyes going wide. This time, my

blow lands, carving through the flesh of his shoulder and down.

My shadows fall immediately because I know something has changed. I blink as I see the silver glint of a sword coming through Drake's belly.

Blane stands behind him, his brother's blood running down his arm.

"Go," he tells me as Drake's body falls to the ground, his eyes dim.

74

CAELYNN

My heart pounds so rapidly it's hard to think. I pass Rev quickly and lead him through the winding cave, able to see better than him. But that thought only gives me anxiety because the Night Bringer will easily be able to move through these tunnels too.

He'll be much faster than the other fae. And we're so far behind.

We sprint hard. My shoulders slam into damp stone several times, but I don't dare slow down. I slip between two slabs, following the magic path of the Night Bringer.

This time, it will be me stalking him.

A high-pitched whimper echoes on the cool stone, and I run harder. Crashing stone and growls of ancient beasts fill the cave system.

Light glows up ahead.

I suck in a breath when I see a large, glowing male wrestling with the beastly form of the Night Bringer.

"Now," I whisper. "We have to do it now."

I don't see any of our allies, but I don't dare take a

moment to search for them. If we don't do the spell, we'll lose and they'll all die horrific deaths. I don't need the distraction of knowing I'm already too late for one of them.

I drop to my knees, pulling the spell book out quickly. We kneel over the open book, and the spell appears on the worn pages.

"Rev?"

His brow crinkles in concentration.

"We don't have time to wait for them," I whisper frantically. "It has to be us."

Footsteps alert us to someone approaching. I hold my hand up, ready to blast anyone who would dare attack us now. I release a relieved breath when I see Raven.

"What's going on?" she asks breathlessly.

"Rev will need to complete the spell."

Raven frowns. "I thought you said Aurora was supposed to do it. That...whoever completes the spell has to stay behind when we destroy the portals?"

"Is she here?" I ask. I already know the answer. She might be near, but not near enough.

"The Light King and Rev both will be a part of the spell."

Rev's silver eyes meet mine, full of resignation.

"Together," I tell him. "We'll stay together."

Tears sting my eyes at that admission. We'll find happiness as some of the only fae left in the human world—forever barred from our homelands. But the Shadow Court...

I shake my head. I won't think about that now. I can't dwell on that now.

Rev places his hands on the spell book, and immediately light blasts from the pages. We suck in collective breaths as the spell comes together quickly. The light flies from Rev's back and latches itself onto the beastly form of the Night

Bringer, whose jaws are clamped around the Light King's neck.

The sound of ripping magic fills the cavern, bouncing off the falls. The Light King's body falls limp to the ground—with his head still in the Night Bringer's jaws.

75

REV

I don't have to see the fight to know what just happened.

Everyone grows still. The battle pauses. Only the heavy breathing of the ancient beast remains filling the darkness. The light of the Ancient King has been snuffed out.

The Night Bringer howls in angry triumph.

"Who is next?" His voice rumbles. He tries to step forward, but his paw stops midair.

I continue forcing every ounce of my power into the spell, stitching itself around the Night Bringer. He didn't notice its claws in his back. He was too distracted to realize that the magic grasping him wasn't just from the Light King. It was from me, from the spell book.

His eyes flare. "What did you do?"

The Night Bringer throws his weight at the barrier in front of him. He pulls at the anchors of magic stuck into his back.

Kari, Ty and Aurora crawl up from a nearby ledge, watching the magical binding with awestruck wonder. They were too late to help. Now we just have to hope we had enough time. That we have enough power to complete the spell.

I roar in pain as the magic begins to rip from my grasp. "The Light King isn't here to complete it. I don't know if I can finish it."

Caelynn pulls a glowing stone from her pocket and holds it out. "Together," she says. Then she places her palm on my chest, hurling as much of her magic into me as possible.

The Night Bringer roars, sending stones raining down on us as he shakes the very foundation of the mountain. Kari and Ty throw their hands up, working the stone above to remain where it is. If he manages to bury us, we'll never complete the spell.

"It's almost done!" Caelynn yells.

"But we're almost out of magic!" I yell back. The Night Bringer roars and claws at the spell. It's not finished. The chains are not complete. I push my magic again but feel the end of it. My well is dry...

No. No, it can't end like this. So close, so very close.

Then, another set of small hands land on my chest.

My eyes flash up to find the little human girl I saved all those months before holding me. She sends her magic into me.

My own magic, gifted to her, flashes into my body.

It's stronger than I expected. The wave of renewed power explodes from the three of us, connecting us, drowning all three of us in light.

And when the wave recedes, the Night Bringer is silent.

The monstrous unmoving form of the Night Bringer is muzzled and bound tightly in glowing white chains.

76

CAELYNN

"It is done."

Chills wash over me as I stare at the beast, my monster, my nightmare, trapped as much as I was, all those years before. Stone inches its way up his fallen body, but his eyes are red in anger.

I spin to find Ty and Kari manipulating the stone together to cover him.

The final look the Night Bringer gives me promises death. But it is a promise he will never fulfill. Kari and Ty complete their project, covering him entirely.

"The Light Ancient died too," Rev says.

"Yes," I whisper, heart aching. I don't know if he knew this mission would cost him his life, like Drake implied.

"He knew. When he saved Reveln, he knew what it would cost to continue the fight. And he was proud to do it. Proud to end his life protecting his creations."

My heart clenches.

"Is that it?" Blane asks from the tunnel a few feet away.

I nod "Are you all right?"

Blane shrugs. His eyes tell me he'll be haunted by his brother's death for a long time.

"Now what?" Kari whispers.

"We leave the mountains. Kari and Ty, can you destroy this mountain entirely? Smash it good so no one will ever find the tunnel that leads here?"

Ty and Kari nod as one.

"Then, you all will go back to the fae realm, and Rev and I will stay behind."

"Why does Rev have to stay?" Raven asks quietly.

"It was his magic that sealed the prison. If he leaves this world, the power binding it could break. Kari and Ty, you'll take the spell book back to the fae realm and destroy the portals—so the prisoner and the key can never be reunited. The Night Bringer will remain encased forever if we do this right."

"But," Raven says uncertainly, "all three of us completed the spell. Do I have to stay too?" Her eyes dart to Aurora, who smiles reassuringly.

"I'm not leaving you behind, my little bird." Aurora snakes an arm around Raven's waist.

Raven blushes.

"The spell only requires one anchor."

I frown. "What does that mean?"

"What?" Rev asks, turning to me.

"The spell book said, 'the spell only requires one anchor.'"

Aurora sucks in a breath. "Does that mean if Raven and I stay here—you two can go home?"

My heart rises into my throat.

"Yes," the spell book says.

My mind spins, and I almost lose my balance. "You're sure? Positive. Like the whole world depends on the answer being correct. If Raven stays because she still holds the power that sealed the prison, the spell will remain solid?"

"*I am positive.*"

"And her power will not fade?"

"*No. She will hold onto Reveln's power for the rest of her life—which will be long.*"

"And if she dies?" I cringe saying it aloud, but it has to be done.

"*Death does not remove the magic. It will be imbued in something else. Usually a child. But it could be a loved one or even an object.*"

My mouth falls open. "So, Rev and I can go home—"

Tears well in my eyes. No, it's not possible that this could actually work. I can't actually get everything I've wanted.

"*Yes.*"

My knees buckle at the word. Rev catches me and falls to the ground, holding me as I sob in relief. I don't have to abandon the kingdom that needs me. I don't have to abandon my mate.

"We can go home," Rev whispers. "This time, it's my home too."

77

CAELYNN

I'm in utter shock as we stand before the portal to the fae realm.

The Night Bringer and Night Terror are gone. Rev is alive. And we get to go home—together.

"It's real," Rev whispers in my ear.

I embrace Raven one last time and thank her profusely. Her eyes are not sad in the slightest, though. "You gave me a lot of hope, Cae. I don't think you realize all the ways you helped me."

"But I also hurt you. And put you at risk and—"

She waves me off. "It's okay. All of it. I'm going to be happy now."

I pull her into my arms one last time. Then, we wait another few minutes while Blane says goodbye to his friends too. They talked about him staying, but then I brought up how he'll technically be next in line for his throne and we'd like to have another good ruler in the fae world.

I still don't know much about Blane, but his loyalty to his friends and our cause gives me hope that he can live up to Raven's kind words about him.

Ty and Kari give us hugs too, mostly to give us encouragement. I still can't conceive that my monster is gone. He's alive, and maybe the slight possibility that one day he could get free will haunt me some days. But I will take each day of happiness as I live it. And I suspect, I will have many.

Destroying all of the portals to the human world will take some time—we'll have to destroy them one by one. But it won't be too difficult of a task. And once it's done, the fae realm will be forever barred from the human realm.

"No one can ever recreate them?" Kari asks as we prepare to blast this portal to bits.

"Not once both sides are destroyed," Blane answers. "And Aurora will take care of the human side."

Kari nods.

"*I have the knowledge and power required to reunite the realms,*" the spell book tells me. "*You will have to guard me well, once your time is through.*"

I frown. *Once my time is through.*

"*In a few hundred years,*" he clarifies.

"We'll talk more about this later," I tell the book. It's... an interesting thought. But one we can discuss in time. Right now, I can barely manage to wrap my mind around winning this battle and saying goodbye to Raven forever.

I sniff and smile at Raven, whose hand is linked tightly with the Twisted fae female willingly leaving behind her own world for Raven. Maybe she too finally has a real place to belong. Raven waves happily.

I say one last goodbye to the world of my banishment. The world of my mourning. And the girl who gave me hope that I am worthy of love.

"Take care of her," I tell Aurora. Her smile tells me she intends to do exactly that. Then, I step through the portal hand in hand with the mate I actually get to keep.

78

TEN YEARS LATER

Every time I've earned everything I've hoped for, my fated mate has burned it all to ash—and then given me so much more than I ever thought to dream of.

I shift behind the shadow maple, pressing my cheek against the rough bark, heart pounding.

"Reeeevvv!" Caelynn calls in a sing-songy tone as she leaps through the trees, looking for me.

It's very challenging to play hide and seek with a Shadow fae, but this time I have back up.

Sprites leap onto my back, sending chills all the way down to my feet but then in only a moment I'm hidden from the world. My lips curl into a smile.

Phantoms dance among the leaves above me. The High Court crown appears in the shadows above, somehow shining and flickering with light, despite the fact that I'm looking at only shadow magic.

A new High Ruler will be crowned today.

And it will not be me.

The phantoms show the silhouette of a fae, marching stoically toward the crown and then stops to face a crowd of awe-struck onlookers. Bodiless hands lift the crown and then place it over the fae's head.

It was never supposed to be me.

Caelynn searches through the shadow palace courtyard, still filled with overgrown shadow maples. It's been ten years since Caelynn took her place as the Shadow Queen. Most of the palace is lustrous and beautiful, filled with Caelynn's power. There are still two wings closed off to the magic and we likely won't open those until a new generation of Shadow fae learn to support the palace's magical structure. One day.

The palace courtyard is wide open to the magic, though it remains wild and uncultivated. I've told Caelynn that a palace courtyard is supposed to be beautiful and inviting to visitors, but Caelynn refuses to trim—or "tame" as she puts it—the trees here. *I won't change who we are for anyone else,* she says. *They can like it or leave.*

So far, the only visitors we've welcomed into our hated court are the expected—Rai, Kari and Ty. Each coming with extravagant gifts. We've also reached out to another "lesser" court and potential ally—the webbed court. Their heir aided me during a very challenging trial and I owe them a favor or two. The queen responded favorably, but we've yet to solidify anything. We have a lot of time, though.

A body presses tightly against my back, shoving me into the tree. "Got you," Caelynn whispers against my ear. I chuckle and push back, twisting so I'm facing her.

Her nose grazes mine, her lips curling into a smile that graces her expression often now. My thumb finds her chin. "I could never hide from you for long," I say.

She chuckles. "You sure tried though."

My lips graze against hers. "That's one battle I don't mind losing."

Her fingers claw into the shoulders of my jacket as she

presses her lips to mine. I chuckle and pull her hands back. "No wrinkles," I chide.

"Yes, because our clothes are going to make such a difference in how the High Courts see us."

Another quick kiss and then I curl my arm in hers and pull her through the trees then into the palace. "If I'm going to embrace my image as the High Court deserter, husband to the infamous Shadow Queen, then I'm sure as hell going to look good doing it."

Caelynn chuckles and pulls me along faster. "Whatever helps you sleep at night."

We march through the shadow palace, the dark walls shining and pulsing with life. The magic has been eager to reestablish itself, like a living being that had been just waiting for the chance to breathe again. The gargoyles now take flight every night and growl when strangers enter the palace.

The shadow sprites bound through the halls like mischievous puppies. The Phantoms have found their way to several of the rooms, including the throne room where they perform for every fae who drinks of the fountain.

Today, the fountain is closed to the public, though. Our advisors stand in front of the chalice, beneath an extravagant chandelier made of sparkling white lumi-stones. Stones that represent my love for Caelynn, and it is not nearly big enough if you ask me.

Some of the shadow court citizens were displeased by the new addition, but Caelynn loves it. She insists that light and dark are partners, and we should embrace them each.

Luscious stands rigid among the advisors, his jaw set. It took him a while to crawl back and beg for forgiveness from Caelynn. After our final battle with the Night Bringer, and all the portals to the human world were destroyed, Caelynn quickly dismantled the shadow rebel society. Some are in prison. Most are simply afraid that the "psychic" queen will find them if they even whisper a word against her.

Caelynn is quick to forgive, though. And of course it helps that she has a spell book to tell her the moment one of her advisors does something naughty. So she took Luscious back, but has made his life miserable, forcing him to prove his loyalty many times over.

There are also two new advisors. The "wanderer" still lives in the Whisperwood but has happily given his aid and wisdom whenever asked. He stands here today, eyes dark and hair disheveled, but smiling. And we also reestablished one of the old families in the northern hills. Their matron is meek and gives nearly no feedback, even when asked, but she is present and that is all Caelynn expects for now. The next generation will be raised to support a strong throne.

One step at a time.

The Whisperwood Queen—we've decided she should keep her title out of respect—will be accompanying us to the High Court today, but she is not alone. Her nephew and his new bride, Tania from the Crackling Court will be coming. Her older nephew has not yet found a bride, but he's still hopeful he can find a strong wife to solidify his legacy within our kingdom. We are also bringing along two young and promising females in hopes they can find a husband to bring home.

I hold my head high, and Caelynn squeezes my hand gently as we lead our party through the front gates for our first official High Court event since Caelynn ascended to the throne. She's lovely in her black silk gown and elaborate lumistone jewelry. I made her teardrop earrings, and necklace that looks like stars dripping down her neck.

I'm fairly certain she only wears them for my benefit, but they do look lovely on her.

Our party stops in front of the newly constructed portal to the High Court.

Though the Shadow Court is not yet part of the ruling courts-- we do not yet have a seat on the council—Caelynn and I know it is only a matter of time. It may take fifty years, it may take five, but Caelynn will have a place there before the end of the century and this portal is proof of that.

Caelynn and I walk through the portal first. I breathe deep, pulling the salty powerful air of the High Court island through my lungs. The magic here is not as potent as it once was now that the ancient king is absent. Part of me wonders if that means the High Court will eventually lose its power and influence over the other courts but it may take several centuries before that is known.

"Are you ready for this?" The Whisperwood Queen leans in to whisper to me. "It will be your first time facing the High Court since your desertion."

I smile. "I am ready." More ready than anyone could imagine. Yes, I will face hatred when I walk down those steps for the first time, but I will be standing beside the love of my life. I am supporting her and there is nothing—nothing-- I could imagine that's better than that.

Before we walk into the High Court palace, I pull Caelynn into my arms. "I love you," she says, beating me to it. I kiss her fiercely. Then I press my forehead to hers.

"I will never regret this. You have made me happier than I could have ever been as High King."

Caelynn closes her eyes. "I don't know how I earned all of this." Then she gently touches the lumistones at her neck. "But I will be forever grateful to whatever fates brought us together."

"I love you too," I whisper with a smile.

Then we both take in long deep breaths and enter into the

High Court palace with our heads high, and expressions full of pride and power.

The winged fae at the top of the palace stairs freezes when he takes us in. But then he straightens and shouts to the crowd below. "The High Court welcomes Queen Caelynn and King Reveln, of the Shadow Court."

Author Note

THANK YOU THANK YOU THANK YOU for reading this series to completion. I loved writing it and I hope that you loved reading it!! I think every author has a love hate relationship with every book they write. I adore these characters and this story, but pushing myself to write it during a pandemic, on and off from work, my son home from school—was rough. I suppose every good thing will come with trials.

Because I nearly burnt myself out writing this series, last year I decided to take a little time off from deadliness but that time off is now complete and I have a new series out now! I'd love it if you kept scrolling for a sneak peak at my new book baby! It has several of the elements you loved in the Wicked Fae series, but set in on Earth this time. While I can't have Cae and Rev pop in based on what happened at the end of this series, there will be some hints about the fae world and how the portals closing have affected things.

You can find me on Facebook, Instagram or Tiktok @StaceyTrombleyAuthor

Or better yet, join my newsletter to get the lastest book news

www.StaceyTrombley.com

Keep scrolling to find more books by me!

A MAGICAL PRINCE WANTS TO DATE ME. BUT THERE'S ONE BIG PROBLEM. THIS PRINCE HAS CLAWS

Everyone at Shadow Hills Academy desires the dark and powerful Jarron Blackthorn. But I'm the only one who has seen the terrifying beast beneath his magical façade.

When my sister is murdered, and the case mysteriously

dropped, I know where to begin my own investigation—Shadow Hills Academy, an elite school for supernaturals. Technically, I have zero magic, but just enough skills with potions to be accepted. Now I have the means to get close to the most likely culprits—powerful people like the demon prince Jarron.

I was friends with Jarron years ago, before I saw his true form, but I'm still shocked when he reacts to news of my sister's death with a fierce determination for vengeance. He has an insane plan to help me get access to Elite Hall, where the most powerful students reside—by pretending to date me.

Dating a demon was NOT how I expected this year to start, but his plan will work. Hang on the arm of Jarron Blackthorn, the heir of the Under World, and everyone in school will be so desperate for my friendship they'll spill their darkest secrets.

I just have to make sure Jarron never learns he is my number one suspect.

Read it now

ABOUT THE AUTHOR

Stacey Trombley is a casino pit boss by night, urban fantasy author by day. She lives in Ohio with her husband, son, and GSD Riley. When she's not writing or reading her husband is probably dragging her along on one of his crazy adventures for this travel vlog or competing against him about who can pick the most Survivor winners in the first episode (hint: she's winning). But mostly, she's probably reading.